CW00852872

MORSELY MANOR

AND THE

MAGIC MIRROR

MORSELY MANOR
AND THE
MAGIC MIRROR

R J WEBB

The Book Guild Ltd

First published in Great Britain in 2021 by
The Book Guild Ltd
9 Priory Business Park
Wistow Road, Kibworth
Leicestershire, LE8 0RX
Freephone: 0800 999 2982
www.bookguild.co.uk
Email: info@bookguild.co.uk
Twitter: @bookguild

Copyright © 2021 R J Webb

The right of R J Webb to be identified as the author of this
work has been asserted by her in accordance with the
Copyright, Design and Patents Act 1988.

All rights reserved. No part of this publication may be
reproduced, transmitted, or stored in a retrieval system, in any form or by any means,
without permission in writing from the publisher, nor be otherwise circulated in
any form of binding or cover other than that in which it is published and without
a similar condition being imposed on the subsequent purchaser.

This work is entirely fictitious and bears no resemblance to any persons living or dead.

Typeset in 12pt Adobe Jenson Pro

Printed on FSC accredited paper
Printed and bound in Great Britain by 4edge Limited

ISBN 978 1913913 359

British Library Cataloguing in Publication Data.
A catalogue record for this book is available from the British Library.

For my sister, who sees the magic in everything.

CHAPTER ONE

On a hillside deep in the Lancashire country sat a lone Manor; the exterior was immaculately kept, and an array of flowers neatly pruned in their designated beds lined the modestly sized garden. A barn and a small cottage sat five hundred yards away where a few animals occupied the space: horses, sheep, chickens and perhaps a few others that couldn't be seen from distance. A gravel road, running over a mile long, led from the bottom of the hill right up to the front door, with its imposing statues and large sash windows that were encased by remarkable stonework, all of which made up Morsely Manor.

You could easily mistake the property as being owned by a family of aristocrats, who would entertain guests in their fancy dining hall and would then retire to the family room for evening activities, songs and joyous occasions.

In actual fact, this could not be anything further than what the eye perceived. No one knows exactly when it happened, but the rather large and beautiful Manor was home to approximately fifty children, ten sisters, two cooks, one gardener/handyman and one very fearsome headmistress.

Regardless of what the house may have seen in its previous years, it was now a children's home. The children were not mistreated and by all accounts they lived a very comfortable life: they were fed, they were clothed and they were educated. However, this did not distract from the fact that they were orphans, and the only family they each now had.

With summer looming, the children spent more time outdoors, as they did every year, and could easily spend hours in the fields that surrounded the property. This was only ever allowed after they had attended their lessons and completed their daily chores, which included helping the sisters with the upkeep of the property, inside and out. If they completed all this to a good standard, their time was theirs to do with as they wished (as long as they stayed within the grounds).

On this particular day that was precisely what they were doing – all except one!

The bell rang! *Is it that time already? Come on, just a bit longer,* she thought to herself. *I'll just pretend I haven't heard. They won't notice I am not there anyway.*

'Isla… Isla,' came the sound of a young man's voice. 'There you are.'

Sat on the edge of a very precarious-looking jetty, Isla barely lifted her head to acknowledge the new arrival.

'You know they would have never come in here looking for you, don't you? The place is a hazard; everything is falling to pieces.'

She returned the boy's gaze. 'Precisely, that was the point.'

He ignored her passive-aggressive snare and returned it with a smile.

'What do you want, Will?' She knew she should not be so blunt with him, but she just wanted to be left alone.

If she thought he had noticed her curtness, he didn't show it. 'I've come to get you for dinner, the bell's gone.' He looked down at her. 'I've sent the others on their way, but when they said they couldn't find you, I guessed you'd be here.'

'Well, congratulations, here I am, you found me,' she said with a sarcastic tone.

'There's no need to be like that, Isla.' Will looked at her, puzzled.

'Well, I didn't ask you to come in here, did I? I didn't ask you to come get me. I was quite alright until you turned up.'

Will held his hands up in an "I submit" gesture. 'Okay, Isla, I give in – you coming now?' He steadied himself for a second round of insults, but they never came. Instead she stood up without a single word, leaving him with nothing but his own baffled reflection.

'Children, finally, your tea is getting cold.'

'Sorry, Miss,' they said one by one as they came trampling through the door.

'Whatever will I do with you?' chirped Ms Pepperin, the largest of the sisters at the home, who also happened to be the nicest and the cheeriest. Short, tubby and rosy-cheeked with the first signs of greying hair, Ms Pepperin was a widower. She had unfortunately lost her husband to an ongoing illness two years before and had not remarried. The death of her husband had hit her hard; however, she never let it affect how she treated the children. In fact, having never had the chance to have any of her own, it only made her love them more.

'Now, shoo shoo, be gone with you,' she said, hurrying the children to wash their hands before tea. Her voice was stern, pretending to be cross, but nothing could disguise the smile in her eyes.

Isla was one of the last through the door, having lagged behind.

'And what's wrong with you?' Ms Pepperin asked, hands on hips, looking down her rather large belly.

'Nothing,' came her short reply.

'Well, it certainly doesn't look like nothing. Your face looks the dead of winter.'

'Oh, she's alright,' burst in Will behind her. 'She's just grumpy because her secret hiding place wasn't so secret after all.' And he gave her a nudge as he passed her by.

Isla forced a smile, deciding it was better to try act her usual self than have too many questions asked at that moment.

'Oh, he wishes,' she called out after him.

Ms Pepperin paused, softening her gaze; she went to say something that Isla felt had more importance than their usual encounters. But she was disturbed before she could get the words out, then, as if being snapped back to reality, Ms Pepperin shooed her along with the others in her usual motherly way.

When she reappeared chatter covered the dining hall and a seemingly much happier Isla joined the table. Sitting next to Grace, a girl similar in age but far taller than she was, by a foot at least, she grabbed some bread; though it was a bit stale, she did not care, for her belly grumbled to be fed.

'Butter?' Will offered from across the table, arm outstretched with a pleaful look on his face, hoping to bring whatever he had done to upset her to an end.

'Did you hear something?' Isla said, ignoring him, looking everywhere but in his direction.

Grace, with her slightly ginger shoulder-length hair, rolled her eyes, snatching the butter from his hand. 'Just take it,' she said in a hoarse tone and shoved it down in front of a very disgruntled-looking Isla.

It was not unusual for the pair to bicker from time to time, and Grace knew all too well not to get involved.

You see, Will and Isla had both arrived at Morsely Manor the same time ten years ago – well, almost, a week to the day on Isla's birthday. Having both lost their parents and there being no other living relative able to care for them, they were sent to the only place that would.

In fact, Will did have an auntie from his mother's side, but she refused to take him in – not because she didn't care for him, but because she could barely care for her own children. And Isla had no one.

So that was that: their fates were sealed; their destinies forever intertwined.

Will had come from a working-class family on the outskirts of London; his mother an embroiderer at the local factory and his father a labourer, they were a happy family. However, due to the nature of his father's work, this meant that he was often away for long periods, grabbing the work wherever and whenever he could.

Will adored his father and missed him greatly when he was away, but when he was home, he was the best father that he could ever hope for. Together they shared a fondness for animals and, as a family, often spent weekends escaping to the countryside. His father taught him all things wildlife, and his mother was on hand to help nurse any injured animals they undoubtedly always came across. She had a way with natural medicine; a skill that she would pass on to her son.

Life was good for the Thatcher family until Will's mother was caught in a fire at the factory. At the forefront of the blaze was his father, who fought fearlessly and the reason why so many were saved that day. Upon hearing that his wife was caught in the lower levels, he and a few of the other men forced their way through the smoky building, following the screams to the basement, where they were able to move enough debris to create a small hole for the women to climb through. Will's mother ensured the younger girls got out first, pushing them one by one into the waiting arms on the other side. She was just about to escape herself when she noticed an elder lady, too scared to move. Will's father screamed for her to come back, but it was too late; she was already gone.

He followed her in, and together they helped the frail lady up and carried her to her freedom. It looked as though there would be no fatalities that day; however, just as they were about to escape themselves, a second blast caused the building to collapse further, blocking their only exit.

Will was not there that day; being a young boy, he was at school. However, he later learned the last words his parents ever spoke were that they loved their son; they were proud of the caring boy he was and the man that he would become. From that day he swore to himself that he would never let them down.

Not much was known about Isla's family – just that her father was a fisherman and they lived in a small fisherman's town somewhere in the south of England. Unfortunately, a tragic boat accident had seen both her parents swept out to sea, and though many attempts were made to find them, they were never seen again.

That was ten years ago.

Isla couldn't remember much of her time before the Manor, just a few flashing memories that didn't make much sense to her. Will, however, liked to keep every surviving memory alive and often talked to the photograph of his parents next to his bed, much to Isla's annoyance. She felt the past should stay in the past, and that's exactly where she kept hers. Needless to say, they differed on this point of view.

The rest of dinner was sat chitchatting about the usual things that one would find themselves talking about in a children's home: teachers, other children, Scampi (the resident cat) and not to mention Mr Stopes, the caretaker/ gardener who had a scar down the left-hand side of his face –

he was a particular favourite amongst the children, who liked to make up elaborate stories of just how he came about to get his unusual scar.

Just as dessert was being served, the doors to the dining hall were flung open and in walked the headmistress.

'Silence!'

To this, everyone automatically closed their mouths, some even too scared to swallow the remainder of their food. All that could be heard was the sound of her footsteps echoing in the large room as she very graciously, but very purposely, walked to the other side to address them.

'Good evening, children,' she said in a poised manner.

'Good evening, Miss Sparrow,' came the reply in unison.

'You will all finish up your dinner and head straight to your rooms for an early night.'

'But, Miss, this is our late night. Have you forgot it's Saturday?'

Everyone looked at the voice coming from the far side of the room, in astonishment that someone had just questioned the headmistress's orders – for that's exactly what they were: orders, not kind requests, not when it came to Miss Sparrow.

Walking back towards the direction she had just come from, footsteps resonating even louder this time, she turned and addressed the culprit. 'Jimmy Jameson, thank you for kindly interrupting me and also pointing out that of what I already know. However, you are under my roof and in my care, and for reasons that do not concern you, you shall do exactly what has been asked of you.'

And without waiting for a reply, knowing the boy understood, Miss Sparrow continued. 'Now, thanks to Master Jameson you shall all do this right away – spoons down, no dessert and head straight up to your rooms.' And as swiftly as she had arrived, she disappeared through the double oak doors without leaving a clunk behind her.

Knowing not to disobey her, no one attempted to have any of their dessert – except for Jimmy Jameson, that is, who shoved the biggest spoonful of apple crumble and custard into his mouth, just as Ms Pepperin was approaching the table.

'Now, children, you heard what she said. Off to bed with you, nightgowns and teeth brushed, please.'

❖

'Someone's not doing as they're told… Again!' Will said as he sat down next to Isla. 'Don't think I've not seen you roaming around the Manor late at night or sneaking off when you think no one is looking.'

'Shhhhh!'

Will looked into the direction of Isla's intense stare. 'What are we looking at?' he whispered.

'How do you think they got in there?' she said without looking at him.

'Who? In where?'

'Miss Sparrow's office. I have been sat up here since we were told to go to bed and I haven't seen anyone enter or leave, yet I can hear voices – do you think that was why she wanted us all to go to bed early?'

'I'm not sure I understand,' he said quizzically.

'She wanted us out of the way for some reason.'

'Are you feeling okay?' Will said, more as a statement rather than a question.

Isla finally turned her head to face him. 'Something is going on, I just know it!'

Will paused, brow furrowed, not sure how he should proceed. 'Isla, I don't hear anything or anyone!'

'What do you mean? Of course you can. I can't make out exactly what they are saying, but it's something about the time, or it's time, or the time is now… Oh! I just need to get closer.' And with that, she was up and down the second flight of stairs.

'Isla, what are you doing? Come back! You know what will happen if they catch you out of bed.' Against every fibre in his body, he reluctantly followed her. 'Isla, what is going on?'

'There are people in there, Will. They're planning something, and I intend to find out what.' She stared at him with her serious face, the face that said "don't push me", but he did.

'Isla, I don't hear anything – what is going on with you? And so what if there are people in there? It makes no difference to us.' Will had been growing increasingly concerned with Isla's behaviour of late. She was far snappier than usual, secluded, withdrawn even, and if there was anything that had not been right, it was her.

Just as Isla was about to protest, the door opened! Having momentarily taken their eyes off of it to get into what would have been another debate, they watched as one of the sisters entered the room. Carrying with her a tray and a teapot for one, she placed it down at the desk where Miss Sparrow sat, *alone*!

Isla's eyes widened at the revelation, her pupils catching the light of the chandelier that hung above her desk, and if possible, her already pale skin became even paler. The room was silent; no one else besides Miss Sparrow occupied it. Isla's eyes darted from side to side in search of evidence of the commotion that she, just moments before, had heard inside, but her efforts were fruitless.

Dressed in her usual evening wear of a loose-fitting burgundy and cream dress – it was the only time Isla ever knew her to wear anything other than her usual black and grey A-lined fitting clothes – Miss Sparrow sat casually at her desk completing what looked to be paperwork. Her almost jet-black hair, that by day sat in a neatly tied back bun, and a curled over fringe was now loose in one single plait resting down the side of her shoulder. She looked a shadow of her daily self and not someone who was or had been entertaining guests.

Where did all the voices go?

Miss Sparrow's study was much what you would expect a headmistress of such prominence to look like. Modestly furnished, velvet curtains hung the height of the room, a large bookcase occupied the wall to her left, a watercolour painting of the Manor overlooked her desk, and two plush armchairs were purposely positioned by the bay windows facing out into the gardens.

All looked normal except for a large freestanding mirror that stood in the corner of the room, which to Isla seemed rather odd. Clearly out of place with the rest of the homely mahogany furnishings, it appeared to be made out of metal, silver even; one could clearly see the craftsmanship that would have gone into the intricately woven design – stunning, but somewhat misplaced. Come to think of it, she was not sure if she had ever seen it before.

Drawn to the mirror, Isla forgot where she was until Will nudged her out of her trance. Not wanting to get into a discussion about how much of a fool she felt at that particular moment, she stood up abruptly. How could she explain this to Will? She knew what she had heard and she was positive there had been people inside, yet where were they now?

He tried to speak, but she cut him off before even one syllable had left his mouth. 'There were people in there, Will. I swear it. I know you don't believe me, but I know what I heard.' Not giving him a chance to respond, Isla turned her back on him, marking the end to their endeavours for one evening.

CHAPTER TWO

Having spent most of the night restless, Isla was already awake before the bell sounded for breakfast. She was glad that it was a Sunday and that she wouldn't have any chores to do.

Ignoring the movements of the other three girls who shared her room – Elizabeth, Sissie and Lexi, the Taunton sisters – she avoided eye contact as they started to awaken for the day.

Lexi opened the curtains, revealing what looked like was going to be another beautiful spring day. Light filled every corner of the room, with the heat of the morning sun instantly warming Isla's sheets.

'Can we go for a picnic today? Maybe down by the creek?' squeaked Lexi.

'Yes, I think that would be a lovely idea. I'll speak to the sisters and ask if we can take a packed lunch out with us,' replied Elizabeth, tightening the sheets on her bed. 'Perhaps the other children might like to join us – we could make a day of it.'

'So, if we're going down by the creek, that means I don't have to brush my hair?' pleaded Lexi hopefully.

'Oh no you don't, you don't get out of it that easily. Now come here. What will it be, a Dutch plait or a French plait?' offered Elizabeth, taking a seat at the end of her bed.

'Oooh,' huffed Lexi, resuming the usual position on the floor, 'two French plaits then, please.'

'Very well,' confirmed Elizabeth, brushing the blonde waves of Lexi's hair. 'Sissie, you're not going to stay in bed all day – it's time to get up, please.'

'I don't want to,' came the muffled sound of Sissie's voice from under her pillow. 'I'm tired.'

'Well, you shouldn't have stayed up past lights out reading then, should you?' came Elizabeth's stern reply.

'Okay, I'm up. Happy?' Crawling under the covers to the end of her bed, out popped the head of Sissie, whose hair was a few shades darker compared to the golden blonde of her sisters. 'But it was a very good book – there were swords and fighting and murder and blood, lots of blood.'

'Hush now, we have a slightly younger, delicate mind in the room,' said Elizabeth, covering Lexi's ears. 'I don't want you filling her head with nightmares and nonsense.'

Sissie ignored the comments of her prim and proper sister, and continued to pull faces at Lexi, who was doing her up most not to giggle.

Finally emerging from her bed, Sissie stretched out her morning stiffness in a rather elaborate way. 'And what about you, Isla, would you like to join us? Seeing as today's plans have already been made without my consult, I guess I can have a say in who comes along.'

'Oh, don't be so dramatic,' sighed Elizabeth. 'But yes, please do, Isla, join us.'

Rubbing away the morning sleep Isla sat up, revealing a set of absent hazel eyes. 'I think I might just stay in today. I feel a bit under the weather, probably best I should rest,' Isla replied.

'Oh, I hope you're not coming down with what Nancy had. Is

there anything we can do for you?' said Elizabeth, automatically jumping into nurse mode – with her kind-hearted caring nature, she would make a pretty good nurse one day.

'Oh no, thanks, I'll be fine,' Isla said swiftly.

'Well, I'll let the sisters know that you are feeling unwell and bring some breakfast back up for you,' she replied.

'That's really not necessary, I'm not that hungry.' Truth be told, she was a bit hungry, having not had the chance to finish her dinner the previous night. Thanks to Jimmy Jameson, her stomach felt empty, but she also wanted to be left alone as quickly as possible and with minimal fuss.

'I insist, you must eat something. You have to keep your strength up,' Elizabeth said with finality.

'Yeah, Isla, you must keep your strength up. We have a surprise for your birthday, so you must be better by then,' Lexi said, now having made her way over to Isla's bed.

'Ssh!' Sissie chimed in. 'You weren't meant to say anything.'

'Sorry,' said Lexi, her big blue doe-like eyes reaching the floor. 'But she looks like she could do with a bit of cheering up, it's why we are doing it after all. I didn't tell her that we were going to—'

'No!' cried Sissie, sweeping in to stop her younger sister from blurting out any other unwanted surprises. 'That's quite enough chat from you. I think it's time to go to breakfast and leave Isla in peace.'

Subsequently, that did put a little smile on Isla's face; she liked the sisters, Lexi especially. So free-spirited, so honest – she couldn't help but smile.

'Come on, girls, time to go. Isla, I hope you feel better, and we'll make sure to bring you back something to eat,' Elizabeth confirmed, ushering the other two out the room.

'Yeah, hope you feel better, Isla,' sang Lexi, humming a sweet-tuned melody as she skipped out the door, then the room fell silent.

Isla lay there thinking about the sisters for a moment; she had spent the best part of six years sharing a room with them.

Elizabeth was eighteen and actually too old for the Manor. However, because of her siblings it was decided that she would stay and help out with the younger children at the home. She was kind, sweet and generous. A pure beauty, with porcelain skin and ruby lips, her hair was long and free-flowing, and she fitted into her role of big sister to everyone perfectly.

Sissie, who from what they had been told inherited more of their father's looks and quirks, was rarely seen without a book or pen and paper in hand, and was the total opposite. Though she shared the same oval face as her sisters, same wide smile and round eyes, she differed in the fact that she had short light brown hair, pale green eyes and wore glasses for reading. Her clothes were torn from her endless experiments, and the sisters at the Manor had given up trying to stop her, so they gave Sissie her own room in the basement in the hope of keeping her crazy ideas contained.

Now Lexi, nine years younger than Elizabeth, shared qualities with both her sisters. She had the beauty of Elizabeth but the inquisitiveness of Sissie; she was fearless, cheeky and always happy. She had an infectious laugh that could brighten up any room, and there was never a dull day with her around.

Isla really couldn't have wished for a better adoptive family and was happy she had spent the last six years sharing a room with them. Especially Lexi, who would have been only two when they arrived and had not understood what was happening. It had been quite scary and confusing for her at first when she cried most nights, screaming for the parents whom she didn't realise she would never see again. It reminded Isla of how she had felt when she first arrived: the blurred memories, not knowing where she fit in. She wanted to reach out to her at the time and make all her pain go away. However, as it turned out she didn't need to. Lexi was stronger than all of them, and though at first it was tough, she soon found her feet and was the first to make Morsely Manor her home.

Pausing her memory, Isla turned her attentions to the door, where the floorboards creaked, letting her know that someone was about to enter, but no one did. She got out of bed just to double check that it wasn't Elizabeth, being true to her word, and may be needing some help carrying her breakfast, but when she looked out into the corridor, no one was there. *Not again.*

SWOOSH!

There was a sudden gush of air that almost knocked Isla off her feet, and upon turning around she could see that the window was open. *Perhaps Lexi did it when she pulled back the curtains.* She went over to close it, gripping her fingers tightly on to the solid wooden frame, slamming it shut, a task that usually took two to do.

Stopping to catch her breath, something odd caught her attention: away from prying eyes Mr Stopes and Miss Sparrow seemed to be having a heated discussion. Miss Sparrow appeared stern, which was not wholly unusual in itself; however, what did appear unusual was that she was also clearly very agitated, not a word that was often associated with the headmistress. Isla watched as a few more words and hand gestures were exchanged before she finally walked away, ignoring Mr Stopes' attempts to keep the conversation (or whatever it was) going. *Does this have something to do with last night?*

Isla's mind wandered back to the night before, with so many questions running around her head. *Who was in that room? What were they planning? Why does it make me feel uneasy? And why was I so horrible to Will?*

Her brain snapped. *Will!* She thought to herself, a sudden wave of guilt – her best friend, her oldest friend.

She wanted to talk to him so much, but she didn't know how, and even if she did, how could he possibly help her when she didn't even know what she needed help with?

Isla could tell that he had noticed that she was not herself, and she knew that he wanted to talk to her about it, but Will – kind, loveable, caring Will – would be tentative around her. He would let her blow off steam and wait for her to come to him. It's how they had always been, but this time she feared she couldn't share the burden; she couldn't share her secret, not even with her best friend.

CHAPTER THREE

It had been almost a week since Isla had pretended that she was unwell and she had managed to keep herself to herself for the most part of that. It was a Friday evening, and she was down in her secluded spot overlooking the meadow that only one other person knew about. And that particular person had taken the hint that she wasn't in any type of mood for talking.

Using the excuse that she still felt unwell had made it pretty easy to remove herself from any social activities and with minimal fuss. Attending classes when she had to, then retreating back to her secret spot, where she continued to block out the increasing unsettling feeling in her stomach.

The Manor had always been home to Isla; it was what she knew, and despite her occasional moments of defiance, she was well liked by both the sisters and her peers. However, it had not gone unnoticed that her spark was somewhat lost as of late, and she knew it. Isla had always been pretty good at covering up her thoughts and feelings, the ones she really didn't want people to know; however, her head was all over the place at the moment, causing her behaviour to be inconsistent. Luckily the sisters put it down to adolescence.

She heard the rustle of branches, followed by a little white flag. Knowing exactly who it was, she rolled her eyes and called out his name.

'Will.'

'Can I come in?' he said, popping his head through the gap.

She turned away. 'You can't hide from anyone in this place.'

'I'm going to take that as a yes.' He made his way in and sat down next to her on the dusty old cushion that must have been there since they were kids. 'I've not been down here for a while,' he said, looking around. 'I like what you've done with the place.' He paused. 'Very rustic, I like it.'

Isla rolled her eyes again; she knew what he was trying to do. He had a childlike quality about him, introducing humour into the most awkward of situations, but in an endearing sort of way.

Dropping her shoulders, Isla released an extended sigh; she couldn't keep her act up any longer and decided it was time for a truce. 'So you missed me then,' she said, in-keeping with the playful tone.

'The mood swings, the bad temper, the insults – and that's just a good day! Of course,' Will joked playfully.

Isla couldn't help but smile; she could never stay mad at him for long, especially when he hadn't actually done anything wrong in the first place.

'I'm sorry, Will.'

This took him by surprise, as it was not often that he ever heard her mutter those words. Isla could admit when she was wrong, but he knew it was not easy for her to do so.

The mood changed; seizing the moment, Will took his opportunity to gather more information while her barriers were down.

'Isla, what's going on? Please tell me, I mean, tell me what's *really* going on?' he said, staring at her with his warm brown eyes.

Isla sighed, shrugging her shoulders, tempted to retreat back into herself, but decided against it. *It's time.*

'I don't know, Will. If I tell you, I think you will think I am crazy – I already think I am crazy, and I don't need you to tell me too.'

Will was stumped as to what could possibly have happened to make her feel this way, but he wasn't going to let this opportunity slip; he needed to know what had been making her act so erratic. 'I'm not gonna say you're crazy. You drive me crazy – my God, Isla, you do – but I'm not going to say you *are* crazy. Now, tell me, I've never seen you like this.'

'You promise to let me finish speaking before you say anything?'

'Yes, I promise.'

Isla gave him a look that said she meant it, which was followed by a deep breath. 'I'm not sure where to start,' she said, crumbling at the first hurdle. This was the first time that Isla would have said aloud the things that had been playing on her mind. The unexplained occurrences.

Will remained patient but urged her to continue. 'Just start from the beginning,' he reassured her.

Isla thought about it; it had felt like it had been going on forever. 'I'm not entirely sure when that was, but I guess it all started with a dream – well, dreams in fact, reoccurring ones. They just came out of nowhere, only the thing is they felt real, too real.' She paused, clearly unnerved, but Will urged her to continue.

'It was weird. Every night I wake up in my bed – in the dream, this is.'

Will nodded to show he understood.

'The only thing is, it feels eerily quiet, like there wasn't even the sound of sleeping, you know. So I look at the girls' beds, but they're empty, then out in the hallway I hear footsteps. Of course, I get up to see who it is, but no one is there; however,

I still hear the footsteps. I follow the sound, for some reason I want to know who it is, but I never quite catch them up. As I walk past the rooms I check each one, but again all the beds are empty. So I start calling out names: Elizabeth, Sissie, Lexi, Jimmy, *you*! The more empty beds I see, the louder I get, but the louder I get, the more it feels like the walls are closing in, then I realise they *are* closing in, which makes me panic more. Then suddenly the footsteps stop, the temperature drops and that's when I hear my name. I turn round and standing at the end of the hallway out from the mist a dark figure emerges. "Isla," it repeats, but this time I don't like the way it says it, so I start backing off, slowly at first, but the thing, whatever it is, seems to have had the same idea, only instead of going in the opposite direction it starts coming towards me. So now I'm running away from the very thing I was trying to chase. I stop on the stairs and look up, but I can no longer see anything, for the mist has turned to fog. I continue to run, making my way to the front door, just wanting to get away. But instead of going for the front door, for some reason I change my mind and go to Miss Sparrow's office instead. I grab the handle, pull the door, swing it open, and as I do so I'm blinded by a bright light and a hand on my shoulder pulling me back. My eyes are closed, I scream and the next thing I know I'm back in bed and the girls are fast asleep in theirs.'

'Wow, that does sound like a bad dream. I can see why that would upset you, but dreams can't hurt you,' Will said reassuringly.

Isla glared. 'You said you wouldn't interrupt.'

Will leaned back, letting her continue; he certainly was not going to do anything to stop her, now that she was finally talking to him.

'That was just the start of it, the dreams. Sometimes I've even found myself sleep walking, like all of a sudden I wake up without any recollection of how I got there. Then things started happening around me. It was as if the dream had really come to life. In the Manor, out in the fields, I'd see things.' Isla corrected herself, 'I *see* things – at first I put it down to my imagination, but now I'm not so sure.' Isla focused heavily on her hands.

Will waited a good few seconds to see if she was going to continue, and when he felt safe to talk, he did. 'I'm not sure I understand, Isla, what kind of things?'

'I don't know, Will, just not normal things, things I can't explain or prove even,' Isla snapped, wishing she hadn't started to tell him now.

'Okay, okay, take a deep breath. I'm trying, Isla – give me an example,' he said, trying to calm her down.

Isla continued, thinking about her words carefully. 'Okay, like things only happen when I am alone. One time I was walking down the corridor, and I felt the presence of someone behind me, as if they were inches from my back, only when I turned around, there was no one there. I've heard whisperings of my name as if someone is trying to get my attention, but again, I can never see anyone. When we were out in the fields last week, I could have sworn I saw someone watching me from the bushes. I couldn't see a face, but it reminded me of the dark figure from my dream – that was right before you arrived.'

'That's why you were so startled and why you were so off with me – because you saw someone watching you?' Will felt relieved he finally had an answer for that.

'Well, I did want to be left alone, but yes, and what could I have said, Will? There was nothing there by the time I looked back, and what would you have done? Nothing.' Isla stared out at the sun, suddenly feeling exhausted. She had kept her secret bottled up for so long she didn't realise how much it had weighed her down until now.

'I've wanted to speak to you, Will, but I just didn't know how, and then with what happened the other night there was just no way you would have believed me. I mean, I don't expect you to believe me now – I wouldn't if it was the other way round – but all I can say is it is happening and I have no idea why.'

Will had never seen Isla look so vulnerable. She was always so together, so independent, stubborn, headstrong – this was a side of her he had never had to contend with before, but she was his best friend, and whether he understood it or not, if she said something was not right then he would do whatever he could to help her.

'I believe you, Isla,' came Will's even-toned reply.

Shocked, Isla's eyes locked with his; she had not expected that to be his response.

'I mean, I'm not saying I know what's going on, or what it is – blimey, Isla, I find it hard to understand, if I'm honest – but I believe in our friendship, and friends stick together, right?'

They stared at each other in a long silence. A wave of emotion that Isla had never felt before came flooding over her. She felt drawn to him, protected, safe. She had always felt that with him, but this time it was different, then she realised what it was. *This is not happening.* Suddenly she sprung to her feet; Isla had far too many emotions to contend with to add this unchartered territory to it as well. It was only a brief moment, but Isla had wanted to kiss Will just then – not a friend kiss, but the kind of kiss that they, that friends *do not* do – and she felt embarrassed.

Will, somewhat confused, examined her. 'Are you okay?'

'Of course,' she said, trying not to make eye contact with him until she felt the redness in her cheeks cool off.

'It's just, you look—'

'I'm okay, are you coming?'

'Isla, I really think we should talk some more about this.'

'I'm done with talking, no more talking.'

'Well, I think we should at least talk about what we are going to do next. I mean, you can't just drop a bombshell like that on me and then pretend it didn't happen.'

'I'm not pretending. Are you coming?' She stormed out of the snug heading back towards the Manor. 'We've got a plan to make.'

'Plan, what plan?' Will questioned, catching her up.

'To break into Miss Sparrow's office, of course.'

He was shocked at how casually she said it; he was hoping he hadn't heard her right, but he had. 'Are you absolutely mad?'

'No, I'm sane, saner than I have felt in weeks,' Isla retorted, keeping up her own pace.

'But Miss Sparrow's office – do you have a death wish? Do you have any idea what she will do to us if she catches us snooping around in there? I mean, if you want to live to see your birthday you'll abort this mission now,' he said, half-joking, half-serious.

'There're answers in there, Will. I don't know what it is or what we are looking for, but my dream, it must mean something.' She stopped and stared him straight in the face. 'I feel it.'

Before Will could add in any further protest about why it wasn't such a good idea, they were interrupted by Mr Stopes as they rounded the corner to the back entrance of the Manor.

'Ah, just the girl I was looking for,' he said, towering over the both of them. 'The sheep have gone AWOL, and I need to catch them before the last of the daylight has gone.'

'Ah, well, I was actually—' Isla tried to say.

'It won't take long, not with both of us doing it, then you can soon be off with your friends,' he said, looking at Will. 'Good evening to you, Master Thatcher.'

'I can help if you like, I'm also quite skilled at—'

'No need,' Mr Stopes said. 'The two of us will be plenty.'

Will looked a little put out but didn't push it any further; it was clear he was either not needed or wanted.

Isla sighed, seeing no way out of Mr Stopes' request; she was, after all, the most experienced rider and the one most likely to help get the job done the quickest. She followed him towards the paddock, looking over her shoulder and mouthing one word.

'Midnight.'

❖

'Just leave that there,' Mr Stopes said as he put his belongings down on the bench. 'You did very well today – have you thought about doing something with horses?'

'I can't say that I have,' Isla replied, looking at the things in his cottage and observing that it felt much bigger on the inside than from what it looked on the outside.

'Well, you should think about it – you have a way with them, they listen to you,' he said, observing her reaction.

'A natural talent, I guess. I dunno, I just feel at ease with them, plus they can't talk back,' Isla replied absentmindedly, stopping at what she thought was a photograph of Mr Stopes, but was instead a very good life-like drawing. It was as good as any photo that she had ever seen, they certainly looked so on the walls, but up close, the individual strokes of an artists pencil could be seen.

The picture was of himself and another man, faces beaming; he was the shorter of the two but every bit as impressive. His hair was slicker than the raggedy mop that was there now and his skin less weathered, but other than that he hadn't changed much. They stood arm in arm, wearing long robes that had a symbol of sorts on the chest. She couldn't tell the colour for it was drawn in black and white, but there was something about the other man in the picture that looked somewhat familiar to her.

'Snooping around, I see,' Mr Stopes said, causing Isla to drop the frame, smashing the glass into two pieces.

'I didn't mean…' Isla gasped. 'I will clean it up.'

'Don't worry about that, young lady, no harm done,' he said, picking it up off the floor, discarding the glass and replacing the picture back to where it had come from.

'Sorry, I guess I've just been a little jumpy lately,' Isla replied, taking a few steps back.

'Is that right? And why would that be?'

For a moment she felt like she should say something; since opening up to Will she felt all she wanted to do now was talk about it, but thought better of it and changed the subject back to the picture.

'So is that you then?' she asked, hoping that he didn't notice that she might have just been about to say something entirely different. If he had, he didn't show it.

'Oh, you mean the good-looking one?' He smiled; he didn't have his most recognisable feature – the scar, but Mr Stopes was a confident man, and scar or no scar Isla had the feeling he would have acted all the same.

Grabbing a cup, he motioned towards the kettle.

'Oh…' Isla paused, 'I think I am going to be late for curfew.'

'Curfew? It's not even late,' he said flippantly. 'Don't worry, you're with me, I'll smooth it over with the witch.' He coughed. 'I mean, Miss Sparrow.'

Shocked by his comment, Isla couldn't help herself from laughing, it was utterly inappropriate, but he didn't seem bothered by it, so she wouldn't be either.

She had never spent so much one-on-one time with Mr Stopes in all her years at the Manor. He was always around, attending to jobs in and around the house; she had helped him with tasks such as tonight before, but usually, this would have included others and she wouldn't have interacted with him as much.

'Well, okay then, if you insist,' Isla agreed, attempting to take the seat by the fire.

'I think you'll find that's my chair, missus. You'll be just fine in the one over there,' he said, pointing to the smaller armchair by the window.

She took her seat and Scampi jumped onto her lap. 'Where did you come from?' she said to the black and white feline. She was never overly fond of Scampi; however, today she welcomed the soft purring of the scatty cat.

Isla observed her surroundings as Mr Stopes busied himself making tea. He had a lot of clutter in his cottage: ornaments, pictures, books, lots of books, a big old armchair that looked as if it had seen better days, a tatty fur rug placed by the fire and low level lamps that gave it a homely feel.

The living room joined on to an open-plan kitchen, though bigger than what she thought, it was still cosy. The kitchen contained a mass of herbs and spices, some of which she had never seen or heard of before. There was a wooden chopping board, which looked like it still had the remains of whatever unfortunate animal had managed to cross paths with him, and a double Aga, where he stood now making tea for two.

He walked over and placed the teapot, two cups, two saucers and a plate of biscuits on the side table next to his chair. 'Thought you might like a little snack before bed – a thank-you for helping me out,' he said, gently pouring the tea.

'Well, I won't say no.' Having missed dinner, Isla was grateful for the offerings.

'What are you doing all the way over there? Bring your chair closer. I know it's spring, but the evenings still bring a bit of chill with it. Warm yourself up by the fire,' he said, ready to hand her a cup.

Isla nodded her appreciation and delved in for a biscuit simultaneously while moving her chair. 'So who is that in the picture with you?' she enquired with a mouth half full of one of Ms Pepperin's famous biscuits.

'A very dear old friend, one of the best,' he replied without hesitation.

'Well, you certainly look happy,' she commented, wiping crumbs from her mouth. 'And what are the cloaks for?'

'The cloaks? A kind of club, I guess you could say – one of a kind. They don't make them like that no more.'

Isla wasn't sure if he was talking about the cloak or the other man who occupied the picture. Still, she decided not to ask any further questions; she guessed she was not the only one who could have secrets.

Isla stayed for a little over an hour until the clocks sounded the time, signalling her leave. 'I must go,' she said, glancing at the clock. 'It's getting late.'

Mr Stopes shuffled in his seat. 'Agreed, else they'll have the wolves out searching for you, and never mind what will be looking for me,' he replied, picking up a torch.

'Thank you for the tea,' Isla started, 'and the biscuits, but I'll be fine to walk by myself – it's only a couple of minutes.'

'Precisely, a couple of minutes. You'll be doing an old man a favour and keeping me company for a bit of fresh air.'

Mr Stopes was far from old, older but not an old man by any means; middle-aged with sandy, greying hair, he had kept his physique and not all his looks had faded. The ladies of the village certainly seemed to like him, always going out of their way for him, bringing him food and cakes, and she could certainly see why now: he was charismatic, funny and full of stories.

Isla saw a different side to him tonight from what she had ever seen before. He had never been rude or unpleasant to her, but she felt he had always certainly been a bit harsher on her compared to the others when it came to the one lesson a week they had with him. A few years prior, the sisters had thought it would be a good idea if all the children learned how to be self-sufficient, so they set up a survival class that Mr Stopes taught one morning a week. Isla had to admit, she enjoyed it far more than she thought she would when they had first made the announcement, but despite her interest in some lessons, others bored her, and he was never overly impressed on these days, once keeping the whole class back until she had got it, which she had never understood.

Their short walk over, they arrived at the Manor to be met by Miss Sparrow as he opened the door.

'Children should not be up and about in the Manor past curfew, especially not walking the grounds at night,' she said sternly, with sharp amber eyes.

Mr Stopes raised his brows. 'Miss Sparrow, I would like to inform you she was with me the whole time and perfectly safe. I have even returned her in one piece.'

Miss Sparrow stared at him coolly. 'My office, please, Mr Stopes, I'd like a word.' She turned and started to walk towards her office. 'And bed for you,' she added.

Isla did as she was told and ran up the stairs as fast as she could; she looked down at Mr Stopes, who gave her a wink as he closed the door behind him. *I would not want to be in his shoes right now*, she thought to herself.

CHAPTER FOUR

'That's not your call to make, Mr Stopes,' she said as he stood staring out into the night.

'She senses something, Eliza, and call me Ed. We're not around the children now,' he replied, not taking his eyes off the window. His whole demeanour had changed since walking through the door; his presence was strong, calm, but all jokes were put aside.

'I prefer to keep it professional. Now, why would you think she senses something?' Miss Sparrow sounded exhausted, and he could tell.

Finally turning away from the window, locking eyes with the headmistress, he walked towards her desk. 'That young girl is not so young anymore; she's a clever cookie and she knows something is not right.'

'That does not mean anything to me. That's just a hunch, and I do not work on hunches, Mr Stopes,' she returned, taking her seat.

'My hunches have never proved me wrong before,' he replied, bearing over her.

'Let me ask you something, Mr Stopes, were you given

overall responsibility of the girl?' she retorted, having regained some of her strength.

'Goddamn it, Eliza, no one cares for that little one more than I do,' he bellowed, pacing the room in frustration. 'We need to tell her something before she finds out things for herself; she takes after her father, that one.'

Rising to her feet in anger, '*You* swore an oath,' she darted at him. 'Do not forget who you are talking to; you are only here because I allowed it. Do not let your personal guilt invade my duty of care and responsibility.'

'Your duty of care and responsibility is to acknowledge the things that are going on around you. Don't think I haven't noticed your disappearances of late. You are worried about something, which means if you are worried the council are too, and if it involves Isla it's time that she knew.'

'*Know your place*, Mr Stopes. You are here for one purpose and one purpose only. You're not my personal advocate and nor do you have a say on how I wish to conduct my business. I decide on what I see is best for the girl and will act in the way that I see fit that subsequently does not involve me breaking my oath.'

'We took that oath ten years ago, Eliza, and you know I sacrificed a lot to be here; it was my moral duty, and it still is my moral duty. But none of us could predict what would happen then, and if times are changing maybe we have to change with them,' he said more as a fact rather than with force.

Before he could wait for her reply, a familiar apparition appeared, and an awkward silence fell between them until Miss Sparrow spoke.

'I believe that is our meeting concluded, Mr Stopes. Now, if you have nothing further to say, I have prior engagements I need to attend to,' she said, walking towards the new addition in the room.

'Actually, I do have one other thing I'd like to add.'

'Yes!'

'That girl you refer so fondly to she has a name – her name is Isla, and I'd appreciate it if you used it.'

Miss Sparrow's back tensed as she mulled over the comment. 'Goodnight, Mr Stopes, close the door on your way out.'

CHAPTER FIVE

I sla waited in the darkness behind a small alcove at the top of the stairs, her partner in crime arriving before the clock had finished its strike at midnight.

'So how do you suppose we get in?' whispered Will.

'Leave that to me,' she replied, the corners of her mouth rising just a little.

'What do I not know about?'

Isla hesitated. 'I may have borrowed something from Mr Stopes' cottage that will help get us in.' She grinned, revealing a set of keys in her hand.

'You mean you stole, Isla, you stole something that can help get us in.'

'It's not stealing if you put it back, and I do intend to put it back.'

'That's not the point – you have taken something that doesn't belong to you. I don't like this,' Will maintained, trying to keep his voice to a whisper.

'Oh, and as if breaking into Miss Sparrow's office isn't already an offence. At least this way we're not breaking in.' She jangled the keys. 'We are simply letting ourselves in.'

'Isla, I love how you can try to justify anything.'

She looked at him with puppy-dog eyes, hanging off his arm. 'But Will, you promised. You said you'd help me figure out what's going on. You said you believed me.'

He sighed but didn't budge.

'But if you are chickening out, that's okay – you go back to bed and I'll go by myself.' This had the desired effect that Isla was looking for: the sensible type he was, but he also was not the type to back down from a challenge.

'This doesn't mean I agree with what we are doing – it's dishonest, it's wrong, it's breaking and entering.'

She cut him off and held up the keys.

'You know what I mean, but just so you know, I'm not doing this because I want to, I'm doing it to stop you from doing anything too stupid!'

'I know – now, are you ready?'

'Let's get this over and done with.' And he followed her down the stairs.

They need only try a couple of keys before they found the right one, slipped in and ensured they locked the door behind them. There was little light, so Isla went to switch them on, but Will intervened before she could.

'*Stop!* Do you want to let them know we are in here already? Just wait a few minutes, your eyes will adjust, then we can put a lamp on if need be.'

'Good idea – see, that's why I brought you along.' She smiled.

'Yeah, yeah, enough with the flattery. Now you've got me in here, what are we looking for?' Will asked, adjusting the curtain just enough so that the moonlight could slice through the gap.

'I don't know, just look for anything that doesn't look…' she paused, 'normal.'

'Not normal – how do you define that, Isla? Can I say we found you and leave?' Now it was his turn to grin.

'Very funny, you know what I mean. Just look around and see if there's anything that doesn't fit in. I'll start at the desk, and you check the bookcase.'

He did as he was told while Isla headed towards the desk; there was nothing on top that didn't look like it belonged there and the drawers were the same. Papers, reports, all very orderly, nothing looked out of place – that was until she reached the last one. Isla tried to pull it open, but it was locked. *That's strange.* Why have one locked drawer? Why not all of them or none of them? She checked to see if any of the keys she had unlocked it but wasn't surprised when none of them did.

'Will, come over here, I need to open this.'

After a few minutes' arguing over whether they should attempt it or not, Will eventually succumbed to Isla's persistence.

'Okay, give me your hairpin. My dad taught me a trick when I was younger, for if I ever got locked out the house.' He continued to mutter the story behind how he come to know how to break into a lock, when: 'There you go, done.' He stood up, rather proud of himself.

Isla bent down to open it. 'Empty,' she said in surprise. 'Why would it be empty? That's strange. I mean, why go through all that effort to lock a drawer and then keep it empty?' she questioned.

'Maybe she took out whatever was in there and through force of habit locked the drawer?' Will offered as an explanation.

'Mmmm, maybe.' Isla felt around in the drawer. 'And here's something I learned: there's always a reason for something, it's never nothing and if someone wants something hidden they will go to great lengths to hide it.' She continued to examine the corners of the drawer until her index finger had found what it was looking for, pulled it, and out popped the base of the drawer. Isla removed the fake lid and revealed the contents inside: vials of liquids and powders each of a varying colour, jewellery, a dagger and some black-and-white pictures. *Such odd things to have.* One by one she took them out and scattered them on the table – she started with the pictures first, they were of the same style that she had witnessed in Mr Stopes' cottage, the same trickery to the eye, which she found intriguing. One was of a group posing in front of a castle, one was of an elderly man by a fire, another of a couple with a baby. Miss Sparrow was in one of them too and the clothes they were wearing, just seemed – different.

'*Hey!*' She picked up one of the pictures. 'That's the same picture I saw in Mr Stopes' cottage – why would Miss Sparrow have the same one?' She went back to the group one. 'And this one – it's the same robes that they are wearing too.' She stopped, paused and picked up another one. It was quite old and the couple (if that's even what they were) were quite young, but there was no mistaking it. Scar-free, it was Mr Stopes and Miss Sparrow arm in arm, smiling.

Isla shoved it in Will's face. 'Look, I was always under the impression that they did not know each other before the Manor, and what's even more strange, look at Miss Sparrow's face – she's smiling.'

'Yeah, that bit is odd,' Will admitted. 'But focus, Isla, I think this is just a box of trinkets and memories that's nothing to do with us. What would any of this have to do with you?' He put down the picture and picked up the dagger, which was about ten inches long, silver, with tiny blue jewels embedded on the handle.

'What do you think of this?' he said, holding it up to her; Isla had been so engrossed in the pictures that she hadn't actually paid much attention to the other items until now. 'Much like the mirror, don't you think?'

'*Yes,* you are right – how could I be so stupid? The mirror, we haven't even looked at that.' Isla took the dagger off Will, remembering how enchanted she had been previously, and continued towards the mirror so that she could compare the two.

'I don't recall ever seeing this in here before, do you?' she questioned. 'Surely one of us would have noticed it at some point because it is not like Miss Sparrow to have such extravagant things.'

Isla did not think it was possible to be more amazed by it than she already was, but here she was, in awe and too occupied to notice the small changes that were happening within her hand.

'*Isla,*' Will hailed.

Instinctively she turned to look to where he was pointing and in shock sent the dagger clanging to the floor. 'What was that?' Isla said, looking at Will for reassurance, who apparently, by the blank look on his face, had none. The initial shock subsiding she picked it back up, only this time was prepared for what she was about to see.

'There must be some kind of sensor in it.' The jewels flickered a pale blue light.

'I think we should put it all back,' Will said, finding his voice again.

'No, not until I've looked at the mirror. You just said yourself we've not looked at it.'

Will huffed. 'Okay, fine, but then it all goes back – remember, this is not our stuff.'

'Well, come on then.'

She motioned and they both took a step closer, Will the first of the two to touch it. 'This really is quite something, I wonder where she got it from?'

Isla smiled to herself; clearly he was no longer worried about getting caught anymore.

They looked it up and down, round the back, examined every inch of it, but it offered no clue as to what Isla might be searching for.

'Okay, you win, we are not going to find anything here.'

'Isla, *stop!*'

'What?' She turned round to face him.

He pointed towards the mirror. 'Move your arm.'

'Why?' she said, somewhat confused.

'Just do it.'

She lifted her arm.

'No not that one, your other one, the one with the dagger.'

'What is it, Will?'

'I… well, I'm not actually sure.'

Impatient at Will's attempt at an explanation, Isla spun round to see for herself. At first, she did not notice what had caused his jaw to drop so far to the floor, but when she did, she was not far off the same reaction.

Wherever her arm was going, the mirror was following her; what had once been a solid firm pane of glass was now a molten marble surface that rippled like a current as she glided her hand across it.

'What is this?' Isla stared back at her distorted reflection, watching her face come in and out of focus. *Is this a dream?* In a daze, she felt as if the mirror was talking to her, willing her to do what she knew she shouldn't, but she couldn't resist. Curiosity got the better of her as she raised her hand; and slowly with the tip of her finger touched it, it wobbled like jelly, so she quickly pulled it away.

Is this real?

Undeterred, Isla tried again, but this time she did not hesitate: her finger went straight through, and the liquid marble clawed its way onto her skin, encasing her arm. She wasn't scared, it did not hurt, and nor did she try to stop it, for the call of the mirror was intoxicating. She was lost, her thoughts were lost, so much so that she didn't hear the voices as they approached and she didn't hear Will trying to get her attention; she couldn't hear anything other than the mirror enticing her.

CLICK!

Then it all stopped.

Isla was alerted to the sound of a key turning in the door and the sound of voices behind it; she quickly snapped her hand back, the mirror returning to its natural state: a solid piece of glass.

'Can't this wait till morning?' they heard Miss Sparrow's voice say.

They panicked; Will quickly put the contents scattered on the desk back in the drawer. Isla flustered and hid the dagger under a cushion, then together they dived behind the chairs just as the door opened.

'I'm afraid it can't,' said Mr Stopes, standing at the door. He followed her into the room, eyes darting from corner to corner as if he was in search of something. Isla and Will's hearts were beating so fast it was a wonder they couldn't hear them.

Isla pointed to the secret drawer's top. 'You didn't put it back,' she snarled at him.

'I didn't have time to,' Will defended.

As they continued to argue under hushed breath, they froze as Mr Stopes spotted them, but he didn't flinch; instead, he turned his attentions back to Miss Sparrow.

'Really, Mr Stopes, it's been a long night, not to mention day. I have nothing further to add to our previous conversation, it's almost 1am in the morning, I have some paperwork to do and I would really appreciate if this could wait until morning.'

'I promise it won't take long, but there is something I really think you should see, Eliza,' he said, taking her hand in his.

'Your charms are lost here, Mr Stopes,' she replied, agitated. 'But if I really must see it, then let's get it over and done with.' She took her coat off the coat stand, where Will had been standing only seconds before, picked up her keys and walked out the office.

'It will only take ten minutes, then I promise to have you back in your rightful place,' he said, loud enough for both Isla and Will to hear as the door was locked behind them.

CHAPTER SIX

'Happy birthday!' Isla woke up to three sets of eyes staring down at her.

'Sorry, we couldn't wait any longer.' Lexi beamed.

'Okay, okay, I'm awake.' She sat up in bed, her heart slowly regaining its natural rhythm and rubbed her eyes. 'What's all this? I don't usually have so much attention for my birthday.'

'Yes, but we thought we would do something special this year – just because we could,' Elizabeth said warmly.

'That's right,' Lexi agreed, and jumped on the bed with a thump. 'We have lots planned for you today, so I hope you got plenty of rest last night because you are going to need it.'

Isla thought about that: rest – she had been sneaking into Miss Sparrow's office at midnight, escaped certain capture had it not been for Mr Stopes and then spent the rest of the night pondering why he hadn't given them away. *What did he know?*

'Earth to Isla,' Sissie said, waving a hand in front of her face. 'Are you there?'

'Oh yes, sorry, I was just thinking... Never mind. So, what do we have here?' she asked, looking at the presents in their awaiting hands.

'Start with mine, please, please, please,' exhaled Lexi, bursting at the seams.

'Okay, pass it here – now, this is rather big.' Isla looked at the flat rectangle present wrapped in newspaper, wondering what it could be. As she opened it she saw the most beautiful drawing: it was of all four of them, and in the corner of it, it simply read "sisters".

'I know we are not really sisters, but we see you like one.'

'Did you do this all yourself, Lexi?'

'I sure did,' she declared, straightening her posture like she had just won an award.

'Yes, that's right, she had numerous attempts, all of which can be found discarded in the basement. Let's say she's been a bit of a distraction to me lately,' Sissie offered, giving her little sister a playful nudge at the same time.

'Do you like it?' Lexi asked hopefully.

'Oh, I love it,' Isla confirmed, holding it to her chest. 'You are very talented.'

'Okay, my turn,' said Sissie, and all three girls sat down on the bed. They spent the next half hour exchanging presents and stories and memories about past birthdays, which had not always gone to plan. Mainly the disaster that happened at Elizabeth's last birthday when everyone had fallen ill and she ended up nursing them all back to health when she should have been celebrating her own birthday. Jimmy Jameson had also vomited all down her brand-new dress, which was horrifying at the time, but they laughed about it now – well, they did; Elizabeth didn't.

They got dressed and went down to breakfast, where Isla received more congratulations, cards and other small gestures. They did not have much money, as it was rarely a thing given to the children in the Manor; however, many of them had gone to the effort to either make or buy something with the little that they had, which Isla was greatly overwhelmed by.

'Oh, come here, my cherry pie.' This was what Ms Pepperin often called the children of the Manor, especially when she was about to give them one of her big, motherly hugs. She took Isla and squeezed her into her arms as tightly as she could. 'Oh, my little darling is growing up. Well, I never. When you first arrived here all those years ago, you didn't speak a word for months, and now look at you.' She took Isla's cheeks into her hands and stood back to marvel her face. 'Such an understated beauty.'

Isla had never been called a beauty before, or an understated one at that; in fact, she wasn't quite sure what she meant by that at all. Other than her exceptionally pale skin that failed to attract even the slightest sun during the summer, Isla felt she looked rather ordinary. Her medium to light brown hair was something of a common nature, and the colour of her eyes did not fare too far either, though hazel would have probably been a more accurate description. Her nose stuck out just enough to know that it was there and her lips, perhaps a little too visible for her liking, framed a wide smile with just a hint of a dimple (which for reasons even unbeknown to herself she did not like).

Ms Pepperin hugged her once more, and as Isla walked away she thought she heard her say, 'They would be so proud.' She really hoped she wasn't talking about her parents, for if there was anything she hated more, it was being reminded that she didn't have any. Which coincidently was what every birthday did, but they were no longer here, that was that, end of story to Isla.

Sitting down for breakfast, it was the same as usual, but what wasn't the same was how much attention Isla received, she was only turning fifteen, which to her understanding was not a significant milestone and did not warrant such treatment. However, by the time breakfast was over Isla realised she had not given anything else a second's thought and the distraction was somewhat welcomed.

'Has anyone seen Will?' she asked the group; he was yet to show himself and it was not like him to miss a meal.

'Ah, don't you worry, he'll be around, or have the two of you had another argument?' Jimmy Jameson teased her.

There was a time when she couldn't understand a word that he said; blue-eyed, brown-haired, baby-faced Jimmy Jameson from Belfast was a hell-raiser. He arrived a few years ago and instantly formed a friendship with Rudy, a Scottish boy, who until he had arrived had been quite shy. As it turns out he was just as mischievous as he was, and an alliance of practical jokes and general trouble-making was formed, and the pair were inseparable.

'You might want to check he hasn't done a runner, Isla,' said Rudy in a thick Scottish accent. 'Maybe he thought you were getting too much attention for your birthday.'

Isla laughed the comment off, but maybe without knowing it, he had a point. *Was what happened last night too much for him?* She hadn't seen him since they left Miss Sparrow's office, which they had done so quickly, and had barely said a word to one another. Now she had not seen him all morning, which worried her.

Before she had the chance to look for him though, Isla was sent to her room, where she was told very firmly by Lexi to occupy herself until further notice, so of course she did not disobey. However, as late morning turned to afternoon with still no word from anyone, she wondered if they had all forgotten about her – that was until Elizabeth turned up.

'You ready for your surprise now?'

Isla shot to attention. 'Yes.' Anything to save her from her own thoughts. She followed Elizabeth down the stairs, who, before they got to the door, gave her an envelope.

'What's this?'

'No need to look so worried.' Elizabeth smiled. 'It is your birthday.'

'Sorry, I just wasn't expecting it, that's all – all of this, you know.'

Elizabeth returned a comforting, knowing gaze. 'It's from Will.'

'From Will?' Isla felt a flutter; he hadn't forgotten about her after all.

'He said you would know where to go, so I'll leave you to it.' Elizabeth nodded towards the envelope then left.

Isla waited until she'd completely disappeared before holding her breath, and daring not to release it until she had read every single word, but as her eyes cast over the first few sentences, Elizabeth was indeed right: Isla knew exactly where to go.

Just below the horizon on the highest point of the furthest place that they were allowed to go stood a lone chestnut tree. Very few frequented it, for most could not be bothered with the long walk or were simply not bothered by a chestnut tree at all; however, back in the early days it had become their salvation and a place where they would go to live momentarily in their own little world. A young boy and a young girl who had had their lives turned upside down finding peace in the company of each other.

Isla ran as fast as her legs would carry her and did not stop until she had reached her destination. She had never felt so unnerved and wanted to make sure that Will was okay, to make sense about what had happened the night before, but more importantly, now more than ever she wanted to let him know that she was thankful, thankful for their friendship, because he was the one that no matter what she put him through was always there and, she hoped, always would be.

Out of breath, she came to a halt; dirt lined the hem of her dress, the one that Elizabeth had insisted she wore – Elizabeth had also insisted that she do something special to her hair. Patiently, piece by piece, she had pinned it up, flattering Isla's oval face, but her efforts were short-lived, for the precisely pinned curls had fallen out and she was now sporting an entirely different hairstyle, one that Isla was sure Elizabeth had not intended.

Isla took a deep breath, recalling every sight, sound and memory she had ever had of this place. She couldn't remember exactly when the last time was that she had been there, but the nostalgia was overwhelmingly comforting and made her wonder why they, or perhaps she, had stopped visiting a place that had meant so much to them. It was in this reverie an even older memory came flooding back to the surface, not because she remembered it but because she heard it:

> "Down by the tree, is where I'm going to be
> Please say you'll meet me down by the tree
> Everything is fine, if you say you're mine
> Down by the tree is where I'm going to be
> Please say you'll meet me down by the tree
> Down by the tree, is where I will be."

'I can't believe you remembered that,' Isla said, surprised. 'How long has it been?'

'About six years.'

'Has it been that long?'

'Yes,' said Will, holding a small parcel in his hand. 'Happy birthday, Isla.' He smiled softly.

But Isla didn't smile back. 'I'm sorry, Will,' she said, not taking the offering. 'This is all just a bit much, so much fuss for my birthday, I don't understand why – it's just all a bit too much for me.'

'See, this is why I wanted to bring you here first. I didn't want you to ruin your own birthday.'

'What do you mean?'

'I know you, Isla, I know you've been thinking about last night, letting it play over and over again in your mind, thinking up stories, coming to conclusions.'

'No, I haven't,' she snapped back.

He gave her a look, knowing this was precisely what she would have been doing.

'So what?' she said defensively, arms folded.

He examined her tenderly, his soft chocolate brown eyes surveying her. 'Sometimes you've just got to let things go.'

Isla suddenly dropped to the ground, knowing she could not lie to him. There was no point, not anymore, not now that he knew the truth. 'But what if I can't, Will?'

He sat down next to her, the sound of grass crunching beneath his hands. 'Do you remember when we first arrived? It was your birthday and you wouldn't talk to anyone – six years old and you already had a mind and, dare I say it, an attitude of your own.'

Isla looked at him in recognition of the memory, but took no offense.

'The sisters had done all they could to make you feel at home: they made you a chocolate cake, everyone sang happy birthday and when the cake was put down in front of you, you just stared at it; you didn't even blink.'

'I remember, but I had just lost everything that was known to me, so I think I can be forgiven for not wanting to celebrate.' She was deliberately being sarcastic, and he knew it. She also refrained from referring to her parents directly, and he made a mental note not to either, not on today of all days.

'Okay, maybe you're right, but what happened after that?'

'You mean the part where you came running out of the kitchen with a massive slab of cake and one of the sisters chasing after you?' Isla smirked; she remembered the look on the sister's face when she'd finally caught up with him flustered, shouting all manner of things, but in the end, had reluctantly left the cake when she saw Isla.

The irony was not lost on her: he had made such a fuss about breaking into Miss Sparrow's office; however, at almost seven, years of age he had not batted an eyelid about breaking into the kitchens and stealing a piece of chocolate cake. But that was just Will: full of surprises, even now.

'You still didn't talk to me though. I couldn't make you, no matter how hard I tried. It was weeks before you spoke to me, and when you finally did, what was the first thing you said to me again?'

Isla smiled. 'Idiot.'

'Yes, you did, that's right. I've not forgotten that, by the way.' He laughed. 'But did you ever wonder why I tried so hard to talk to you in the first place?'

Isla shrugged her shoulders. Truth be told she had not given it much thought; she presumed he was just as lonely as she was, and they were both new at the Manor.

'I never understood what my mother had meant by people having auras – that was until I met you.'

'Auras?'

'Yes. It's a colour, or rather an energy that surrounds a person, tells you a bit about their personality – are they warm, cold, loving, angry? That sort of thing.'

'So you see colours?'

'Well, not so much see – I feel it; I feel your energy. You are built for something great, Isla, you truly are, and one day you will see that too, but until you figure out what that greatness is, don't shut yourself off from the world.'

Isla could see where he was going with this speech now; she did not quite understand the greatness part, but that was just Will, taking things over the top. She understood the message, though. She had been so tense, so isolated, and with good reason, but in doing so, she had lost a part of herself, or her aura, as Will would have put it.

'You trusted me then, so trust me now. Let it go. I am not the only one to notice your distance either, the others' have too. It was Lexi's idea to make such a fuss for your birthday and you wouldn't want to let her down now would you? Just for one day, forget about everything else that goes on in that little head of yours and enjoy yourself, give yourself permission to have fun. You remember what fun is, right?' He dug around in the soil until he found what he was looking for: two stones no bigger than a small coin, perfectly smooth. He brushed them off and passed one to her. 'One for you and one for me; as long as we each have one, we will always have each other.'

This was possibly the best present that he could have given her: reassurance that she was not alone, that no matter what he would indeed always be there and no matter what, parents or no parents, she had a family.

He held out his little finger; Isla reciprocated, holding hers out too. They linked fingers and leant in towards one another.

'Always,' they said together. For always they had never been apart.

Isla's surprise had been a party, and one that had gone off with great success. Much to Will's reassurance, Isla had relaxed and indeed enjoyed her day; now everyone had exhausted themselves they were heading back to the Manor for a much-needed late supper.

'I'll meet you there – I've just got something I need to do quickly,' Isla informed the others.

'Okay, but I can't promise they'll be any cake left. I'm ready for seconds,' Lexi announced.

'Me too,' Jimmy Jameson agreed.

'That's okay, you go ahead, just make sure you share.' The two looked at each other, positively sure there would be nothing to share once she returned.

Isla walked tentatively towards Mr Stopes' cottage; she had never turned up unannounced before and wondered how he would receive her, especially after what had happened the night before.

Her heart thumped so loud it practically knocked on the door itself, and as she stood there nervously waiting for him to open it, she already regretted her decision. *What if he doesn't want to see me?* But too late: the door had already swung on its hinges. *Nowhere to run now, Isla.*

He invited her in. She couldn't read his expression: was he mad? Angry? Sad? None of the above?

'No need to look so nervous,' he said, returning with what now felt like their customary pot of tea.

'I'm not nervous,' Isla said, more defensively than she had intended to.

'Okay,' Mr Stopes replied, holding his hands up in surrender. 'But call me Ed, please. We're not in lessons now, so I think that would be okay.' He took his seat and poured their drinks. 'So to what do I owe this honour?'

'Honour?'

'Why are you here?' he explained further.

Isla swallowed; he wasn't going to make this easy. 'I… well… sort of…' *Get a grip.* 'The thing is…' *Deep breath.* 'Miss Sparrow's office.' She paused awkwardly.

'What about it?' He raised an eyebrow, sipping his tea. 'You mean the breaking-in part?'

Isla cringed.

'Well, I must say it would have been quite a shock to see the two of you in there if I hadn't already seen you sneak in there earlier, which I'm sure you have a perfectly good explanation for?' He raised another inquisitive eyebrow.

Isla wasn't sure how to respond. *How much does he know?* He didn't give anything away, so she felt quite unnerved.

'Well… umm… we…' She fumbled for the right words until a brainwave made her almost shout poor Mr Stopes off his seat. '*It was a dare!*' She lowered her tone. 'You know, before my birthday, it was a stupid one, but…' She trailed off, not knowing what else to say.

'Hmmm, well, I must say I struggle to see William ever taking part in a *dare* such as that.' He made a point to highlight the word dare.

'Well, that may not have been the only reason.' *Shut up, Isla.* 'But we didn't take anything, I promise – it was all my idea. I forced Will into it,' Isla blurted out. *Stop saying so much.*

'I thought as much.' He rubbed his chin. 'He's very fond of you, William is. Good friends are not easy to come by, Isla.' At the mention of his name she squeezed the stone that he had given her earlier; Will was right – she could feel him there with her. Mr Stopes was also right – good friends were not easy to come by.

'Soooo, does this mean we…' she corrected herself, 'I am in trouble? Are you going to tell Miss Sparrow?'

Mr Stopes guffawed. 'If I was going to tell her, I would have let her catch you two red-handed and save me a job. No is your answer to that, but I trust you won't be so reckless again.' He winked.

'No, I promise.' Isla gave her best impression of a scout's honour salute, even though she wasn't sure if she was doing it correctly, for she had never taken part in any sort of group like that before.

'SO,' he clapped his hands together, 'now that's out of the way, how was your birthday?'

Somewhat perplexed by the sudden change of subject, but also very relieved that it appeared there would not be any repercussions for their sleuthing antics, Isla happily went along with the new line of questioning. 'It was great, thank you. I'm not sure what I have done to deserve it, but really, they have all outdone themselves, and to keep it a secret even more so – I had no idea.' Isla continued to reel off the events of the day, down to the tiniest detail, from the food, the decorations to the presents. 'Oh, and they even organised a treasure hunt, though I am not sure that was entirely for my benefit, but still.'

'No?'

'I'm sure Sissie and Lexi would have been behind that one – they love problem-solving, Sissie especially.'

'And you don't?'

'Well, I would rather not have any problems to solve,' Isla said, thinking her response was quick-thinking and witty; however, Mr Stopes did not seem to agree, for he stood up abruptly and walked towards the window. *What now?*

From where Isla sat she could see that dusk had arrived quickly during the short time that she had been inside his cottage, for the sky was now a deep red and Mr Stopes looked a solemn figure against the crimson backdrop that seemed to match his sudden change in mood. His hands were rested on the countertop, and she could see the rise and fall of his chest as he took in long, lengthy breaths.

'Are you okay?'

'Yes, I'm fine, but come join me, Isla.'

She wasn't sure what to make of his sudden change of demeanour. *Was it something I said?*

He appeared to be battling with himself but finally spoke, choosing not to look at her as he did. 'Life's full of secrets and many hidden treasures, Isla. Some will remain lost forever, but some, some want to be found,' he had something within his hand, which he pushed towards her. 'Happy birthday,' he said gently. 'I think it's time now.'

Isla looked down at a small-laced handkerchief; it was old and musty and not present-like at all, but a present it was meant to be. Something caught her eye, and she could just about make out the same crest that she had seen in the pictures that were both in Miss Sparrow's office and Mr Stopes' cottage. Isla opened the lace and revealed a heart-shaped necklace inside; she touched it and momentarily a vision of it hung around a women's neck entered her head. *Have I seen this before?*

'I don't understand?' Isla said, confused; it really was beautiful but looked far too expensive a gift, especially from a caretaker to a student. 'Why are you giving me this?'

'Sometimes we have to go with our gut feeling, the same gut feeling that led you to Miss Sparrow's office and the same gut feeling that is making me pass this on to you.' He turned to face her; he looked as if a burden weighed heavily upon him. 'Sometimes we have to set our own path, even if there are people telling us we shouldn't. The hardest thing we can do sometimes is to go against the wind, but even the wind can change its course.'

He was speaking in riddles; Isla had no idea what he meant, and Mr Stopes saw her confusion. He clasped both his hands round hers and spoke. 'I have watched you grow from a child to a strong, independent young lady. If there are answers that you seek, find them.' And he closed her hands with the necklace inside.

Isla had no idea what to say; she had never heard him speak this way before, yet every word he spoke somehow resonated with her, and she had no idea why. He released his grip and stepped back. 'It's getting dark – you should probably return to the Manor now.' He forced a smile.

'Umm. Okay, yes, thank you.' There was so much she wanted to question him about on this overly exuberant gift and why he had given it to her, but at the same time she felt like it already belonged to her. *Which is impossible.*

Isla picked up her bag and checked that he was not looking before she reached inside and pulled out the keys, the other reason for her visit that evening.

'Just leave them on the table by the door.'

Isla froze. *How did he know? Did he know all along?* But now was not the time to ask any more questions; she did as she was told and dared one more glance at him before she closed the door.

CHAPTER SEVEN

Isla woke the next morning with more questions than answers, yet she still felt a sense of clarity, a newfound direction.

She opened her drawer and pulled out the ancient-looking lace. She ran her fingers tenderly across the crest, wondering what it stood for, and couldn't shrug off the feeling that there was a sense of familiarity about it.

'What ya doing?' Lexi jumped up from behind her.

She jolted and quickly hid the necklace under her pillow. 'Just thinking how lucky I am to have family like you.'

'Well, I know that,' Lexi said.

'No, I mean it, you are very precious to me – you all are. You do know that, don't you?' Isla said, suddenly very serious.

'Are you okay?' Lexi quizzed, eyeing her cautiously.

'I'm fine.' Isla smiled, easing the built up tension in her features. 'I just want you to know, that's all, and no matter what, I will never ever forget you.'

'You are talking as if you are going somewhere; you know you don't have to leave; now they raised the age limit, right? Elizabeth is still here – in fact, I don't think she will ever leave.'

Isla pulled Lexi into a hug. She had to admire her innocence; Lexi had no idea the things that had been going on with her, and there was no reason why she should. 'I know, I just wanted you to know. Is that okay?'

Elizabeth arrived at the door along with Grace, interrupting their conversation. 'Come on, we have to be quick, we're told our lesson with Mr Stopes has been changed to today as Miss Bugglesworth is unwell.'

'Probably all the cake she ate yesterday,' Lexi commented. 'Did you see how much she had?' Lexi demonstrated with her hands and pulled a funny face, puffing her cheeks out.

'Come on, you.' Isla laughed, ushering Lexi off her bed. 'Time to get moving.'

As the day's lesson had not been planned, they all got stuck in, with Mr Stopes quick to do the organising and delegating of his never-ending list of things to do.

Isla had hoped that being busy would have been a good distraction like it had proven to be the day before, but only this time it didn't work – because this time yesterday, she didn't have the necklace. So while everyone was preoccupied she snuck off towards the place where she was sure she would be left alone.

The door closed with a heavy thud, making her jump. She cursed herself for being so skittish and briefly rested against it. 'Hello,' she called out to no one in particular, then peeled herself off, walking towards the four sets of eyes now staring back at her.

'What?' she said as if she had just been rumbled. 'Am I not allowed to come visit you?' She knew what they were thinking: *You've not visited us for a while. You don't speak to us anymore.* And she felt guilty; if they could talk, that would have been a fair assumption. And she had no excuse for it either – that's what made their disappointing gazes feel even worse.

'I promise to make the effort, okay?' She directed this mostly towards Lancelot, a pure white thoroughbred who was particularly stubborn and would not forgive her negligence so easily.

Isla loved horses; she loved spending her time with them and she loved these four horses in particular, even Lancelot with his uneven temperament. They understood her more than most humans ever would, and she made a mental note that despite how she was feeling, they, her innocent companions, should not have to suffer.

Adjacent to Lancelot the stubborn was Bernie, the youngest and the most energetic of the four, and a complete contrast to his sister, Ash, who was named aptly after her colour. Then there was Sorrow, Isla's favourite, the oldest but by no means the slowest; she was strong yet calm and still had speed.

'How's my favourite girl today?' Sorrow stuck her head out from the stable door; Lancelot huffed and turned his back on her, his hoofs moodily scrapping the concrete. 'Sorry I haven't been around for a while, girl,' she whispered, stroking her mane. Isla drew a deep breath in; she missed her smell and the smooth touch of her golden coat. Sorrow instantly reciprocated the affection, nuzzling down into her neck, flicking her hair – her way of saying that she had missed her too.

It was an embrace that Isla had very much needed, but she had barely had the peace of ten minutes before she heard the handle to the stable door lift up off its hinges and the door swing open.

'Said she would be in here,' she heard Will say.

'Indeed, well, it's almost break time, you two had better make a move,' Mr Stopes instructed, picking up a trowel.

'Can I stay?' Isla replied, stroking Sorrow's nose. 'Please?'

He looked at her and then at Will. 'Why don't the two of you go out for a ride? It will give me a chance to muck out their stables, plus they haven't been out in a few days – that will be two things off my to do list.'

'Really?' Isla's face brightened. 'I thought we were not—'

He cut her off and tapped a finger to his nose. 'I won't tell if you don't, plus you're both experienced riders, so you'll be fine. Just take them long enough to get their joints moving and be back before the class ends.'

'Of course, we'll be sensible, I promise.' Isla unhooked Sorrow from her stable, bringing her out into the sunshine, and took no time in setting off. It had been a while since Isla had felt the wind through her hair at this speed and it was the first time in a long time Will had seen her so happy.

'Come on, slow coach,' she shouted, the wind slicing through her words, muffling them so Will could not hear.

'Just you wait till next time,' Will challenged breathlessly when he finally caught up. 'We won't be so kind to you.' He slipped himself off Bernie and left him free to graze on the grass for a well-earned snack, then walked towards Isla, intending to help her off, but as he did he tripped on an upturned root, causing Sorrow to flinch and subsequently Isla to fall down clumsily on top of Will, where together they tumbled down the hill.

They came to an abrupt stop, both laughing uncontrollably, Will's hair tousled, looking like he had just rolled out of bed, and Isla's even worse, for it had almost completely fallen out of its one singular plait. They laughed some more until their bellies hurt and untangled themselves, lying side by side so that the warmth of the mid-morning sun was beating down on them.

'There's no hiding them,' Will said, poking at her playfully.

'Don't!' Isla said coyly.

He was referring to her dimples, to which she unsuccessfully tried swatting him away. 'Hey!' He caught her hand in his and leaned closer, too close for Isla's comfort.

'What? What is it?' she asked quickly.

Will paused. 'Hmm.' Then he laid back down.

Isla perched up on her side, staring at him, waiting for an explanation.

'I've never noticed before, that's all.'

'Noticed what?'

'Your eyes.'

'What do you mean?'

'Maybe it's the sun, but they just looked a little green.'

'And now?' She stared at him intently. 'What are they now?'

He looked at her; they were close, just a breath apart, closer – was his heart beating faster? He coughed and quickly pulled away. 'Brown, they're brown,' he said hastily.

Isla sat back, disappointed. She didn't know what she was expecting; she thought maybe it might have been significant, but then she was reading a lot into a lot of things lately, and she couldn't be sure what was and what wasn't. Anyway, what the colour of her eyes may or may not be wasn't important; what was important was the tiny object that she had been carrying around with her all day.

'Will.'

'Yes.'

'Can I show you something?'

He sat up, giving Isla his full attention.

'After the party last night, I went to see Mr Stopes.' She paused, waiting to see if he was going to comment, but he didn't. 'I was worried that he might have said something or might be going to say something to Miss Sparrow,' she added for clarification.

'I am sure he would have said something that night if he was going to. I'm surprised as you are he didn't, but hey, I'm not complaining, and I am not going to rock the boat by asking. You shouldn't either.'

'Well, I did, and he didn't seem surprised or annoyed that we had been in there – in fact, he saw us go in there and never stopped us. It was like he wanted us to.'

'Why would he want that?'

'I don't know, but that's not what I wanted to talk to you about – look.' Isla handed over the necklace.

'Where did you get this from?' Will enquired, but by the look on Isla's face he could guess. 'He gave this to you?'

Isla nodded, confirming his suspicions.

'But why?'

'A birthday present, he said – well, at least that's what I understood.'

'An overly expensive birthday present.' Will had a good look before handing it back to her. 'Remind you of something else?'

Isla returned a look of acknowledgement that she too had indeed thought the same.

'Do you think they're connected?'

'I don't know, but I am going to find out.'

Will sat up, suddenly turning very serious, wishing he had not asked the last question. 'Isla, do you not feel that you should leave well enough alone? Last time was a lucky escape.'

'Yes, but—'

'You said the dreams stopped, right?'

'Yes.'

'And the strange feeling of someone watching you – has that gone too?'

Isla thought about it; she had not seen or felt anything since the time down the pond. 'Well, not for a week or so.'

'So then I am saying this for your own good: please, leave it alone.' Will was not saying this to cause friction or because he didn't care; it was because he cared, too much.

'So you think I made it all up?'

'No, I didn't say that, Isla. I just think that if it has stopped, then why pursue it? You said yourself it made you feel uncomfortable – scared, even. So isn't it a good thing that you are no longer seeing these things or having weird dreams?'

Will was right; why did she feel the need to keep persuing it? She had got what she wanted: the strange occurrences had stopped and her eyes were no longer deceiving her.

'If it happens again I'll be here. I don't know what we will do, but we'll do it together. However, until then can we just enjoy the summer? This will be one of our last.' He was referring to the fact that it wouldn't be long until they would both move on and would have to leave the Manor and make way for actual children.

Isla decided to drop it; she shouldn't have expected him to understand. He had done his best, and if he had seen or felt the things that she had, he would have felt differently, she was sure of it, but he hadn't. As much as it frustrated her, she knew that he was only doing what he thought was right for her. She made a decision right there and then to not get him involved any further, not to get anyone else involved; it may have calmed down for now, but something told her that this was not the end of it.

Will was relieved that Isla didn't kick up a fuss and accepted what he said; all he wanted was his friend back, and it seemed to him that just might be exactly what he was getting.

'It suits you, you know.'

'What?'

'The necklace – it would suit you. Are you not going to wear it?'

'Oh.' She automatically put her hand to her neck. 'Later on, perhaps. Come on, think we better head back now.' Isla signalled for Sorrow, who diligently obliged. They both jumped up on their horses, with no accidental falls this time, and rode the whole way back in silence; the silence that Isla felt was only the calm before the storm.

CHAPTER EIGHT

'It's been ten years. A week since her birthday, she is now of age and there has been no sign of any changes – I say we should let our men rest. Too long have they fared far from their families,' came the voice of a man short in stature but not in presence.

'I don't think any of us disagree with you, Lord Lestrone. However, she does not know who she is, and we cannot take for granted his determination to find her.'

'Yes, you're right, Lord Teline,' said Miss Sparrow, addressing the room. 'I agree with you. We all knew this day would come – she is of the age of enlightenment, but without her pendant, this cannot be fulfilled. We can assume her safety for a little while longer; however, we cannot take for granted his determination to find her. This is an unknown path we walk now. We've all witnessed what unfathomable devastation he is capable of, some more than others.' She nodded her head in acknowledgement to a redheaded lady sat on the far side of the room, who in turn returned the gesture. 'It's too early to tell. We appreciate your men, Lords Lestrone, Havenray and Clementine.' She nodded to each man individually. 'They have continued to uphold the king's oath, and enough gratitude can never be repaid.'

'*This is ridiculous*,' shouted Lestrone, rising from his seat. His leather-bound cape and white fur hood flew ferociously into the air as his arms raised in protest. 'We have honoured our oath and more – many of my men have not seen their children, their wives, for years, and some have never even met their children. Yet they have still done their duty. You talk about gratitude – what gratitude have you shown them? We kept what little men we could to protect our own, but many towns have fallen over the years, and only Lestoris stands now. Too many years I have left my own people to suffer, but I will no more.' He sat back down in his seat, the colour slowly draining from his face, clearly exhausted from his unexpected outburst.

Lestrone, with his sunken eyes, broad nose and greying hair, was a man of honour, a warrior in his day, but he was getting old now, too old to fight in any battle. He knew his days were numbered, and though he still looked a man of authority, by night, his body suffered from whatever illness was betraying him. And while he managed to keep up some appearances, his trimmed facial hair did little to disguise his leathery pale skin and broken veins. However, where his body had failed him, his mind had not, and if there was one thing he could do before he died, he would return as many of his men to their families as he could.

'He's right,' said another who had been silent until now; his name was Learhorn, a leader of a small yet strong clan of men. He was sat with his associate; both were tall, tanned and broad, with Roman noses and long dark hair to match their masculine physique. Learhorn's hair, however, had the addition of two plaits that fell free either side, signalling his higher position within the clan.

'We should be using Isla to our advantage. If she holds so much power, why have we kept her away for so long? We should be enhancing her, making her stronger – I say we use her to our advantage and free ourselves from the darkness once and for all.' The words lingered for a few moments, this thought perhaps having crossed others' minds in the years that had passed.

'*That* is not an option; I will not allow that. I repeat: *I will not allow it.* Only I was given the grace from the king as her guardian. I swore to protect his kingdom and in so doing his daughter. I do not want to sever the good relations we have between this council; however, if you or any other jeopardise this kingdom or his daughter and bring onslaught to our lands, I will hold no shame in doing what I see is right.' As stern as ever, Miss Sparrow stared her company down.

With this there was uproar: men stood from their seats, shouting at one another, taking opposing sides. Fingers were pointed, arms were flung, fists were shaken; it lasted a couple of minutes until a piercing ringing could be heard in the room, forcing them all to cover their ears and look in one direction.

The redheaded woman Miss Sparrow had addressed earlier was sat poised in her chair; she wore a simple green dress with a golden trim, which, close up, held a very delicate hand-stitched pattern. Draped over her left shoulder flowed a golden cape that skimmed her body to form a puddle on the floor. All eyes were drawn to her, though they were not interested in her hair or what she was wearing; it was the now illuminous glow that shone from her hands and the obvious conductor of the melodic chime in the room. She did not speak until everyone had silenced themselves.

'It is not the fate of one man, woman or child to salvage our world from the devastating depths it has fallen to. We all had a part to play in its demise. Either too greedy, ignorant or idle to realise the powers that grew within, too blind to notice when they surfaced. We took for granted what we stood up against until it was too late. And that is not a mistake I shall ever make again. Now is not the time to attack each other; a shift has already begun.' She rose with purpose, her angular jaw and fierce eyes penetrating those that dared meet her eye; it was easy to see she was a woman of command. She was a cousin of Lord Clementine – they looked so alike they could have passed for brother and sister; however, she was his advocate, a strategist and a fighter. She possessed both warrior and pure blood, which made her quite a formidable force.

'We cannot burden one *child* with the weight of our world; one that she does not even know exists.' She emphasised the child part, pausing, her face softening. Then Miss Sparrow heard her speak the words she hoped she would never have to hear.

'Though I fear it will not take her long to find out.'

CHAPTER NINE

Everything had returned back to normal: the decorations taken down, the birthday cards put away. Talk had turned to summer, and the normal schedule resumed. Except Isla did not feel normal.

Since her last chat with Will, they had not spoken about what had happened; that was because there was nothing to talk about. Her dreams had ceased completely, and she no longer felt the eerie presence that someone was watching or following her. The only evidence that any of it had been real – or real to her, at least – was the item that lay under carefully positioned books.

She had thought of many places of where to hide her newly acquired item; she had even considered wearing it but didn't want to risk bringing attention to herself. She had thought of hiding it under her bed, but that was too obvious; then her secret snug, but she felt uneasy about it being so far away. In the end, she had settled on the drawer next to her bed, as no one had any need to go in there and it was easily accessible for the moments she dared to take a look.

Today was one of those days.

Isla had decided to return to her room in between lessons; having seen the other occupants all busy with their own individual tasks she felt quite confident that she would not be disturbed. Lexi was playing with the other younger children, Elizabeth was assisting one of the sisters, and Sissie – well, she wasn't quite sure what she was doing, but she seemed rather preoccupied with a pile of books and some rather questionable-looking ingredients.

Shuffling herself until she had reached optimum comfort, Isla finally settled onto the cushions that lined the bay window. Staring out to the haze of blue and green, fondling her necklace absentmindedly, Isla mulled over the weeks that had passed and her feeling of complete isolation, even when she was in a room full of people. She had thought on a few occasions to perhaps go back and speak to Mr Stopes and ask precisely what he had meant by finding answers – was she meant to be doing something, and if so, what?

But every time she made the walk down to his cottage, her courage soon depleted, and she would talk herself out of it. Therefore, this meant the only interaction they had had was in his weekly classes, where she was treated no different and he had acted no different, Mr Stopes was his usual charismatic self, and the necklace was never mentioned again.

Isla felt at a loss of what to do: should she just forget everything that had happened? Save the necklace as a nice trinket, which she might look back on with fond memories in years to come? It would surely make life easier. She imagined that's what Will would say to her anyway – well, he'd as good as said that. But surely not. Surely there was a reason, right? Or was she just hoping there was?

Isla had never been unhappy at the Manor, yet she had never felt complete; there was always a part of her that felt lost. Would this lead to the missing piece of her own puzzle?

Isla had been so deep in thought that she had not noticed

Lexi calling her until she felt a tap on her shoulder. 'Isla, are you there?'

'Huh?' She looked up.

'What's that you're holding? It looks pretty.'

Isla looked down at her hand and quickly put it inside her pocket. 'Ah, nothing, just a present.'

'It looked like a really nice present. Did Will get you that?'

'For me? Um, no, it was just a gift,' Isla replied evasively, not sure what to say; however, luckily Lexi did not pursue her line of questioning any further.

'What are you doing here, anyway?' Isla changed the subject.

Lexi giggled. 'Well, it is my room.'

'Yes, sorry, I mean, why are you not outside playing with the others?'

'Break time is over, silly. It finished fifteen minutes ago. I've been sent to retrieve you immediately,' she said, standing to attention as if she had successfully delivered her information like a soldier.

'It's over?' Isla looked at the clock on the wall; it was small but certainly not unnoticeable. She couldn't believe she had been sat there for almost forty-five minutes; it had only felt like five.

'Mrs Bugglesworth said that you are to come immediately.'

'Of course, I'm coming now.'

'I'm sorry I am late, Mrs Bugglesworth,' Isla confessed straight away; she had thought about trying to just slip in and hope to go unnoticed, but that was pointless seeing as the door to the classroom was at the front and Lexi was also with her.

'Yes, yes, just sit down. Ms Pepperin will be assisting us today. Now, Isla, as you are behind, please can you go to the back of the class so she can set you up with the items that you need. You will also stay behind if you are unable to finish.' Isla had barely put her books on her desk before she was ushered to the back of the room, where an array of materials, scissors, ribbons and string lay on the table.

Isla had come to learn over the years that her education at Morsely Manor was somewhat different from what was taught at conventional schools. Well, certainly from what she had heard and seen from the local children. They occasionally visited the villages around them, for mostly what was educational outings or local volunteering projects, and had never ventured any further than a ten-mile radius. The only one she had ever known to go further was Will, who occasionally saw his aunt and uncle in London; there may have been others over the years, but to her knowledge, there had only ever been Will. Other than that the only time the rest of them got to mingle with children similar to their ages was at the yearly summer fete; this was where she gathered most of her intel that they led somewhat a sheltered but also a privileged life at Morsely Manor.

Seeing as there were only approximately fifty children, there didn't seem a need to split them up into year groups – this being something she understood they had in conventional schools. The age you were determined what group you were in, meaning ten-year-olds would be with ten-year-olds and fifteen-year-olds (such as herself) would be with other fifteen-year-olds; at times she wished they had that option.

In these schools, they were taught maths, English, science, physical education, philosophy, French (she wondered what they ever would they need French for?). Here, yes, they were taught maths and English, but they were also taught how to grow things, fix things and make things; they worked with animals, they cleaned, they had weekly chores – which she presumed the children in conventional schools also had in their family homes. Sometimes over the years as she had grown up, she often wished she was one of these children. The ones who said goodbye to their parents were given a packed lunch, would walk to school, complete a very ordinary day of lessons, arrive home late, receive a telling-off from their parents to then sit down to a supper with their rather annoying brothers and sisters. As the years went by she thought about these scenarios less and less; in her world, there was no such word as normal, only what she knew, and what she knew was neither good nor bad.

'How are you, my dear?' Ms Pepperin asked, waiting for Isla to acknowledge her. 'Away with the fairies lately, aren't you?'

'Huh?' Isla looked up from the items she had been staring blankly at on the table.

'Not like you to be late for a lesson. You seem a bit like your mind is somewhere else. Is something troubling you, my dear?' Ms Pepperin said, placing a warming hand on her forearm. The act of kindness made Isla feel comforted, so much so that words started to tumble out of her mouth without permission; however, luckily, or unluckily, for Isla a jolt from behind caused her to drop everything on the floor, and subsequently her necklace out of her pocket, which she quickly picked up before anyone other than Ms Pepperin noticed.

'You silly boy,' came Ms Pepperin's stern voice. Jimmy Jameson had been swinging on two legs of his seat (clearly not interested in the lesson at all), lost his balance and fallen back into Isla.

As Jimmy continued to receive a telling-off from Ms Pepperin Isla took the opportunity to swiftly return to her seat and, under the disguise of the commotion, she clipped the necklace around her neck, where she felt it was the safest place for now.

For the remainder of the lesson, nothing else eventful happened. Isla had soon caught up so that she was able to leave on time, which they were all doing now.

'I shall expect you not to be late again, Isla, we do not tolerate tardiness here,' said Mrs Bugglesworth over the top of her brightly coloured glasses that were just a little too big for her nose. Mrs Bugglesworth was not a large lady; Lexi was right, it was well known she had a sweet tooth, but she was nowhere near as significant in size as what her appetite might suggest, and it was a wonder where she put it all. Her hair was short and unruly, being the kind that was hard to tame, and spent most its life in a half-up, half-down sort of style, often pinned back with the clip attached to her apron, one that Isla was sure was not actually meant to be used for hair but did the job all the same.

'One word to Miss Sparrow,' she reaffirmed then picked up the work that Isla had been working on. 'I'm sure there are plenty of others who would be happy to take your place here.' Though Isla knew she would not do so, the sisters did like to use Miss Sparrow's name as a weapon to ensure they meant business, though it was hard to take Mrs Bugglesworth seriously with black smudges across her face that Isla was sure she did not know was there.

'Hmmm, though a little rushed, not bad, though I expect perfection next time.' And she added Isla's stitch work to the pile. 'Now *this*, this is outstanding again, and will make a fabulous addition.' She said with pride.

Isla knew Mrs Bugglesworth was no longer talking about her own work; she was referring to Grace's very delicate, very detailed masterpiece, a complete opposite to its master in every way. Grace was not feminine in the slightest in looks or in personality. Still, there was no denying her natural flair for needlework. *Perhaps it's something to do with her long, slender fingers*, Isla thought.

'I just do it to keep them off my back,' Grace said to Isla. 'As if they think I actually enjoy doing this stuff.'

'Oh no, of course, I wouldn't think such a thing,' Isla responded.

'As if!' Grace huffed.

Isla had to laugh to herself, especially as she could see what suspiciously looked like a pair of needles sticking out of the top of her bag.

CHAPTER TEN

'Knock knock!'

'Come in.'

Ms Pepperin opened the door to Miss Sparrow's office. 'I'm sorry to disturb you, Miss Sparrow, but I wondered if you had a moment?'

Miss Sparrow looked up from her paperwork. 'Of course, take a seat.' She motioned towards the vacant chair on the opposite side of her desk, moving her paperwork to one side.

'New arrivals?' enquired Ms Pepperin, pointing to the files. There looked to be a rather large pile of them, each with a photo of a child on the front.

'Yes, well, not all of them, as we only have space for two at the moment. Just reading to see who will be the most suitable for our residence.'

'I wish we could take them all. Hardly seems fair that we have to judge them, poor little blighters, they're all in such desperate need of a home.'

'Indeed, but the fact remains: no matter how sad you find it that we can't have them all, it's just a decision that needs to be made, and attaching emotion to it doesn't make it any less so.

Now, Ms Pepperin, I'm sure you did not come in here to talk about our possible new arrivals – if you wouldn't mind.' And she motioned to the still-vacant seat.

'Oh yes, my apologies, I wanted to speak to you about Isla.'

'Yes!' Miss Sparrow gave her full attention.

'I have been here since the Manor opened as a children's home. When you employed me you asked me to pay special attention towards Isla, to report anything that I thought may be strange, or not usual, childlike behaviour, as you put it. Over the years I have done just that, and I have never been overly concerned. Yes, she has had her moments, but dare I say it, she is growing into a rather remarkable young lady and I have grown rather fond of her.'

'Please reach your point, Ms Pepperin.'

'Yes, sorry – well, recently I have noticed a change in her behaviour. Nothing really in particular so I can't put my finger on it, but she just seems different to me. Today she was late for class, and I don't think she meant for me to see it, but she had a rather impressive-looking necklace – to be honest, it looked much like your mirror over there.' Ms Pepperin bowed her head slightly, took a breath and continued. 'I wouldn't want to accuse any child here of misgivings, as I don't think any of them are capable of that, but I am not sure how she would have acquired such a piece. I suppose that is all I wanted to say – not much, I know, but you just get a gut feeling sometimes. I know these children.'

'I see. Well, thank you for passing on your concerns to me, Ms Pepperin.'

'Would you like me to do anything? I could speak to her, perhaps?' She went to continue further, but Miss Sparrow cut her short.

'That won't be necessary – leave it with me. Now, I must continue with my work.'

'Honestly, it is no problem, I don't mind at all. I know

71

sometimes she can be stubborn, but I'm sure she will open up to me.'

'Please, if you wouldn't mind.' Her papers already back in hand, Miss Sparrow ignored her offer. It was not only the children of the Manor who knew when their time was up with the headmistress but also the sisters.

'As you wish, Miss Sparrow.'

'Oh, one more thing, if you wouldn't mind, Ms Pepperin – this necklace, was Isla wearing it?'

'Um, no, I don't believe so. It fell out of her pocket, that I know for sure.'

'Thank you, that will be all.'

Ms Pepperin did not hear before she closed the door, but had she listened closely, she would have heard Miss Sparrow breathe a sigh of relief.

CHAPTER ELEVEN

'Your turn, your turn.' Along with Elizabeth, Isla had been roped into keeping the younger children of the Manor entertained for their late-night Saturday routine and for the best part of an hour had been playing various games, and now it was time for the ultimate, their favourite: hide and seek.

After Mrs Bugglesworth's lesson, it had been nonstop with chores and garden duties. They had dug weeds and cleared shrubs; summer was now in full swing, and there was a project to restore life back into the old walled garden. She had no idea how after all their hard work they still had the energy, and she would have quite happily sat this one out. Had it not been for the insistent begs of Lexi she would have.

'Okay, I'm counting – one, two, three, four, five.' She heard a scatter of feet fleeing in numerous directions. Through the cracks in her fingers she could already see a small, childlike figure behind the curtains; she'd make a point to miss that one out on her first inspection of the hall before widening her search to the rest of the Manor.

'Ninety-eight, ninety-nine, one hundred! Coming, ready or not.' She did exactly what she said to herself she would do: she looked under a few tables, behind a few curtains and casually ignored the not-so-silent giggle as she exited the room.

Before long she found the twins hiding behind some boxes under the stairs; a few others were also found in not-so-original places, and Jimmy Jameson was in plain view as he and Rudy were kicked out of the kitchen with faces full of biscuits. 'Out! Out!' They laughed at the now evidently stressed cook, before admitting to Isla that a game such as hide and seek was far too dull for them. She watched them go back into the dining hall, grabbing what looked suspiciously like more treats out of their pockets.

Just then she saw someone run across the stairs on the second floor. 'I see you,' she shouted, and ran up them, hoping to find which room they had ducked into; she checked behind a few doors but nothing.

'Isla,' she heard, and turned round just in time to see a shadow fly up the next set of stairs.

'This is meant to be a game of hide and seek, not chase.' Suspecting it was Lexi, she followed the voice up the stairs. She reached the top and stopped, hoping for a sign as to which direction she had gone.

'Come out, come out, wherever you are.' She crept along the corridor.

BANG!

A door slammed, causing a judder of nerves through her body, followed by a whisper. She was getting a bit annoyed now; even if it was Lexi, she wasn't up for this game to last any longer than was necessary.

'Okay, I give up. Where are you?' There it was, repeated again, her name – and again, it was just a whisper.

She heard a creak as if something had moved and was drawn to the door that led to the attic. The attic was only ever used for storage, and no one ever had any need to go up there other than to collect things such as Christmas decorations, sports equipment and the like – it wasn't a place that any of the children particularly liked to go, for it was dark and full of cobwebs.

Still, she decided to go investigate, and sure enough, as she pulled the door towards her, she heard the exact same distinctive sound. Isla switched on the lights with a flicker and left the door open, for something told her that this was not Lexi. She would be too scared to go in there on her own; in fact, something told her this was not anybody from the Manor at all.

She climbed the stairs, instinctively holding her hands to her chest; it was at this same moment she also clutched on to something else. Isla had completely forgotten that she had been wearing her necklace all day and pulled it out from under her clothes where it had been hiding. She was surprised to see that the little specs of gems started to glow. *Is this happening again? The same as what had happened with the dagger?*

'Hello.' Isla reached the top of the stairs, but instead of it getting brighter, she could feel the room becoming colder, darker. 'Is anybody there?'

'Isla!'

The lights still flickered, making it difficult to see where the voice had come from. She kept the necklace firmly within the clutches of her hand, feeling safer of its presence.

She tapped at the light bulb above her head, hoping to encourage it to stay on; dust particles fell into her eyes, momentarily blurring her vision. *Was that...?* No, she must be seeing things.

She rubbed at her eyes with both hands, squinting away the dust. 'Look, I know someone is in here, so you may as well come out.'

'Come to me, Isla.'

She spun around quickly, looking into the shadows. The lights were still blinking, so she was only able to see the outline of boxes piled one on top of the other. Her necklace was still glowing, feeling heavy upon her chest.

'Come to me.'

She really was at the end of her tether now. *Who the hell is this person?* It wasn't even funny. 'I'm already here. I'm asking you to show *yourself!*'

'Isla, Isla!' she heard coming from all directions; the lights were flickering too much now for her eyes to focus on anything. But what was that, by the window – was it a person, a shadow? They flicked on and off again – gone!

'Come to me! *Isla! Isla! Isla!* Come to me.'

'Arrrragh! *Stop!*' she screamed.

BANG!

Darkness – all the lights broke, scattered in pieces on the floor; even the glow of her necklace died out. She took a moment to catch her breath, holding whatever solid furniture was next to her with both arms.

Breathe, Isla, just breathe, she told herself, arms still tense. *Breathe, breathe.* The thud in her chest eased. 'Okay, get yourself together. You're alright.'

But the calm did not last for long; something was not right. She felt shaky – was the room moving? Then she looked down and realised it was her necklace; it was vibrating. The gems started to glow again, but this time it was brighter than ever before. She felt the weight lift off her chest and pull her into the direction of the window. Dust covered the pane; she could not see through it from where she was, but gravity was pulling her in its direction, and she let it.

SNAP!

The pendant broke free from the chain around her neck and stuck itself to the window. *What the...?* She wiped her hand across the dust-encrusted window and there it was. There was no denying the necklace was trying to show her something, and that something was a tall, slender figure dressed all in black, and that figure was heading straight towards Mr Stopes' cottage.

CHAPTER TWELVE

The cool air of a late evening breeze skimmed the back of his neck; Mr Stopes paused from what he was doing. 'To what do I owe this pleasure?'

'Don't play games with me, Ed.'

'It's Ed now, is it?' Mr Stopes replied, amused, as he took a seat in his best armchair. This was his territory, and he was not about to be bossed around in his own home.

'Where is it?'

'Where is what?'

Miss Sparrow paced the cottage floor. 'Where did you even get it from, how?' she said, partly to herself, partly to Mr Stopes.

'Eliza, you are going to have to be a little bit clearer. I'm not sure I understand you.' He was very calm and casually placed a lump of sugar into his tea.

'You shouldn't have had such an item.' Again she said this mostly questioning herself rather than directing it at him.

Mr Stopes was not sure he had ever seen Miss Sparrow so untogether, and a part of him was enjoying it.

'*Do not* play me for a fool, Mr Stopes.'

'Ah, we're back to that now.' He rose from his chair, knowing that she had made the change from Eliza to Miss Sparrow.

'Where did you get the pendant from? And most importantly, how did it make it from your possession to Isla's?'

When she had walked in unannounced, he hadn't expected this to be the nature of her unexpected visit, and now he understood the reason for her erratic behaviour. He wondered when he would have to explain himself, though; to be honest; he'd thought it would have happened sooner than this.

'Ah.'

'*Ah* – is that all you have to say for yourself?'

'Nope. First of all, I would like to say thank you for correctly using her name this time.'

'Now is not the time to test my patience, Mr Stopes. If I could I would have you sent back without a word, but as that is not only dangerous but also impossible, it looks like I am stuck with you and your downright idealistic and foolish behaviour.'

'I don't know what you want me to say.' He paused. 'Miss Sparrow, the pendant was a gift to me, and I gifted it to Isla.'

Seeing that she was not going to get anywhere with her approach, Miss Sparrow mustered every bit of strength in her body to stop herself from cursing him there and then. She knew this man all too well, more than she cared to remember sometimes, and her stern approach would not work on him.

'Mr Stopes, I know that you are fond of Isla, but I need to know how and where you got it. Do you not understand? This could affect her very safety here and defy everything that we have worked hard to keep her from. So I will not ask you again: please, tell me?' Her face was placid; she showed no signs of anger, only those of someone wanting to know the truth.

'She gave it to me.'

'Who?'

'You know, *she*.' He nodded towards the picture of himself and the other man that Isla had seen the very first day she had entered his cottage.

'I don't understand?'

'I know you take me for some reckless fool – a reckless fool you used to admire once, may I add – but I am not a complete Neanderthal. They trusted me and I proved my worth on more than one occasion.' He pointed to the scar on the side of his face. 'Do not think you were the only one that they believed in, Eliza. It's still so clear in my head, even after all these years, and the memory will never fade from me.'

Miss Sparrow did not have time for sentimental nostalgia; time was of the essence. God knows what irresolvable damage may have been done; she did not know how long Isla had had the necklace for or what kind of pendant hung from it, and it was gravely important that she knew now. However, she held back her increasing urge to throttle the man that had just put them all in danger so he could get the rest of his story out.

'It was right before, you know, the end, the end of our lives as we knew it.' She softened her gaze towards him. It was true; she had once admired this unruly, charming man. He had brought her out of her box, being so full of character. There was a moment in her life when she had relaxed, not taken everything so seriously, but that time had gone. *And quite frankly*, she thought to herself, *for the better*.

'Before I failed at my duty, she gave it to me, in the midst of a battle; she took it off from around her neck and gave it to me. "Promise, promise me," she said, "you will keep this and give it to her when the time is right." "How will I know when the time is right?" I asked her. "You will just know," she told me. I tried to return it to her. I didn't want it; I knew its importance. How could I be responsible for something like that? I knew what it was and what it could do. Yet she made me take it, and I made my promise.'

Miss Sparrow stood in silence. *Could this story I'm hearing really be true?* And if so, how come she had never been informed?

'So let me get this clear: what you are telling me is the woman who gave birth to Isla, right before she died, gave you the very thing that could have saved her?'

He could hear the doubt in her voice; no one had been more shocked at her decision than him, but it was true, as true in his mind as on the very day it happened.

'Yes, that is exactly what I am saying: in a room, surrounded by the screams of fighting and dying men, a room that was crumbling and shaking down around us, Isla's mother took off the very thing that could have kept her alive and entrusted it to me to do what was right. To keep it safe until the day came to pass it on to her daughter, my goddaughter, and I have done exactly that. I have done just as I promised; her fifteenth birthday was the right time, and no one, not even you, was going to stop me from fulfilling my promise.'

Miss Sparrow was stunned; she had no reason to doubt what he was saying was true. *But why him, and why at all?*

'I don't understand – why would she do that? Her last fighting chance, and she willingly gave it away, *and to you!*' That was it; she could no longer hide her anger and frustration. 'All this time, all these years you've had something as important and as dangerous as that, and you didn't think to tell me?'

'I know exactly what you would have done: you would have taken it, locked it up and Isla would never have had a chance to have it!'

'All for good reason. You know exactly what that is; if she wears that, she might become enlightened, which means he will know exactly where she is. He will be able to find her and then be able to finish what he started.'

'This is all just theory; you do not know that for sure. The enlightenment may not work if she hasn't walked the path to

Elethrul herself – also, enough protection has been put on these premises, and she has us.'

'*Do not fool yourself!* We are not strong enough to fight what looms in the dark we are proof of that fact for the very reason that we are here. You better pray that she has not worn it, you have put *everyone* at risk with your selfish behaviour.'

They squared off with each other, both believing that they were right, their complete contempt for one another heightened.

'She has a right to know; she's always had a right to know. We should have never kept it from her for so long.'

'That was what was agreed by the whole council as the best thing to do; no other way out could be seen, you know that, and I am only doing what is right for her and everyone's safety, as I always have, and now you hinder me from fulfilling my duties correctly.' She positioned herself towards the door, ready to make her exit.

'What you have done, what we have all done, is hinder Isla from finding out who she truly is. I may have agreed once that this was what was best for her, but I do not agree now.'

'You cannot change the rules just because your conscience tells you to; we still have a job to do, and, quite frankly, in my opinion, you have let your king down. Now I must check with the council at once if she has at any point worn the necklace. If she has there could have been movement on the other side, and *you*, Mr Stopes, you had better retrieve that necklace!'

CHAPTER THIRTEEN

'There you are.' Isla bumped into Will. 'Everyone gave up on you. Jimmy said he saw you go upstairs and not come back down again – you could have told them you didn't want to play anymore.'

'I've got to go, Will.' She pushed past him.

'Whoa, go where?' He followed.

'I need to get in there, and I have to do it now.'

'Get in where? This is not about the game, is it? Because they all gave up when you were no longer searching for them.'

'It's not about the game, Will – Miss Sparrow's office.'

'What, why?'

She ignored him and carried on down the stairs.

'Look, Isla, wait, not in this state. If you make this much racket everyone will see you.'

'*I don't care – I don't care if Miss Sparrow sees me herself.*'

'Isla, what's got into you? Talk to me, please – clearly you are upset about something.' Will watched the frustration in her face as she tried to do the same trick as he had done before, but without the same success.

'Here, give it to me.' He took the crooked pin out of her shaking hands and within seconds unlocked the door.

'Thank you!'

'Right, we're in here *again*! Now explain.' He stood, arms folded, in front of her.

'I don't have time for this, Will,' Isla protested.

'Well, make time!' He maintained his stance and refused to move; he was not going to go through all this again.

'Just now, I saw Miss Sparrow go into Mr Stopes' cottage, okay?' She tried to get past him, but again he stopped her in her tracks; he wasn't going to have her walk away from him this time.

'So? That's hardly unusual.' He looked puzzled and held his arms out so she couldn't get past.

'Would you get off me, Will?' She tried to shrug his arms off her, but he kept a firm grip.

'*No!* Not until you explain to me what has got you like this.'

'*Fine!*' Isla pulled the necklace out from her pocket. '*This!*' she said, which of course offered him no further clarity. 'I could hear someone in the attic calling my name, okay? So I went to see who it was, but other than hearing my name repeated over and over again, I saw nothing, and then the lights exploded!'

Will saw tiny shards of glass in her hair and stepped back to check that she was okay.

'Don't you see, Will? It's back. Whatever had been trying to contact me before, whatever had been in my dreams, it's back.'

'How do you know that?'

'Because of this. When the lights went out, my necklace started glowing, just like the dagger. It pulled me to the window, snapped off my neck and stuck itself to the glass, and what did I see? Miss Sparrow. That was no coincidence, Will. It wanted me to see it.'

'So what are you saying, this is some kind of magic necklace now?'

'Yes – no. Oh, I don't know, but you saw what happened before. You explain it.'

Will stuttered, 'I can't, but it's quite an assumption to think this all comes down to Miss Sparrow. Look, Isla, we shouldn't be in here. Let's find somewhere quiet and we can talk about this, think it through.'

'Look, Will, you asked to know, I've told you and now you don't believe me. Stay, go, I don't care, but I'm getting into that drawer and you're not going to stop me.'

'I didn't say I don't believe you, Isla – just... I'm worried about you, you don't stop.'

'Well, *go* then, I don't need your help!' she cursed him.

'*Yes*, you do, but this is the last time – this must stop!' He opened the drawer for her for the second time.

Scrambling inside, Isla dropped the contents onto the table; she searched through the pictures, picked out the ones that looked the most interesting to her and shoved them in her pocket.

'She'll notice they're missing,' Will said as a warning.

'I doubt it – she obviously wants this stuff hidden, so I doubt she ever goes in there, and if so, how will she know it's me? It's not like she can start asking around now, is it?'

'Well, true, but still, this is not you, Isla.'

Isla ignored him; she was being uncharacteristically rude and blunt, even by her standards, but he was too honest for his own good sometimes and now was not the time for his conscience.

She picked up the dagger and held it next to her necklace. 'See? They're the same: a necklace given to me by Mr Stopes and a dagger hidden by Miss Sparrow – that's no coincidence, Will.' Isla paced around the table, reeling off theories; she hadn't understood how frantic she had been until she looked at Will's face and realised she had been shaking the dagger right at him. She lowered it to her side and apologised.

'Look, all I am saying is this has to mean something; even you must admit that this doesn't add up.' She looked for any signs that he agreed, but his face was somewhat stunned; she couldn't tell if it was because he agreed or because he thought that she had completely lost her mind.

'*What is the meaning of this?*' They both turned to see Miss Sparrow and Mr Stopes in the doorway. 'How did you get in here?'

Isla backed off as Miss Sparrow walked closer to them. 'Stay where you are,' Isla instructed them all; she needed to gather her thoughts before she was bombarded.

'Where did you get that from, Isla?' Already knowing the answer, she took a slight glance to her left and could see her drawer half opened.

'You know where I got it from, but what I want to know is what it has to do with me?'

'Please, Isla.' Mr Stopes made a slow move towards her, his hands in clear view. 'Pass it to me, come on now.'

Her eyes surveyed the room. 'Not until someone explains what this is, and what it has to do with me.' She held it up with the necklace for them all to see, too angered to notice that this time they did not shine – well, not bright enough for any of them to see, including Isla.

Miss Sparrow glared at Mr Stopes; it was entirely his fault that they stood where they were now, and she wanted him to know it. 'Isla, have you worn the necklace?' She pressed, 'Isla, I *must* know: have you put that necklace around your neck?'

Isla was confused. *Why ask such a question?*

'What does that matter?' she replied bewilderedly to Miss Sparrow.

'Because it is important, that's why.'

'No, what is important is that someone tells me the truth, and I am not leaving here until someone does.' The whole time Isla had been talking she had been unknowingly backing off in the direction of the mirror, and suddenly she caught sight of the dull light creeping through her fingers. She remembered what happened before and spun round to face it.

Will did not need her to say anything to know what she was thinking of doing. '*Don't* do it, Isla,' he said.

'Do what?' Miss Sparrow demanded to know.

'Please, Isla,' Will pleaded; he was too far away to stop her from doing what he knew she was about to do.

'I'm sorry, Will.' And just like that she was gone: one step and she had disappeared through the mirror.

CHAPTER FOURTEEN

She had walked straight into darkness.

The drop in temperature wrapping itself around her in an instant. *Did I really just do that?* Her heart pounded in her ears; only seconds ago she'd stood in Miss Sparrow's office. It had been a split-second decision, one she had not thought about; had just acted on, and she was already regretting her decision.

'Hello?' She spun around, frantically in search for the mirror, but it was nowhere to be seen – gone! But what she could see, now that her eyes had adjusted, was a rotten rundown street; derelict – lifeless.

'Hello,' she called out again, keeping the contents of her hands very close to her chest. 'Is anyone here?'

The place was dreary, colourless; in daylight she could tell it wouldn't have much more to offer. It was as if the soul had been taken away from what once could have been a charming place. But any signs of a previous life looked as if they had faded long ago.

'Come here, child.' She saw an elderly lady frantically ushering for her to come towards her, illuminated by a soft glow. 'Quick, before they catch you.'

'What do you mean, catch me?' Isla didn't move.

'Be quick now, come inside.' Isla went on to say something. 'Sssssh, don't speak,' the old lady said, and moved her fingers to her lips and mouth. 'Slowly.'

Isla thought about her situation – should she trust this elderly figure? Her gut said yes. Still, her brain said no; either way, she started to feel very uneasy outside on her own in a place so silent, so still.

She decided to trust her gut; the old lady looked harmless enough. She started to move. 'Slowly,' she repeated, holding her hands up. 'Try not to make any noise.' Isla did as she was told, and not another word was spoken until she was safely behind the closed door.

The old lady pulled down her hood and stared at her intently. For a second she regretted her decision – that was, until she spoke. 'Are you hurt?'

Isla shook her head.

'Did anyone see you?'

'No.'

'Did you see anyone?'

Again. 'No.'

Though her questions were short, they were said with concern.

'Please, sit,' she said, pointing to the vacant chair. There was one larger chair already occupied by a child no more than eight, who twisted strands of mousey curly hair through her fingers whilst staring curiously at Isla.

'Here, you must be starved, though you don't look like you have missed a meal.' She handed Isla a hot drink and something that looked like a cross between bread and a biscuit. 'Sorry, we don't have much, but we get by.'

Isla wasn't hungry, but, not wanting to be rude, she took a sip of the drink, which instantly warmed her insides. It did not taste of much but tasted nice all the same.

'Thank you.'

Now that she was sat opposite her, she noticed that the old lady was not so old after all; in fact, she looked much younger than she'd first thought. The hair that had looked grey was not actually grey; much like the child's, it was wavy but covered in what she could only guess was ash. The hooded cloak, now removed, had made her appear far more fragile than she actually was; it had definitely seen better days, much like the rest of her clothes, but the body that wore them, though slim, was strong.

They sat in silence, so Isla continued to sip at her drink. The little girl remained seated and said nothing, while the lady kept going to the window anxiously looking outside; after about ten minutes she finally settled down.

'What were you thinking?' she said to Isla.

'What do you mean?'

'What I mean is, what were you doing out there, in the middle of the street, in the dark? You should have been inside hours ago.'

Isla wasn't sure how to respond; she couldn't exactly say the truth. 'I got lost,' she finally said.

'Where is your home? You won't be able to leave tonight, but first light we will make sure you get there. I will try and get word to your parents that you are safe, they must be frantic, but I cannot promise; it will be very risky at this time of night.'

Isla didn't know what to say; she had no idea where she was, and she couldn't exactly say that she had walked through some magical mirror to get there either.

'My name is Andrina, and this is Kelina,' she said, pointing to the little girl, 'my daughter,' to which she stroked her hair. 'Kai should be home soon.'

Isla said hello to the little girl, but she didn't say anything back, she just stared at her blankly, her button nose slightly pinched.

The lady who had now identified herself as Andrina asked a few more questions, which Isla kept as aloof as possible; all she said was that she'd got separated and didn't know her way back.

'Not to worry, my dear, we will wait till morning. Your family will be sure to be looking for you, but until then you are safe here.' Andrina went over to the tiny fire where old, discarded pieces of coal and ash lay on the floor, which explained her grey hair. 'We ran out a few days ago,' she said in explanation of the unlit fire.

The house was small and basic; heavy, coloured blankets covered the hard wooden furniture. The sitting room and kitchen were pretty much as one, and to the far side of the room a ladder led up to a mezzanine level which was about half the size of the ground floor, she guessed that was where they slept, but being such a small room she wondered how it fit them all in; she was surely used to more space at the Manor.

The very thought of the Manor made Isla feel sick; she had only been gone five minutes, and she missed the comfort of its walls already. *Why had I been so determined to prove something was being kept from me? Why hadn't I listened to Will?* And at the thought of his name, her heart sank again.

A noise was heard from somewhere within the house. 'Ah, that will be him.' She got up and moved towards the kitchen. 'We have a guest,' she called out.

Isla heard a little more shuffling, then a tall, slender boy entered, or perhaps he was a man. She thought he looked similar to her age anyway.

He ignored both her and Andrina and went straight over to the little girl, who jumped up into his arms.

'Kallon,' she cried; they were the first words that Isla had heard her speak since arriving, and she now sported the broadest smile that changed her demeanour completely.

'Have you been behaving?'

'Yes,' she replied.

'And been practising?'

The little girl looked up. 'Ummmm.'

'I shall do some with you tomorrow. Now it's time for you to go to bed.' He put her down, walked towards Andrina and gave her a gentle kiss. 'Mother,' he said, 'I thought you may have run out.' He placed a bag of logs on the floor next to her.

Andrina smiled and placed a gentle hand to his cheek then looked at her daughter. 'She's been waiting up for you.'

'I'm sure she has, but it's late – off you go.'

And, unwillingly, the little girl disappeared to bed.

'Kallon, this is Isla. Isla, this is my son, Kallon, Kai for short.' It was hard to believe that this was her son; apart from the same grey eyes, that was about the only thing they had in common. The little girl, Kelina, was a spitting image of her mother and no doubt what she would have looked like at the same age. However, he had lighter hair, shaved at the sides and tied back into a knot. He had milkier skin and longer limbs; his jawline was on the way to being developed, though his face was not as square as his mothers. Nor was his personality, for he looked at her with discontent as soon as his mother had introduced the two of them.

'She's been separated from her family and will be staying here for the night.'

'Who's your family?' he questioned immediately.

'Um, we are not from around here. We were travelling, and I got separated from them.'

It was clear he did not believe her. She couldn't blame him; her story was hardly iron-clad. Isla was surprised that Andrina had believed it herself, but by all accounts she appeared to, or was too polite to say otherwise.

'How did you get past the watchers?'

'Watchers?'

Kallon raised his arms in protest. 'Mother, she doesn't even know who the watchers are and you let her into our house.'

Andrina did look a bit puzzled that Isla did not seem to know who they were or what they did – it was very much common knowledge that they had been stationed to enforce curfew and had authority to punish those who were caught not obeying rules – but unlike her son, she was far more forthcoming when it came to helpless teenage girls in evident need of help.

'It's been a tiring day – you must be exhausted, Kai. Let's all get some rest, and we can discuss this in the morning.'

Kallon didn't say any more; Isla could tell he was none too happy about her staying the night, and the deathly stare he gave had just sealed the deal.

CHAPTER FIFTEEN

It was late morning by the time Isla woke. Andrina had put her in a small but comfortable room, which she later learned was Kallon's. It was basic but had all the amenities that a room needed: a bed, a small desk and a lamp, which she was told to use sparingly as it was powered by oil, and it was hard to come by. She felt a little uncomfortable sleeping in a boy's bed, especially one that had taken such an instant dislike to her, but eventually sleep had won, and she slept without a dream.

'Morning, my dear.' Andrina smiled brightly. 'Would you like some breakfast?' she said from over the kitchen sink, scrubbing away at her laundry.

'Thank you, but I am not hungry at the moment.'

'As you wish, but if you change your mind let me know. Kai is just outside with Kelina at the moment; once they have finished we will look to help you find your family.' She smiled to herself. 'Kai has been away for a few weeks, and his sister has missed him terribly. Being the only man around the house now, he is the only father figure she really has.'

Isla wanted to ask where their father was and presumably

her husband, but she didn't want to ruin Andrina's happy moment at having her two children reunited.

She looked out the window to the compact space at the back of the property, which looked as if it was a communal one judging by the other doors that opened out into it. There was not much to see: the ground was dried mud, the kind that was crumbly and flakey; a washing line ran across the length of it; and the late morning sun had just about crept its way through.

They were making quite a racket and Isla was surprised she had slept through it. Kai was showing Kelina how to fight with a sword, one that was small and clearly blunt; it would have been a shocking sight for anyone to see; yet for some reason, it did not shock her. This was not something that they would have done at the Manor, yet it felt completely normal. Watching them both enjoying each other's company, Kelina hanging on Kallon's every word, she was touched by the closeness of these two siblings. Will was the closest thing she had ever had to such a relationship, and she wondered if she would ever have that connection again.

'Go join them,' encouraged Andrina, who had been watching Isla. 'They won't bite.'

'I don't want to disturb them.' Isla twisted at her hands, something she did in times of discomfort.

'You won't disturb them; they will be happy for the company.'

Isla seriously doubted that, especially following the welcome she had received the night before, but feeling she couldn't think of a better reason not to, she did as Andrina suggested. She was careful not to make much of her entrance and kept close to the wall, hoping they wouldn't really notice her and she could get through it without bringing attention to herself.

'Kai, that's cheating!' yelped Kelina.

'It's not cheating – I'm just bigger and stronger than you.'

'Exactly,' she cried.

'Come on, find your way out.' Kallon had her compromised: one hand was held firmly down by her side while the other (which held her sword) he had high up in the air. Kelina laughed in frustration as she struggled to free herself.

'Come on, what are you going to do?' Kallon teased.

'*This!*' With her free leg she lifted it as high as she could and sent it crashing down on Kallon's foot; he instantly let her go, and she was free.

'Ouch! Now that is cheating. Come here!' he said, chasing her around on one limping foot.

Isla found herself immersed in the moment and joined in with the laughing. It reminded her much of something that Lexi would have done, and the feeling of familiarity made her feel comforted.

They both suddenly glanced her way but didn't say anything and continued with their own conversation.

'I wish I had something proper to practise with,' Kelina moaned, holding up her sword. 'I can't do anything with this.'

'Precisely – it's a practice sword and keeps all my fingers and toes intact,' Kallon reaffirmed, positioning her for yet another round.

'But it's boring – I want a real one!' she huffed again.

Isla had to admit, the one she was using did look especially dire. Most certainly it would have seen better days, and before she realised what she was doing, she found herself offering up her own dagger for Kelina to use.

They both backed off; Andrina had also picked that precise moment to enter the courtyard with her freshly cleaned laundry. 'Where did you get that from?' she gasped, dropping the washing to the floor.

'What, have I done something wrong?' Isla said, wishing she had not got it out by the looks on their faces.

Andrina picked up one of the clean sheets and threw it over Isla's hand, which still held the dagger, and ushered her inside.

'See, I *knew* there was something not right about her. She should never have stayed; you should never have let her in,' Kallon said to his mother.

'I didn't know,' replied Andrina. 'Kelina, go to your room, please.'

'But I don't want to,' she protested, remaining by Kallon's side.

'Not now, Kelina, we must talk. Go to your room.'

She reluctantly did as her mother told her and climbed up the ladder to her room, where she undoubtedly could hear everything that was being said anyway.

Isla stood in a state of shock, the dagger still under the sheet in her hand; she felt thankful it had not done anything weird this time – she was not sure they could have coped if it had. 'I'm sorry, I didn't mean to upset anyone. I will go now; I didn't mean to cause you any harm.'

'*No!*' shouted Kallon. He put two firm hands on her shoulders; this was the first proper interaction they had had, and Isla didn't take too kindly to it. 'You *can't* go!'

'But you just said I shouldn't be here. I don't want to put you and your family out any longer.' Isla shoved past him. *Who is this boy anyway?* he was arrogant to say the least; she was beginning to dislike him just as much as he evidently disliked her.

'Kai's right – you can't leave now, Isla.' Andrina put a calming arm around her. 'It's safe now.' And she took the sheet off Isla's hand and stared at it.

'Here, would you like to hold it?' Isla offered; she didn't want it, not now, not after so much drama had been caused over it.

'No, no, I mustn't.' She held up her hands so Isla couldn't give it to her. 'You can put it on the table.'

Isla did just that, glad that it was no longer in her possession.

'How did *you* get that?' Kallon demanded to know; he bore

96

down on her waiting for an answer. Isla decided that now she really did not like him.

Andrina moved him to one side. 'Kallon! There's no need to be like that. Can't you see that she looks scared?'

Isla didn't think she looked scared – shocked, yes; uncomfortable, yes; wanting to run away from this family a million times, yes. But not because she was scared but because she was confused. She straightened her back and made an effort to hold her own; she didn't want them to think she was scared, especially not him.

'I don't care – we have no idea who she is; we have no idea where she came from. Look at her clothes – whatever she has told you, she certainly is not from around here. All I care about is why she has brought that into our house; I most certainly do not care about her or what happens to her.' He glared in her direction, ready for another attack.

'Isla, he may be angry, but he is right. It is not normal for someone of our calibre to have that – where did you get it from, darling? Are you in some kind of trouble?' She sat down next to her and placed both hands on top of hers gently.

Isla took a moment to respond; she looked at Kallon, scrunched up her face, then returned her gazed back to Andrina. She was nice, she had been kind to her and she trusted her. Isla decided all she could do was answer their questions; she needed them right now. She had no idea where she was or, in reality, where she would go if she left.

'I know you think I am a bad person,' she made a point to direct this to Kallon, 'but in all honesty, I don't know what this is. It is true, I did get lost, that I have not lied about, but I have no family – not here, anyway. The truth is, I don't know where I am at all.'

'What do you mean?' replied Andrina.

Kallon clearly did not believe a word, for he stood stoic with his arms folded, looking sceptical.

'I mean, I'm not from here.'

'We know that!' interrupted Kallon. 'Now tell us something useful.'

'*Stop it!* Kai, let her speak.' Andrina showed her son that despite him being the man of the house, she was the mother of the house, and he would show her respect. 'Carry on, my dear.'

'I don't really know where I am from – well, I know where I am from, but I don't know where here is, or exactly how I got here.'

'I'm not sure I follow,' said Andrina.

Kai rolled his eyes, clearly impatient.

'I don't think you would believe me if I told you.'

'Try me, my dear – we're used to our fair share of strange things around here. We might surprise you.' Isla dared another glance at Kallon; if anyone wouldn't believe her, it would be him, with his judgemental eyes just glaring at her, but she liked Andrina and wanted to tell her the truth.

So she told her – not the whole story, just the point from Miss Sparrow's office. How she got the dagger – she also showed her the pictures – how she went through the mirror, that it had brought her here, and that's when she had seen her, she had come into the house and, well, they knew the rest.

Andrina looked at the pictures. She was silent for a long while and was careful Kallon did not see them. 'And these, you say, came from this Miss Sparrow? Did she know the people in these pictures?' She pointed to one with a group of men, the one that included Mr Stopes.

'I don't know, but this one,' Isla pointed to Mr Stopes, 'he's the caretaker at the school, though he is older than that now. I've also seen him in a picture with this man.' Isla pointed to the man that had also been in the picture that she had seen in Mr Stopes' cottage. She thought about telling them about the necklace. However, she decided to keep that part to herself;

even though she trusted Andrina, she still didn't know her, and some things were just best kept to yourself.

Andrina carefully placed the pictures back on the table, which she made sure were face down. 'Thank you for telling me that, Isla, that was very brave.'

Isla wondered why she thought it was brave, but she returned the acknowledgement anyway.

'And I apologise for my son's behaviour towards you – with his dad not around, he gets very protective of us.' She motioned for him to do the same, which he begrudgingly did, though it was clear to Isla that her story had not done anything to lessen his dislike towards her.

'Isla, I'm not sure you understand what this all means; in fact, I believe you have no idea at all, or what we are going through here.'

'I would like to know if you have answers that can explain why I am here. If you know anything at all that could help me to understand how this all connects to me or how I get home, I would be very grateful.'

'Oh, my dear.' She held her hand. 'I am not sure I have those answers, and I don't believe that I can help you get home either, but I do, however, believe that it is you that you can help us.'

Isla looked confused. *What does she mean?*

'I believe, Isla, that you are the one that we have been waiting for – what I believe, Isla, is that you are the prophecy.'

CHAPTER SIXTEEN

'Mother, surely you can't think that *her*, this girl, is the prophecy?' He smirked.

'Yes, I do, Kai, that is exactly who I think she is.' Andrina left Isla's side and stepped towards her son. 'One day a stranger would arrive and with them, they would carry something from the Valeyan line, and that is something from the Valeyan line, is it not?' She pointed to the dagger that still lay on the table.

'Yes, most likely stolen, or better yet a fake. Look at her – she doesn't even know how to yield that thing. I doubt she has ever lifted a finger in her life; she is probably from Lestoris, living a life of luxury while the rest of us fight for pitiful scraps. It's a load of rubbish anyway, Mother, something that was said to give the people hope, but I tell you it will take more than some stupid prophecy to win this war; it will take men, men who have strength and determination, not some girl!'

Isla was in shock; she had no clue what they were talking about, but whatever it was, she certainly did not like it. She shot up, no longer confused, just angry, and she wasn't going to take any more of this, not from him, not from a boy – for that's exactly what he was: a boy, not a man.

'I'm not sure what this prophecy is or what you think it has to do with me, but I can assure you that it is not me.'

'See, she agrees.' Kallon gave her a sarcastic seal of approval.

'*And* I don't care for your tone either, despite what you may think of me. I did not come from some privileged upbringing; I have not run away – well, not intentionally, anyway. I am an orphan, and everything I have told you is true, and I don't have to listen to any more of this.' She grabbed the dagger, leaving the pictures behind, and didn't give them a chance to speak. 'Thank you, Andrina, you have been most kind to me, more than I can say for your son. However, as it is clear I am no longer welcome, I shall be leaving now.' Isla stormed out the door as quickly as she could, leaving it open behind her.

'Isla, wait, come back!' Andrina shouted. But she didn't listen; within seconds she was lost in the sea of people. Isla had no idea which direction she had left in but guessed it didn't matter, for she had no idea where she was. The only thing she wanted to do was get as far away from that house, as far away from him as possible; Will would never have treated anyone like that.

Isla passed maybe a dozen houses before she slowed down to catch her breath. Everything appeared different in the daylight, and though it still looked moody, the town was full. There was a certain electricity about it. With every kind of stall seller there was – from bric-a-brac to food, weird potions and lotions – she saw it all, though the food looked out of date at best, which was somewhat worrying. Voices shouted out their selling items in a currency she had never heard of before, all trying to compete with one another. Women offered themselves to passing men, most pushing them away; one woman was pushed so hard she fell into the mud, but this didn't seem to stop her. She just spat at the man and carried on.

A few yards up a racket could be heard as a group of men

were pushed out from an inn – The Whispering Warrior, she could see it was called. Drinks still in hand, they shouted some abuse at the innkeeper until he yelled at them not to return until they had sobered up.

'Gentleman, how about some pleasure to round off your exciting day?' said an overly large man with a grubby beard and a bulbous head just a few feet away.

'Got anything a little less haggard?' one of the men asked, looking at the group of women.

'Here!' Isla felt a pull from the back of her neck. 'How about this fine one? She's new, not yet broken in and therefore she will be double the price.'

Isla tried to break free, but with just his one hand, he was already stronger than she was. The other man inspected her, including trying to lift up her top; Isla kicked him hard.

'And she's a feisty one too.'

'Meh, too feisty for me – she ought to learn some manners.' He glared at her; half his teeth were missing and the ones that were there were so black he would have been better off without them. He drank the rest of his drink and threw the empty container to the floor. 'Normal price and I'll have her showing a bit more respect.'

Isla continued to struggle. 'Get off me! I am not for sale – not to him, not to anyone.'

'Shut up,' the fat man growled, grabbing her by the hair.

'*Hey!*' Isla felt another push, but this time she was free. 'What do you think you are doing?' It was Kallon, and he had squared himself up against the fat man, who tried to grab her back. 'Get off her!'

'What's your problem?' he growled.

'That's my cousin!'

'Didn't know you had a cousin, boy?'

'Yeah, well, I do, and she's not for sale.' He pulled Isla towards him. He was strong, stronger than he looked, yet gentle.

'It's just business, boy!' he said, the cheeks on his bulbous head wobbling and the sound of his laugh trailing them as Kallon hurried her away.

Once they were at a safe distance, Isla shook his arms off her. 'I've had enough of being pulled around for one day.'

'Don't thank me then – do you have any idea what they would have done to you? Everyone is desperate for money round here. Food is scarce, and what there is is expensive; they would have not cared what happened to you, so long as they continued to get paid.'

Isla knew he had helped her, but she didn't want to show gratitude to him, especially as he was someone who'd so openly showed such a dislike towards her. 'Yeah, well, if you hadn't have butted in, I would have got away myself – why did you do that anyway?'

They rounded a corner where the streets had grown quieter and far fewer people roamed.

'I don't believe you or your story, and I would have let them have you, but you have something I want, and I want to find out if it really is what my mother says it is.' He leaned up close to her and said in a whisper, 'I know a man who will be able to tell us if this is a fake or not.' He grazed the side of Isla's thigh, where her dagger was hidden beneath her clothes. 'So if you want to prove you are not a liar, you'll follow me.'

Isla felt a jolt of electricity run through her body; her heart raced a million times faster. *Who the hell does he think he is, ordering me around?* He infuriated her, yet somehow she couldn't find the words to protest.

They stared at each other for a few seconds until he grinned. 'And keep up – if you get into any more trouble I will not be helping you this time. I'm not babysitting you!'

CHAPTER SEVENTEEN

Two cool steel eyes bore into Will's. 'Speak!'

He was so stunned into silence that he found he couldn't – had what he'd just witnessed really happened? His best friend walked into a mirror and vanished?

'I-I...' he stammered. His brain was struggling to make sense of it. *What was she thinking? How was it possible?*

Miss Sparrow patience was wearing thin. 'Will Thatcher, I am going to ask you some questions, and you shall answer them promptly, is that clear?'

'Um, I...' He straightened his back. 'Yes, Miss Sparrow.'

Mr Stopes leaned forward. 'I think you should go easy on him – remember, he is not used to seeing the kind of things that we are.'

'Your advice is the last thing I will be taking right now, Mr Stopes. You would do wise to keep your opinions to yourself.' And he did just that, realising there would be no talking to her right now; he took a step back, leaving her to her interrogation.

'You are aware of who I am?' She directed this at Will.

'Yes.'

'And you are aware that I am the very reason that you have a roof over your head, food in your stomach and clothes on your body?'

'Yes,' replied Will again, sounding unsure.

'That means you are also aware that I am the very person that can take that all away. Now, with that in mind I suggest that when I ask you a question you respond with the truth – is that clear?'

Will nodded that he understood.

'Why were you and Isla in this room?'

Where should he start – from the beginning or just from today? He decided from today was the better option. 'I saw Isla – what, only about fifteen minutes ago. She looked flustered, angry and maybe even a little scared. She wanted to come in here; she said it was important. She had been up in the attic, and something or someone had seriously startled her – she wasn't talking much sense.'

'But why my office?'

'She said she had seen you go into Mr Stopes' cottage.'

'I expect a far more thorough reason than that to have my private quarters broken in to – now, speak up.'

Will paused, debating whether he should continue with the next bit; he wasn't sure that they would believe him, but then again, they had all just witnessed the same thing.

'She said that someone had been calling her name, but no one was there, that her necklace had somehow guided her to the window; she said it wanted her to see you – I know it doesn't make much sense, but I can only say what she told me. She was quite frantic. Even for Isla this was out of character, but she was sure about what she had seen, and I had no reason to not believe her.' He raised his voice. 'I don't understand this – what has happened to her?'

Miss Sparrow's face was taut. 'Remember, I will be asking the questions.'

'Yes, but—'

'I am speaking. Now, the necklace – tell me what you know about it.'

Will dared a glance at Mr Stopes, waiting for a sign that it was okay to proceed. He returned his confirmation with a nod.

'It was a birthday present,' he hesitated, 'from Mr Stopes. She wasn't sure why, but I guess she felt some kind of connection to it; we spoke about it briefly, but I have not seen it since, and nor have we spoken about it until today.'

'Did she say if she had worn it, or have you seen her wear it?'

Will thought for a moment. 'I can't say that I have, but I couldn't be sure.'

'*Think*, Will, it's of the highest importance – I need a yes or a no.'

He shuffled his feet, feeling a little more uncomfortable. 'No, I have not *seen* her wear it, but I can only assume that she has, considering it snapped off when she was in the attic, so I guess that would only imply that she has. I'm not sure how this is going to help – did you not see what I just saw? Isla walked through a mirror like it was some kind of door. She's gone, disappeared, we don't know where and the only thing you seemed to be concerned about is a stupid necklace.'

Will surprised even himself – he knew his place, and he had never spoken out of turn towards Miss Sparrow before, but her lack of concern towards the situation and the fact that some kind of magic mirror was in her office frustrated him. He just wanted to find Isla and save the questions for later.

'Will, if I may,' Mr Stopes stepped forward, finally breaking his silence, 'it is not that Miss Sparrow does not care – despite her demeanour I can assure you that she is most certainly concerned. However, the necklace holds something of great importance, something that may actually be able to help us find Isla. I know the questions may seem a bit odd to you, and I promise we will explain further later, but you may know things that you don't realise could help.'

'Yes, but I don't see how one necklace could do that. Why not look at the reasons why Isla has been acting strange these last few months? Her obsession with someone watching her, hearing voices, seeing things that weren't there. Why not start with that and then maybe, just maybe, we will find out who or what or why she has gone?'

Miss Sparrow jumped in. 'What do you mean, hearing and seeing things – what did she tell you?'

'I don't know exactly, I was never there, but she said that she had been having strange dreams, ones that felt real. That she often felt like someone was watching her; it took a while for her to tell me. I knew there was something wrong, I could tell, but she didn't know what to do – she was convinced that something was being hidden from her and after today I've come to the conclusion that she was probably right.'

'How could we have not seen, known?' Miss Sparrow questioned Mr Stopes. 'When did this all start?'

'I don't know exactly, but it had been some time before her birthday.'

'Her birthday! And we didn't notice a change in her? The council didn't see a change. How could we have been so foolish? How could I have let this slip by?' Miss Sparrow questioned herself now.

'I did say she suspected something, that she had a right to know.' Mr Stopes made sure he drove his point home.

'Know what?' Will demanded. 'What should Isla have known? She was right, wasn't she? Something has been kept from her.'

Miss Sparrow put her hand inside the pocket of her long black shawl. 'I think we've heard all you have to say, Will, but if there is anything else we should know, now would be the time to tell it.'

Mr Stopes firmly took hold of her wrist and stopped her from pulling out whatever she had intended to that was inside.

'Don't,' he whispered.

'I shall do what is necessary,' she whispered back.

He kept his hand firmly in place. 'Will is Isla's closest friend – if you want any hope at finding her, I would not erase his memory. We know of the powers she has; she may not know about them now, but if she is where we think she is, I bet it won't take her long to find out, and who do you think will be the first person she will want to contact?'

Miss Sparrow released the grip of whatever was inside her pocket. 'I do believe, Mr Stopes, that is the most sensible comment that has come out of your mouth all evening.'

CHAPTER EIGHTEEN

'Where are we going exactly?' They had been walking a while, and he was right: Isla did indeed need to keep up. They had left the main part of the town behind them and had not stopped – just a few hellos from people in passing, none of whom enquired about who Isla was, thankfully, even though she clearly stood out like a sore thumb.

'You'll see when we get there.' That was it: he didn't look at her, didn't stop to say it to her face, just plainly said it over the back of his shoulder. That was all she was worth, wasn't she? A mere thorn in his side, an inconvenience. She wished she could give him what for; she disliked his presence just as much as he did hers. Yet here they were, in the company of each other – well, company may have been a bit strong. That would imply the willingness of two people conversing and enjoying said time with each other. This felt more like a hostage situation, so why was she following him? She supposed she had a choice – a choice to leave, a choice to have said no – but then where would that have left her? Nowhere, but what was better, to be nowhere with someone who knew where they were, or to be nowhere on your own? *It's a fine line*, she thought.

'We're here.' They turned onto a short lane and stood just a few feet shy of a wooden door with iron bars. The houses, if possible, were even narrower, overbearing and claustrophobic than where they had been previously. The ground was undisturbed, but she guessed that was because fewer people frequented there, and she could see why. It felt eerier compared to the area where Kallon's house was; a deathly sound of hollowness clung to the walls, and she did not like it. Where the lane reached its end there was the starting of a field – not the green rolling hills of the Manor but a vast expanse of grey that eventually faded into woods in the distance.

She fought the rising feeling in her stomach that told her to leave. *"Run, Isla!"* it said to her. *"Run while you still have the chance."* But before she could act on her gut feeling the door opened and they were greeted with a warm smile.

'He'll be down in a moment,' said the young woman who introduced herself as Alexis. She was neither extraordinary nor ordinary; she was plain yet had a certain something about her. She had long straight brown hair, fair skin and the curves of a blossoming young woman underneath her drab and unflattering clothes.

'We've not seen you around these parts for a while, Kallon. Grandfather will be pleased to see you, though if I had known we were going to have guests I would have prepared – I'm afraid I cannot offer you much.'

'We won't be stopping long, please do not go to any trouble for us,' Kallon replied, returning a gentle smile her way.

'Well, whatever your reasons, he'll be pleased to see you, as am I.'

Isla noticed that Alexis looked at Kallon with warmth. *Is there or had there been something between them?* She rarely lifted her gaze from him as they indulged in further small talk. *Did he return her feelings?* Perhaps he did.

The inside furnishings offered a far more pleasant

atmosphere compared to the street outside; however, little light fought its way through and a dreary presence still clung to it. Much like Kallon's, the kitchen-come-living room all became one with a staircase just off centre. A collection of weird and wonderful items hung from ceiling to walls, some beautiful, some ugly, some useful and some – well, some she couldn't have given a use for at all.

'My boy.' An elderly man with long, grey hair entered; he walked with an outstretched arm while the other covered his face. As he drew nearer, Isla could see that a cloth just wide enough to cover his eyes was wrapped tightly around his head. He smiled as he approached them, clearly pleased by Kallon's unexpected visit, who returned the same happiness as the man embraced him with a firm hand to his shoulder.

'You are becoming strong, my boy, they've been training you well.'

Kallon didn't say anything but looked humbled by the comment. Perhaps the lack of presence of a father had impacted him more than he cared to let people know, for in that very moment he looked every bit the boy and the man he was. On the one hand, he was tall, slender and toned; he exuberated strength and discipline. But in comparison with his new company, he looked like the boy who sought approval, advice and guidance.

'How are you?' Kallon asked, throwing Alexis a sideways glance. 'I take it there has been no improvement since we last saw each other?'

'Ah yes, I'm afraid my health, as it seems, is failing me, but that is not for a young man to worry about – how is your mother? Keeping well, I hope. She must have her hands full with that sister of yours.'

Kallon laughed. 'Yes, she certainly does. Kelina is eight now.'

'My gosh! Growing up faster than I remembered.'

Kallon responded with the same jest. 'She is certainly growing up faster than I would like; she has a good spirit too –

too eager at times. She wants to go everywhere I go, but I much prefer her to be at home with Mother, where I know she is safer.'

Isla wondered why they always talked about being safe. *Safe from what? What is going on in this place?* She pondered their conversation until she felt all eyes were on her.

'Now, how rude of us, you have not introduced me to your companion. What is your name, young lady?'

Isla was surprised that he had managed to know exactly where she was without her having said a word since he arrived. She rose to her feet and took his outstretched hand.

'My name is Isla. It's a pleasure to meet you, sir.' She didn't know why she spoke so formally to him; it just came out that way. Not knowing the man – or anyone, for that matter – it felt like the right thing to do.

He clasped another hand on top of hers and replied, 'It's a pleasure to meet you too. My name is Arnaurd, and I presume you have already been introduced to my granddaughter Alexis?'

'Yes, I have – it's a pleasure to meet you both.' She looked at Alexis and then at Kallon, trying to gauge some kind of reaction, but she could not see one.

'Now, you've come here for something, my boy – perhaps it's about time you told me what it is for?'

Kallon looked at Isla, giving her a 'let me do the talking' look, and joined him at the table where he now stood. 'We've acquired an item that I was hoping you would have a look at for us. It's somewhat rare, and I believe your expertise could help confirm its authenticity.'

Arnaurd looked curious, taking a seat ready to receive this rare item.

Looking at Isla, Kallon indicated for her to hand it over. She hesitated; she didn't know why, but something made her not want to share it with this man.

'Isla!' Kallon repeated under a strained breath. She didn't look at him; he was starting to irritate her again, and she didn't want to give him the satisfaction of knowing that he could boss her around. If she did something, it was because she wanted to, not because he told her to. She joined Arnaurd at the table and reluctantly handed him the dagger still wrapped in a piece of cloth. He began straight away with his assessment: delicately placing it on the table, he ran his fingers from top to bottom, feeling every groove, jewel, and inch of it with such admiration and attention. He balanced its weight on his two forefingers and let it sit there a moment before placing it back down on the table.

They all looked at each other, waiting for him to speak. Isla's heart started to race; one part of her wanted it to be nothing more than just a simple dagger, to forget everything that had happened and go home, but the other part of her screamed for adventure, for a purpose. She wanted so desperately to prove Kallon wrong.

'Where did you get this from?' he asked, though it was not Isla who replied. 'Sorry, my boy, but I wasn't asking you – Isla, where did you get this from?'

She froze, not knowing what to say. When she hesitated to give an answer, he asked her if she would join him at the table.

'Would you mind doing something for me, please?'

'Ah, yes, sure,' Isla agreed, confused.

'If you wouldn't mind just holding out your hand?'

Oh no. Not this, anything but this. Isla hesitated.

'Please, if you could humour an old man.'

With all eyes on her, she felt she had no choice, even though the same ill feeling was still telling her that they shouldn't be there. Despite every bone in her body telling her otherwise, she reached out, closed her eyes and gripped it tightly. The immediate gasps told her what was happening, and when she opened her eyes, they confirmed it. Sure enough, as she had expected, through the cracks of her fingers, a bright blue light was emitted to every corner of the room.

'So it is true.' Arnaurd did not need his eyes to know what was happening; though they were covered up, he could still feel the power penetrate them. He rose to his feet, ready to speak again, but the smile that was on his face rapidly disappeared; his fingernails clawed at the table, and he began to choke as if something was stuck in his throat.

Isla dropped the dagger on the table in front of her and the room was plunged back into near darkness again.

'Grandfather,' Alexis ran to him, 'fight it.'

He pushed her away; Kallon tried to reach him, but he too got pushed with more force than Arnaurd appeared to have. The coughing and the choking stopped. There was a moment of silence, followed by a low, ominous laugh; under his breath, he muttered the words, 'Come to me.'

Did he really say that? Isla knew that voice all too well; she had heard it once before, but how was that possible? There was no way this could have been the man in the attic, but she wanted to see his face; she wanted to see him say it again. She got closer to him so that only a few feet separated them.

'Arnaurd, what did you say?'

The air was cold, deeply cold, as if she was having an out-of-body experience. Then it happened too quickly for her to react; she hadn't noticed him remove the cloth from around his eyes. He grabbed her, with two hands tightly wrapped around her neck.

'*I see you!*' His eyes were a swirl of a blue-grey mist, the laughing consistent and menacing. '*I see you!*' he repeated.

Isla tried to break free; she was struggling to breathe. Whoever this was, whatever it was, it was not Arnaurd; it was not the man who she had been speaking to moments ago, and she was scared. He slowly began to lift her up, her feet scraping the ground, trying to find her balance. Isla clasped both her hands around his, trying to loosen his grip around her throat. Breathe, she needed to breathe.

'Arnaurd,' she choked. Isla could feel herself fading, her body becoming lighter – perhaps this was how it was meant to be, her heart beat slower like a soft drum as if she was going to sleep. Was this what she was doing? Was she sleeping? Oh, how she wanted to sleep. Fading. Fading. Fading...

With great force, Arnaurd was knocked off his feet and Isla fell to the floor. 'You're too late, boy!' They ignored the words that came out of his mouth, and while Kallon held him still Alexis replaced the cloth back over his eyes; instantly his breathing lowered and his strength dissipated. He was now back to the kind, frail old man that he was before.

'*What was that?*' Kallon demanded to know from Alexis.

'I don't have time to explain – they are coming.' She thrust the dagger into his chest.

'I'm not leaving until you give me some answers.'

'Please, Kallon, you must go.' When he refused to budge she reluctantly spoke further. 'Why do you think his eyes have been covered up? It's not because he is losing his sight; he has done everything he can to stop them, but they have spies in every town. Normal people, just like you and I, they use our eyes as a window as a portal, so that he, the one can see through them. Once they have you it's impossible to break free from them, and now they know that you are here – now they know *she* is here... She is the one they have been waiting for – you must leave. Now!'

Kallon knew exactly what was coming for them, and he had never known fear like it. 'Come on, we've got to go.' He picked her up as if she were as light as a feather.

'Run for the woods – your best chance of losing them will be there. You know them better than anyone,' Alexis urged.

'Kallon! My boy!' Arnaurd was a fragile heap on the floor; he spoke in barely a whisper. 'I'm so sorry,' he cried. 'I'm so sorry. I tried to fight it, but he... the darkness... his spirits... they were just too strong, and now I've led them straight to you.'

Knowing what was coming for him, Kallon didn't want to hang around any longer.

'It's her, Kallon, she's the one. No matter what, you cannot let them have her – you have to protect her… The prophecy – it's true. They must not get her.'

Kallon didn't say anything and made his way to the door.

'Please forgive me, my boy, please forgive…'

The pained look on Kallon's face said that he did, but he couldn't bring himself to say it; he risked one more glance, then they were gone.

CHAPTER NINETEEN

A drop fell on Isla's cheek, followed by two more, then the sky fell through.

'This way.' Kallon grabbed her hand and pulled her quickly. If she hadn't been so shocked by the unexpected invasion of her personal space, she might have protested, but at that very moment when she felt scared and vulnerable, the comforting firm grasp of his hand helped calm her pounding heart.

'SCREEEEECH!' In the streets behind screams could be heard, too close for comfort, and Kallon knew he had to rethink his plan.

'When I say go, you run – you run as fast as you can, you do not look back. No matter what happens to me, you just keep going, okay?'

Isla stared at him, willing the words to come out her mouth, but nothing came; her mind was still in Arnaurd's house with that voice, the voice she had heard before, and it sent chills down her spine.

Isla!

She nodded to show she understood what he had said,

but what she didn't understand was why. *What's got Kallon so frightened? What's coming for us?*

The rain fell harder that Isla could barely see; her hair stuck to her face like glue and her eyes stung from the endless stream running through them. Kallon moved her under an archway, where she felt a brief reprieve from the sharp, icy drops, and firmly clasped his hands around her face.

'Isla, listen to me – it is important that you do not look back.' He pulled her face up gently so that she was forced to look at him. 'Do you understand? Promise me you won't look back.'

With the adrenaline coursing through her body and Kallon practically shaking her back to life, Isla managed to fight her way out of her dream-like state. 'What are we running from? I don't understand.'

He dared a brief look down the street to Arnaurd's house then back at her. 'Please, Isla, we do not have time for this.'

'But I need to know!'

He still had his hands around her face. He locked his eyes with hers – they were dilated, intense, but the rest of his face was calm; it reminded her of the way Will looked at her sometimes.

'Do you trust me?' he said in a tone that was somehow reassuring yet urgent all rolled in together.

Isla thought about it: he irritated her; she found him rude and offensive, self-righteous and egotistical. However, despite all of that, she felt that she could – there was something honest about him.

'Isla, do you trust me?' he asked again.

'Yes!'

'Then trust what I am saying. I promise I will tell you everything that I know, but if you don't do exactly what I say, then neither of us will get the chance.'

She agreed and for once didn't push the matter.

He kept looking anxiously up the street, but she heard it before he saw it: Alexis screams and Arnaurd's protests that he didn't know anything. Her immediate response was to go and help them, but Kallon shouted, 'Now!' and they were off. Only Kallon didn't run with her; she slowed down to see where he was going. They spilt in a V shape: she headed one way, he the other.

'Remember, run for the trees and don't look back.' He turned his back on her and ran faster; after a moment's hesitation, she did the same. Mud splattered up her legs, the pools of water under her feet made it harder to run, the rain blasted against her skin and her lungs fought for oxygen.

A bolt of thunder rippled in the darkening sky above, followed immediately by another; there was no escaping the storm, nor, it would seem, their looming capture. She strived to keep going. She'd promised she wouldn't look back, but she couldn't help it – it was instinct. She needed to know what she was up against. She risked a glance, and even though it was hard to see, she could just about make out the silhouettes of some grey hooded figures headed straight towards her.

But what if she just stopped?

What would they do? She hadn't done anything wrong; she was merely in the wrong place at the wrong time, and still, really what had any of them done? She could stop; she could stop running. She was tired, tired of secrets, tired of being told what to do, so she did!

Isla stopped dead on her feet.

She didn't know exactly how many, but perhaps there was seven or eight of them. Between the rain, the thunder, the lightning and the blood rushing to her head, she wasn't sure what she could see, but she knew what she felt, and what she felt was complete and total fear – the kind of fear that makes you freeze – and in that moment she knew she had made a horrible mistake.

Stuck, it felt as if a pause button had been pressed. Everything around her froze: raindrops stopped in place, her hair floated in mid-air, and her breath danced in front of her. She was completely frozen, but the grey hooded figures were not, they kept moving closer and closer towards her, while all the time she couldn't even manage a blink. Another step – only a few feet between them now. Then something strange happened: they did not attack her, grab her or seem to even notice her at all; they, in fact, went straight past her as if they hadn't even seen her. *Is this right?*

Deep in the depths of her pocket Isla's hand wrapped tightly around the necklace; she heard a faint, soft voice telling her to go, that she must continue. It felt familiar, safe. She didn't want to leave, but the voice told her she had to, then it was gone, and the rain was falling once again.

'Hey! ...Hey! Over here.' It was Kallon, and now she understood why they had passed her entirely. 'Over here – this is what you are looking for.' He was waving the dagger around in the air. *What the hell is he doing?*

He had already made it to the treeline, and before she could see anything else, he dived into it, and they followed.

Isla ran in after him, but was she too late: she couldn't see or hear anything, just the noise of the storm. She called out for him: 'Kallon! *Kallon!*' But she heard nothing in reply. She frantically searched; she didn't want to be left alone. What had she done? Why had she stopped? Why hadn't she just done what she was told? Perhaps they would both be all right now.

Then she saw one, searching, gliding across the forest floor; it didn't have to climb the fallen branches like she did. It was eerie how it moved – she could hear its breathing like each breath was the end of life, then it sniffed the air, a long, drawn-out sniff, and quickly turned in the opposite direction.

'Kallon,' she whispered. She saw him, but there was no time – there was one on his trail. They were coming at him from all directions now; she wanted to scream to warn him, to distract them, like he had done for her. She was about to when all of a sudden the words were stopped from ever leaving her mouth; a hand had come out of nowhere and smothered her words. It was firm, not violent, yet they held her still; one was over her mouth, then one was placed around her waist, pulling her away. She tried to break free, but she felt more hands keeping her still. She fought hard, but her body was too weak, too exhausted – still she kept trying; she couldn't let them get Kallon. Her breathing accelerated, her lungs burst, then she realised that she was not only fighting to break free she was fighting for air; one more gasp then all went black!

When Isla woke, she found herself inside and away from the storm; she had been laid down on a bed that was so thin it was barely even good for use. She could tell she was not in a house, for the walls were made of stone and went from floor to ceiling. She was near freezing, and could still hear the sound of rain. It was a dwelling rather than a home, and perhaps somewhere she shouldn't plan on staying.

As she slowly came to, Isla could hear she was not alone: the muttered whisperings of a group of men gathered around a fire talked about her in hushed voices. They hadn't noticed her stir, which was good, as it gave her time to figure out what to do. She couldn't see a clear way out and with the men blocking the only source of light; it made it that much harder for her to see. There was nothing of interest: just a few beds, a table, some barrels and that was it. She was beginning to think there was no hope, that maybe she was going to die with these strangers and never see the Manor again – that was until she noticed a sword propped up against the table not far from where the men stood.

Maybe she might be able to reach it in time, grab it and demand that they let her go; she knew she didn't know what to do with a sword, but if she was going to challenge a group of men a weapon would be better than nothing. That was it; she decided she was going to do it. The more time thinking about it was more time wasted. She needed to go find Kallon; he hadn't particularly been kind to her, but if anything happened to him because of her – because she didn't, couldn't do what she was told and had put them both in danger – she'd never forgive herself.

She saw her moment when they all appeared to be listening to something that was coming in the distance. *Right, it has to be now*, Isla told herself, *before more company arrives*. She moved so quick that she even surprised herself but was equally surprised at how quick they were too; they were all on their feet just as she managed to get one finger round the sword. They probably could have stopped her, but they didn't.

Isla held it up and demanded they let her go. 'I don't know who you are or why you have brought me here, but I will be leaving now, and I suggest you do not stop me!' She hadn't anticipated how heavy the sword was going to be, and she struggled to hold it up. No wonder they all laughed at her, including a few women amongst the mix that until now she had not noticed.

'I don't think this is funny – you have taken me against my will. This is called kidnapping, and I will cause harm to anyone who comes close to me.' Isla tried to wave the sword around as a warning, but this only resulted in them laughing at her more.

'Okay, okay, that's enough.' One of the men stepped forward from the group with his hands held up, and when they didn't stop he raised his voice and they all did as he commanded. He was of medium height, with thick black hair down to his ears that was wet from the rain and a beard that was equally as long. His hands wore fingerless gloves and his nails were dirty; his face was smudged in mud and his clothes were not much better either.

Isla pointed the sword in his direction, but he did not flinch; he just stopped so he could talk to her.

'We're not here to hurt you, I promise,' he said in a voice that was deep yet calm.

Isla looked at him – despite the rough exterior he did appear kind. His eyes were tired like they had seen a lifetime of worry, but they were kind.

'Why do you expect me to believe you?' She thrust the sword at him again.

'Because if we wanted to harm you, we could have – we would have done so by now.'

Isla still wasn't so sure; she felt intimated by the many glaring eyes. She had no idea what to do – if she gave up her only source of defence they could be lying and she might give up her only way of escape, but on the other hand, her arms were growing tired and her time was running out either way. Luckily, she didn't have to think about it for much longer.

'What are you doing?' They all turned around. 'Put that down before you cause yourself any damage.' She immediately let the weight of the sword drop her arms to the floor, then her heart smiled a beat.

CHAPTER TWENTY

'Give that here – you'll poke someone's eye out.' Kallon took the sword off Isla and handed it back to the man who had just been trying to negotiate with her.

'I'm sorry, Henri, she doesn't quite know her manners.'

Henri placed one hand on his shoulder and took the sword. 'That's quite alright, brother.' There was a murmur of low laughing and grumbling from behind them. 'Come, let us talk.'

Henri led them to a corner away from the rest of the group; it was getting colder by the minute and water trickled down the stonewalls. Having moved from the warmth of the fire Isla shivered, gripping herself tightly. She was still wet from having been out in the rain and her clothes were cold against her skin. Fresh droplets trickled down Kallon's face, though he did not seem to be bothered. Isla watched as the two of them exchanged a few words and it was now she could see just how toned he actually was. As wet clothes clung to his skin, they outlined every crevice, highlighting the curve of his muscles, and the strength that she had felt before now made sense – how he could so easily lift her up as if she weighed nothing. It was evident that he was stronger than he first appeared.

Kallon noticed Isla shivering. 'Perhaps we should wait until we've all had a chance to warm up – do you have any spare clothes she could wear?' This was the first time Isla had actually seen Kallon show any real concern for her.

'Yes, I think I can find something, for you too, Kai.' Henri looked at Isla, clearly confused by her current items of clothing, then left and walked away.

Isla and Kallon, now left alone, stood in silence. Kallon was unnervingly quiet, and it made Isla feel uncomfortable. She had half expected him to shout at her, ask her why she'd put them both in danger, make some kind of dig or sarcastic comment, but he didn't.

'It's cold, I hope he hurries up. I don't think I can feel my body anymore.'

Kallon looked around; Isla realised he was searching for something to start a fire with. He found what he needed, and it didn't take him long to get one going. Isla crouched down next to it and let the prickling sensation take over her hands. She looked at Kallon, who still had not said anything since Henri had left them.

'Thanks,' Isla said to him.

He nodded at her to show that he had heard but still didn't speak. This was not like Kallon to have nothing to say; in the short time she had known him she had not seen him like this. He could be silent in the moody kind of way, but this was not it. Guilt eating away at her, she couldn't handle the silent treatment a moment longer.

'I'm sorry for what I did – I didn't mean to. I know you said to keep going, to not look back, and I swear that was what I was going to do – I was doing that. But I just had to know what was after us. I took a quick look, no more than a second, and, well, after that I had this urge to stop. I regretted it instantly. I don't know what happened – I was frozen, stuck, then the next thing I knew everything was moving again and you were there, shouting.

I tried to catch you up, but I was too late. I tried to help, Kallon, I swear I tried to help, to do something like you did for me, but I was grabbed. I tried to scream to do whatever I could, but I just couldn't. I thought that was it; I thought they had got you and that something terrible was going to happen, then I woke up here.' How Isla managed to say that all in one breath, she did not know, but she felt lighter for speaking her truth.

'Something terrible has happened.' Kallon saw the hurt in her eyes and drew a deep breath. 'It's not your fault, Isla, it's what they do, the grey hoods – you let them get close enough and they make you question your existence, make your fears become reality. They get into your head. That's why I said don't look at them – they eat away at you bit by bit until you are a mere shell of yourself. Every time you come in contact with one, you lose a part of yourself. I have been in contact with one before, and it is not something I want to do again.' He prodded at the fire, encouraging the flames to grow.

'I didn't know,' Isla whispered quietly.'I don't know anything anymore.'

Kallon sat down next to her, the colour having already started to return to his face. 'Isla, listen to me – it's not your fault; none of this is your fault. This has been going on for a long time, long before you turned up. Don't give yourself so much credit to think you caused all this. I'm here, no one got hurt and they can't get us – not for now, anyway. You have to stop thinking about this; you can't let them keep hold of you.'

'What do you mean, keep hold of me?'

'Like I said, it's what they do – long after they are gone, their effects still stay. They're darkness, Isla, and if you let them, they will leave you in the dark.'

Isla looked even more confused.

'You had little contact with them today, so their effects won't last long – you're lucky. But you need to think of a happy place. That's what I was doing – I was concentrating on my memories.

I was blocking them out, but you have to concentrate on that and only that.'

She closed her eyes and thought back to the last time she'd felt happy, safe and happy with the person she always felt safe with: Will. Memories of them on the hill under their tree came flooding back – a lifetime of memories, all the years moulded into one. Laughter, she could feel the laughter within her as if he was with her now. Oh, she so wished he was with her now; he would know what to do. She thought back to her birthday, when he had been so eager to make her happy, to do anything for her, then she thought back to the very last time she'd seen him: they had argued and he'd done his best to calm her down, but she wouldn't listen. She had been too stubborn; she had left. Then the guilt crept back in once more. *What must he think? What must he have seen?* He wouldn't know where she was, and he would be worried; she knew it.

'Isla, Isla!' Kallon was trying to get her attention. 'Remember, happy thoughts – concentrate.' She opened her eyes, and for a brief second, it was Will's face in front of her. She smiled contently, comforted by his familiarity. However, the moment of bliss faded rapidly as Kallon's face started to come into view, the awkwardness instantaneous.

'Here, I found something – it should fit,' Henri said, breaking the silence. 'There's something for you too, Kai. Unfortunately we don't have any changing facilities. I cannot offer you any homely furnishings here, but there is some privacy over there.' He pointed towards a collection of wooden doors lined up against one another.

'It's my private area, so no one will disturb you there. Take this with you.' Henri gave Isla a lantern so that she could light her own way, then turned his attention to Kallon. 'Kai, my brother, you've been missed.'

❖

With dry clothes and a warm fire, Isla felt much better than she had done half an hour ago.

'Get this down you – it will help.' Henri passed them both a wooden bowl that looked as if it contained some kind of broth, but Kallon waved his away.

'Do you have a spoon?' Isla asked.

Henri laughed. 'We don't have such luxuries around here.'

It was the first time that Isla had seen him smile, and it suited him; he was fairly handsome (for an older man), and his laugh was haughty and wholesome.

Kallon took the other bowl. 'Here, like this.' He gently blew the frothy top then took a sip.

'Oh,' Isla replied, embarrassed.

'So, pleasantries out of the way, perhaps we have some things to discuss?' Henri said, bringing the conversation back to the matter at hand.

Isla looked down at her feet, feeling a bit shameful for her previous behaviour. 'I'm sorry for waving a sword around at you.'

Henri belly-laughed again. There it was: that smile, as captivating as the rest of him. 'Not to worry, you gave my men and women a laugh at the very least. Anyway, it shows you have some fight in you – we'll make a fighter out of you yet.'

Isla gave a meek smile and set about sipping at her broth; she had gone from having so many questions to having her mind almost completely evaporated. She let the two of them take the lead while she mentally worked on her happy thoughts; Kallon seemed to be almost back to normal, but she still felt empty – or perhaps not empty, just lost.

'I managed to lose them in one of the hideouts. I am sorry for bringing them to your doorstep, but I had no choice,' Kallon explained.

'It's okay, brother, I am sure you would not have done so if you had seen any other way. But why were they chasing you – why were they around these parts?'

'I have a lot to tell you – action must happen, and soon – but I,' Kallon corrected himself, 'we shall need your help.'

Isla's ears pricked up at this; she presumed he meant her by "we". He was referring to them as a collective now, not Kallon and some girl.

'Hmmm.' Henri scratched at his chin. 'Okay, well, let's start with how you two come to cross paths, then you can explain about the grey hoods. Somehow I think there's more to you than just waving swords around.'

Isla felt her cheeks burn; she didn't like being the centre of attention or being spoken of as if she didn't have a clue, but then again, that wasn't entirely untrue.

'There most certainly is, but there are things she does not know. She doesn't know who she is, Henri.'

Isla's face dropped; any concentrating she had been doing thinking of her happy place now stopped. She listened intently as Kallon went from start to finish about the events of the last twenty-four hours, most of which was correct, though he missed out the part about how unwelcoming and rude he had been to her.

'And so that brings us here, with this.' He pulled out the dagger. 'My mother is right: she's the one, she has to be. I believe it now.'

Henri took the dagger and looked at it in awe. 'It cannot be.' His eyes widened. 'I have never seen…'

Kallon turned his gaze. 'She is. I'm sorry I have given you a hard time, Isla – truly, I am. But perhaps when I explain everything, maybe you might understand my hesitation.' The fire's embers were reflected in his grey eyes, and she could see that he genuinely did mean what he said; however, it did not excuse how he had treated her, and she was doubtful that whatever he had to say would change her mind.

'I want to know about the grey hoods and this prophecy everyone keeps talking about, and how apparently you think it has something to do with me?'

Henri raised an eyebrow; she didn't mean for it to come out as bluntly as it sounded, but she just wanted answers and clear ones at that.

'Okay, okay, one thing at a time, but first you must understand, we never used to live like this. We were once civilised people – everyone lived happily aside one another. Our hills were green, our skies were blue, food would grow from the ground and freshwater would run down the mountains. It really was a beautiful place, but now everyone is out for themselves and life has been hard.'

Isla tried to imagine what it must have looked like before, but with what she had experienced so far she was struggling to see it.

'I know it's hard to imagine, but that is what it once was.' Henri finally moved his gaze from the dagger. 'It is true what he says: this place was a place of beauty, of life, though you will find no life here now.'

Isla looked at him. 'So what happened? I don't understand.'

Henri didn't respond to Isla's question. 'Please excuse me – you do not need me for this part. I must be with my thoughts,' He placed the dagger at Isla's feet then walked away.

'Was it something I said?'

'No, you have not said anything. He has lost a great deal, and he does not need to be reminded of the story I am about to tell you.'

'I see – so why is everyone living in fear? What is everyone hiding from?'

'Before I tell of the dark ages we live in now, I must tell you of a time before; this will help you understand. Centuries ago, a woman by the name of Ilandrya, a seer, was bound by oath to her master – he was a greedy man who sought riches and fortune. He spent most of his days drunk and surrounded by women. He would call upon her to see his future, to which she obeyed. She lived in terrible conditions and was mistreated. That was until, luck would have it, one day she met a man; they instantly fell in love and managed to keep their love a secret for many years – they even bore a child together. Despite the burden of their secrecy, it was their love for one another that kept them going; that was until her master found out and had her husband and child slain. He bound her by chains and tormented her with their deaths. As her grief grew, so did her power, and she managed to break free and slaughter her master. Consumed by the grief for her dead husband and child, she embarked on finding a way to bring them back. She delved into things that she shouldn't have done, and as her grief grew, so did her anger. She got more and more involved with dark magic until it had all but consumed her, and she sought only power and eternal life. She finally succeeded: eternal life was hers, though she was still not happy; she wanted every man to suffer, women and children too, if they were to stand in her way.'

Isla held her breath. *How could a story be so sad?* She let Kallon continue, not wanting to interrupt.

'It is said that she was in possession of five runes. These runes build up our fundamentals of life: earth, fire, water and so on. All the things we need to survive. And with each rune was a guardian, a dragon – how much of this is true I am not sure. I have never seen a dragon, but this is how legend tells it. Anyway, when she was defeated, the runes were divided amongst the realms so that not one sole person could ever have that level of power again. A leader of each quarter attended a meeting held under the guidance of the elders – the grey hoods. They are thirteen priests of the thirteenth circle; they serve no one other than the balance of life. No one knows who got what or where they took it, but they all did as they agreed, and for years everyone lived in peace and harmony. That is until the darkness came.'

'What happened to her, the seer?' Isla asked.

'No one knows for sure: some say she turned to dust and evaporated with the wind; others say she was banished, exiled, never to be seen again.' Kallon prodded a stick into the fire to keep it going.

'Why let her go if she caused that much devastation?' Isla questioned.

'She had been punished enough with the torment of the loss of her husband and child, plus without her runes, she was powerless, a mere seer again. There was not much damage she could do, and I guess the elders took pity on her, if it is true that she still is alive.'

Isla could see why they would have done that.

'So the elders, they are the grey hoods, yes? I thought you said they served no one?'

'This is true; it was true, but then a new darkness came, one we fear is more powerful. A man, by the name of Akos – a pure blood, he too was lured by the lust of power and eternal life, turned them. Well, some of them – the ones that you saw today. It is not known what happened to the others – in hiding somewhere, I suspect.'

Isla was struggling to take this all in; she still didn't quite see what any of it had to do with her.

'So Akos – where is he now?'

'He is at the City of People, where he has remained since the great battle.'

Isla looked even more confused. 'Great battle?'

'Okay, this is another story entirely – move a century forward and we find ourselves at the mercy of Akos. He is a descendent of the Vale, which means natural magic runs through his veins; he took these natural gifts and abused them. Secretly he had been working on dark magic and had become stronger without anyone knowing. He went in search of the five runes, destroying towns far and wide. As his search continued, he grew an army – some joined willingly, while others were forced. It ended in a battle at the City of People, where he was not destroyed, but the fighting suddenly stopped, and to this day no one knows why. Unfortunately, the king and queen vanished that same day, presumed dead, and he took up their residence, where he has lain dormant but plagued our lands ever since.'

'But if you know where he is, why can't you just go and stop him?' It seemed obvious to Isla.

'Don't be fooled, he has built himself a fortress. The City of People is not how we knew it to be, and he has spies in every corner. Animals, people, all feed back to him, and he has the grey hoods doing his bidding – you have seen what they are capable of. He still has strength – no army of our size could rise against him – but he is scared of something. Some say it's the prophecy, some say he is still in search of the runes, but the runes are only a myth – no one can know for sure. But all I do know is that we have never been free of him since.'

'This is all very interesting, but I still don't get what this has to do with me, Kallon. You still have not told me what this has *to do* with *me!*'

'Okay, okay, you needed to understand the history first. After the great battle was over, rumours began of a prophecy. Someone would arrive out of the blue and with them they would carry something from the the Valeyan line and it would mark the beginning of the end.'

'So?' Isla shrugged.

'Don't you see? What you have is just that – this is not your everyday item, Isla. Only someone with Valeyan blood can be in possession of such an item, or yield it, even. Have you not seen how it answers to your call? Don't ask me how, but you are of the Vale, or a descendent at the very least. *You*, Isla, *are* the beginning of the end.'

CHAPTER TWENTY-ONE

'What?' Isla's mouth dropped. 'The beginning of the what?'

'The end, the one to help us end this, to stop it once and for all.'

'You have the wrong person, Kallon,' she said, astonished that he could think such a thing. 'I'm sorry, but I can't help – whoever you are looking for, you have to believe me when I say that it is not me.' Isla uncomfortably pulled at her hands, not sure what else she could say to strengthen her case.

'Isla, I know it's a lot to take in. I wasn't so sure myself at first, but I believe it to be true now.' He looked at her reassuringly.

'To be true, *now?*' she said sarcastically. 'What stopped you from believing it before? Is it because you took an instant dislike towards me?'

'Isla, I said I'm sorry, but it's not as simple as that.' He seemed to genuinely mean what he said.

'Well, I'm sorry to have got your hopes up for nothing I'm just your average girl from a little village in Lancashire. I come from a children's home, and that is about the only special or abnormal thing about me. I hold no magical powers, no hidden talents, and certainly, I am not capable of helping you bring some dark evil to its end. This person, the prophecy you all speak of, I am telling you now, it is certainly not me!' She was stuck between a feeling of uncertainty and rage; unsure of what else to do she stood up, hoping a change of position might calm her nerves, but it didn't: she still felt the same numb feeling.

Kallon took hold of her, his resolve instantly soothing. 'Please, Isla. I know this must be difficult for you, but you asked me to tell you what I know, and this is what I believe to be true.' They let the silence separate them for a moment, his hands a solid yet gentle touch against her skin.

'Look,' Kallon knelt down and picked up the dagger, 'hold this.' Isla was hesitant; she wished she had given it to Mr Stopes when she had had the chance, to be rid of it, to be rid of everything that came along with it. But Kallon insisted, and she gave in, just like she had done in Arnaurd's house. They exchanged knowing glances of what would happen next, only this time it didn't. They waited and waited for the familiar light to show itself, but it did not come; all that was there was Isla's hand and a dagger that had lost its spark. She thrust it back at him, slightly disappointed.

'See, it's not me.'

Kallon didn't look discouraged; he just gently guided her to sit back down. Isla couldn't bring herself to look at him. She wasn't sure if it was because she was secretly disappointed or that once again she'd felt that tingly feeling shoot up her spine at the connection of his skin against hers.

He tilted his head so that he could look up into her glazed-over eyes; she tried to hide them, but it was no use – he had already seen. 'Isla, you have to believe me; you have to believe in it. It won't answer your call unless you trust it.'

That all-too-familiar pool of water of late threatened to release itself once again; it was not like Isla to cry, but she was finding it increasingly harder to keep her emotions at bay lately.

Fighting the urge to break down, to admit her failures and find comfort in the closest arms to her, she took a deep breath, willing her eyes to dry.

'I just want to go home, Kallon.'

He felt for her and, besides her best efforts, her vulnerability too. 'But what if you are home? What if this *is* your home, Isla?' She finally met his eyes. 'What if this is where you are meant to be? Think about it – do you think it is coincidence that brought you here? Because I don't.'

She broke away from his touch. She needed to; the feeling of his surprisingly warm hands against hers was too distracting. 'So what if I am this person, the prophecy, *what am I meant to do, Kallon?* Tell me. Even you said yourself it would take more than one person to beat this. What is one girl meant to do against the darkness?' She had him there; he hadn't quite thought about it. He was still coming to terms himself with the fact that the prophecy was true. He had thought only of one course of action, the immediate action, but after that, he was unsure.

'I don't know,' he said in all honesty, 'but I guess it is something that we will figure out.'

Isla rolled her eyes. 'Figure out? I thought if I was the one, the prophecy, you would have some idea of what it was that I am actually meant to do?'

'That's not how it works. I don't know, okay, all I know is the stories that were told, and now you are here!' They started to raise their voices hastily, which caught the attention of the others.

'Alright, you two, you are giving my crew something to talk about.'

They both paused mid-sentence as if they had been caught doing something far worse.

'I apologise, Henri, it won't happen again.' The old Kallon was back once again; his demeanour had shifted, and he motioned that Isla should say the same, but she didn't, for she was not sorry.

'Now is not the time for arguing. We must come together – only as a united front are we stronger.' He held the back of Kallon's head and bowed them both together. 'I take it you have shared with Isla our story?'

'I have told her what I know, yes.'

Which wasn't much, Isla thought to herself.

'Then you know what we must do?'

Isla couldn't help but feel the cold distance that had suddenly formed between the two of them once again; it frustrated her that he could flick from being one thing to another. Will would have never treated her like that; he was always good to her – too good sometimes.

'We must make our way to Lord Lestrone. He is the largest of our cities left and has managed to hold his fortress – with our men and his men, there is hope.' Henri was pacing, scratching at his chin.

'Are we sure he will let us in?' Kallon questioned.

'Yes, he is a fair man, he will agree to see us, and once we show him who we have with us, he will agree to work with us. We may not be of the king's guard, but we are just as skilled and resourceful, and together we can put up a fight.'

'Once you show him who you have with you? I presume you are talking about me? Before I am taken anywhere, I should like to know where exactly you are taking me.' Isla's inner strength came bubbling back to the surface, and with every cold stare from Kallon, it only urged her to pursue the point more.

'Isla, I apologise. I do not mean to speak as if you are not here. You, of course, more than anyone have a right to know where we are going – come.' He took her to a table and smoothed out a map on top. 'Here, this is where we are.' He pointed to the edge of a wood, which she saw was named Norridian. 'This is where you and Kallon have come from.' And he pointed to another small dot on the map named Branstown. 'We are one of the many towns and villages within the valleys of Weststoria; we are surrounded by hills and mountains that separate us. Most of these towns and villages have either been raided or live in fear of the darkness and their followers. And this is what we do, my men and women: we support the weak by hunting for food when they can't. We track grey hoods and warn towns in advance; we protect the weak from the darkness and give hope to those that fear the silence, and in doing so, we are recruiting. We are creating a resistance; it has taken a long time, but we are growing in numbers.'

She looked at Kallon, realising that he too must have been doing this and this was why he had been gone for weeks, why his sister missed him so much. Was it not for his stony look and self-righteous attitude, she would have admired him for it.

'And here, this is Lestoris. Besides the once City of People this is the largest of them all and where Lord Lestrone resides.' He stopped to see that she was with him so far. 'And this is the City of People – I presume Kallon has told you what lies there?'

She nodded to say that he had. Isla looked at the map. 'What are the coloured dots for?' she asked.

'The black ones are areas that have succumbed to the darkness over the years. Green are places that we know are generally safe, like us, and red are places we are yet to travel but hear there are those that seek a way out.'

Isla inspected the map; it made her feel sad for what she saw. 'But what about the people that still remain in those areas?' She pointed to those marked black.

'There's nothing we can do for them now. If they chose to stay, they chose the darkness; if they didn't leave when they had the chance, it is too late for them,' he replied.

'And the ones marked red? They have no one to help them?'

'I'm afraid not – not all of them, anyway.'

'But that's not fair – how can you choose to save some and leave others? I thought you said you have been helping people?' She didn't know why, but she felt overwhelming anger for them.

'Isla, you must understand: we are but mortals and some of these places are hundreds of miles apart. To get to these places we have to travel on foot and not be detected. I will do what I can, but I will not foolishly put the lives of my men and women at risk.'

She reasoned with herself and said more pleadingly, 'But there must be something that can be done? All these people living in fear, day by day, starving, not knowing what will happen from one day to the next – no one should live like that,' she said, inspecting the map.

'I admire your passion, but advertising our presence will serve no one and will end only in slaughter or imprisonment. These things, they have to be carefully planned, but Lestrone, he has many more men. Together we can rescue many more, and the more we save, the bigger we can grow. Together maybe, just maybe, we might have enough strength to defeat the darkness and get our lands back to what they once were.'

Isla took a couple of seconds to think this through. 'Do you believe that I am the prophecy?'

Henri scratched at his beard again; he seemed to do this when he was thinking. 'I believe you have a part to play, yes, but what that part is I do not know. My gut tells me you are capable of so much more; however, if I may speak plainly, you are blind to it.'

'How can I be blind to it when I don't know what it is I am meant to do?'

He rolled the map up and put it back into its holdings. 'You are not blind to it up here, but blind to it in there.' He pointed to her heart. 'And until the two work as one there's no going forward. We all have our paths to follow, Isla – you must not be afraid to follow yours.'

The words stunned her to silence; everyone seemed to believe in her, yet she did not herself. What was she so afraid of? She could feel Kallon's eyes observing her, penetrating her skin, but she dared not look at him.

'Come, we must rest now; we will make our way to Lestoris – that is the path we all shall follow next. Get some sleep, and we can discuss this further tomorrow. I shall have some beds prepared for you, then we will leave at first light.'

Isla didn't say any more; neither did Kallon. It was clear they both felt enough had been said for one night.

'Isla! Isla!' She woke up to Kallon shaking her. 'Get up, we've got to leave.'

'What?' she replied groggily. 'What do you mean, we've got to leave? What time is it?'

Kallon was shoving some things into a bag. 'They've found us – we've got to go *now*!'

'Who's found us?' Isla said, rubbing her eyes. She had surprisingly nodded off straight to sleep once Henri had shown them to their beds and had been in a deep sleep.

'The grey hoods, and they have company.'

Isla shot right up at the mention of their name. 'They're here? Where?'

He handed her a set of boots. 'Quick, get these on.'

She fumbled around with the laces, trying to get them on as quickly as possible, but they were not shoes she was used to; she was struggling, so Kallon helped her.

'They are outside – Henri's men are holding them back, but they won't last long.'

'What are we going to do?' Isla heard her voice tremble.

'We are going to get out of here.'

Henri came running over; he was bearing a sword and a bag. 'Quick, follow me.'

They followed Henri down a short passageway that opened up into another cave, the only source of light from the lantern within his hand. There was a draught coming from somewhere; she could feel it as they got closer, though she could not see it until Henri stopped at a small gap, barely big enough to fit a child through.

'You must go – we will do our best to cover your trail, but you must move quickly.'

'Where are we going?' Isla asked, flustered.

'Make your way to Lestoris. You must speak to Lord Lestrone – you *must* make him listen,' he said, directing this to Kallon. He grasped his shoulders. 'You cannot get caught – keep her safe at all costs, Kai. Keep her safe.'

Kallon took the sword and bag from Henri and placed them over his shoulder. 'I understand. I promise I shall keep her safe.'

They bowed heads again, and Henri patted Kallon off.

'Do not speak from here on out – not until you have reached a safe distance. Move quickly, but quietly. Now you must go.'

Kallon wriggled his way through the gap. Isla hesitated; she wasn't overly fond of small spaces, and she could feel herself starting to hyperventilate.

Henri faced her in his calm manner, even in a time like this. 'It's your path, Isla. You must trust it.' Then he was gone, running back towards the commotion.

'Isla,' Kallon whispered, 'we've got to go.' She bent her body in a way she never thought possible and came tumbling out the other side, her feet landing into a pulsing stream. She wished he had mentioned this before she went through because now she had two wet feet that could have been avoided. Though she was relieved to see that they had entered somewhere much larger – that somewhat made up for it, even though their path was still tricky, slipping on the moss-covered stones as they followed the walkway to the end of the stream.

When they reached the end she could see the moonlight was out in full view reflecting off a waterfall, which was now the only separation between them and what lay on the other side. Kallon held a finger up to his lips, indicating she needed to be quiet; he motioned for her to follow and to copy him.

They were able to manoeuvre their way around the waterfall without getting wet, and Isla was thankful to see that the storm had passed. Kallon crouched down behind some bushes before heading out from the cover of the cave. The sky was still dark and worked in their favour; they made a dash for it, and their first challenge was done: get past the open expanse from the exit of the cave to the thicket of trees. They kept low and moved a couple of paces at a time before Kallon would signal to stop so that he could check their surroundings. They were just about to move again when they heard a branch snap. Kallon held his hands up to say do not move and gently guided Isla back to the protection of a tree. He had one hand on the helm of his sword and the other on her shoulder. Isla's heart was beating faster than she could keep up with; even Kallon looked flustered.

There was just one man. He didn't look like one of Henri's; therefore, he must have been one of the followers Henri had spoken of.

'There's just one of them,' Kallon whispered. 'We'll wait to see which direction he goes, then we will move. Are you okay?'

Isla nodded, not wanting to speak, for she feared if she spoke, she might not stop.

'You need to slow your breathing. With me: in, out, in out.' He helped focus her enough to level out her breathing to the point where the beats of her heart started to subside, and she began to breathe normally again.

She was about to say thank you when: 'Kallon!' Out of nowhere, a man appeared from behind him. He turned around just in time to miss his sword and Isla ducked, missing the aftermath of the swing. Kallon wrestled him to the ground, but he was large – slow but large and with a lot of weight behind him. Isla watched as the two fought, neither of them winning. Kallon tried to cover the man's mouth so that he couldn't call for help, but he bit him, which made Kallon jump back and gave his attacker the advantage. He put two large hands around his neck, taking joy in watching Kallon struggle. Isla ran at the man, but with his sheer bodyweight, he was able to shrug her off. She landed with a thump and hit her head on something hard. Disorientated, she dragged herself off the floor, bringing with her a rock in her hand, and with all her might she hit him over the head as hard as she could. The man dropped to the ground, not knocked out but momentarily dazed. She rushed to Kallon, who was clutching at his throat, willing the oxygen to fight its way back in, gasping.

'Come on, we've got to go,' she said, pulling him up. He didn't argue, but she did not know what direction to go in, so they just ran away from their assailant.

'Hey! *Hey!* Over there!' The man had got to his feet. '*Get them!*' he said, stumbling on foot. The others caught wind of what he was pointing at, and now their quiet escape was a full-on pursuit.

Isla was still dragging Kallon along; the man had almost squeezed the life out of him, but luckily for them, his large frame was not fast on its feet, and they could still outrun him. That was not the same for the others, though, who were quickly closing the gap.

'Kallon, come on, you've got to keep moving.' She grabbed his arm tighter, and he allowed her to help him. They were headed into low branches; twigs and leaves scratched at their faces as they fought their way through, barely able to see a foot in front of them. The men continued to yell, and barks of dogs could be heard amongst the midst.

'That's it – keep going, keep going, Kallon.' Isla had her head turned, so she didn't notice her foot had travelled further than she expected it to. She focused her attention forward, but by then it was too late: her footing was gone and so was she.

'Whoah.' One of the chasers held his arm out to stop another from following the same fate as Isla's. 'Don't go any further.' The man slipped a little but managed to hold a branch to steady himself.

'They went down there?' he questioned, staring into the abyss. 'What are we meant to do now?'

'Nothing,' the other man replied. 'If the fall doesn't kill them, the cold will.'

CHAPTER TWENTY-TWO

The initial shock over, things still remained tense at Morsely Manor, and the elapsed time had not done anything to settle Miss Sparrow's nerves, the uncertainty was gruelling; even Mr Stopes felt on edge.

'Have they heard anything?' Mr Stopes enquired.

'I have not been informed of any sightings, but I am due to meet with the council tonight.'

'I would like to attend,' he said, making her stop in her tracks. Though Miss Sparrow was often stern and of hard face, she was not completely devoid of emotion, and agreed on this occasion that she would allow his request, though she made it clear that he was not to speak or interrupt: he was to listen and only listen. She was very firm about that. He agreed to her terms, knowing that he was not likely to obey them, not if there was news of Isla – if there was news of his goddaughter.

They spoke no further on this and continued walking in silence, for this was not the reason for their encounter on this early summer's morning. Though Miss Sparrow and Mr Stopes faced a crisis for all other pretences, the Manor continued in the same way, which they had become wearisome of maintaining a double life. Amongst the piles of paperwork and the general overseeing of the Manor Miss Sparrow had spent every other waking hour trying to locate Isla. And had the walk been for different reasons, she may have enjoyed the fresh morning breeze in the now-restored garden, where lavender, marigolds and daylilies sweetened the air.

'What news do you have of Will for me?' she finally asked.

'He had no other information to add of any significance,' Mr Stopes confirmed.

'And what did you tell him?' It was unlike Miss Sparrow to task someone else with such a big responsibility, but during a time like this, she couldn't split her concentrations. Will was an unnecessary distraction, plus she had only one response when it came to matters like this. A more tactile approach was probably a far better one, and there was no one more suited to this than Mr Stopes, though she would have never admitted this to him.

'The truth!'

'Hmmm,' she questioned.

'He's a smart lad – I wouldn't have been able to brush him off. I gave him a watered-down version, though I have to say he accepted it quite well. Luckily, he is more concerned about just trying to find Isla. He doesn't care about the things he cannot explain.'

'Yes, well, any fool can see that he cares for her, but I cannot afford emotion. If his feelings for her get in the way, I will do what I should have done in the first place.'

They were back at the entrance to the garden and began the walk back towards the Manor.

'Eliza, why do you fear love so much? He would follow her to the ends of the earth just to know she was safe – I know I did.'

Miss Sparrow's amber eyes flickered brightly as Mr Stopes placed one gentle kiss on the palm of her hand. For the briefest of moments, there was an understanding of solitude between them, but it was short-lived.

'Eherm.' She cleared her throat. 'Love only clouds one's vision to see clearly, and I do not need clouded fools on my side right now,' she said, abruptly pulling her hand away.

'Eliza.'

'I trust that you will keep an eye on Will and inform me immediately if anything changes.'

'Of course,' he replied, still hoping that he could reach out to her.

'Well, in that case, I shall see you at 10pm sharp. I will also pretend that I have not just heard you call me by my Christian name. You shall, as always, address me as nothing other than Miss Sparrow at the meeting tonight, though you should not have a need to talk – are we clear?' She walked off ahead of him, having now almost made it back to the Manor.

'Eliza,' he shouted after her. 'There was a time, Eliza, and that's never gone away, you know it.'

She didn't respond or turn her back. She kept her long firm strides, though if he were able to have seen her face, he would have seen that it was not as strong as her posture.

Miss Sparrow's usual stern yet level-headed demeanour was escaping her. 'I *cannot* believe you went against my explicit instructions – what part of keep quiet did you not understand?'

'They were not coming up with anything constructive. In case you hadn't noticed they were attacking you!'

'They were *not* attacking me; they were giving their opinion, which as leader of the council I *have* to consider. It is not up to you what I take into consideration or not.'

'Oh, come on, Eliza. They were evading responsibility, and you know it.'

'How many times – it is *not* Eliza! We are not friends, Mr Stopes, and you cannot address me as such. And they were not evading responsibility, as you put it; they were being cautious, which in all honesty, as much as I may have different opinions I cannot blame them.'

'You know as well as I do that they should have all men out searching for her already – why are they waiting to hear news? By the time they hear anything she most likely would have moved on or worst, and God help us if that happens.'

Miss Sparrow let the anger dissipate from her body; she was too exhausted to keep arguing. 'I am not disagreeing with you – in fact, God forbid I agree with you – but they have all given so much over the years, while we have lived in relative safety, and we must not forget that. They have fought every day with the aftermath of the great war. Akos, though dormant, still darkens their way of life, and living with that fear they have still carried out the duty of the council. I cannot blame them for wanting to protect their own people first; I dare say I would be doing the same. But I need them – you know this. We cannot lose them now, and I fear if I push them too far that we will.'

Mr Stopes eyed her carefully – was this the Miss Sparrow that he knew? He swore the Miss Sparrow he knew would have demanded they'd done what's right and wouldn't have taken no for an answer, but here she was, almost defeated. He did not want to argue with her – quite the opposite, he wanted to help her – but he couldn't if she wouldn't let him in.

'Eliza, I have known you to be short – dismissive, even. You are assertive, strong and just a bit stubborn.'

She shot him an icy stare.

'But this? You can barely hold your temper. You just accepted what the council said just then, yet you are getting angry with me even though you know I am right. What are you not telling me?'

'There is nothing I am not telling you – just, some things have to be dealt with more delicately.'

'Delicately?'

'Yes, delicately. We have no idea where she is or what it is even like on the other side now; neither you nor I have stepped foot in there for ten years. And while yes, I agree everyone should be looking for her, I also do not want to bring attention to her. Perhaps while no one knows nothing she is safer; perhaps whatever she is doing she is safer going unnoticed.'

'Do you really believe that?'

'Yes…' she paused, 'and no, but until I can find a way back, until then, I cannot protect her.'

'Surely there must be a way to break the spell?'

'You do not understand – there are things you do not know about.'

'Like what? Just tell me, Eliza, maybe I can help you.'

'You cannot help – no one can help. I never saw this happening; I didn't think it was possible, yet it worked for her and not for me, and now I have failed him. I have failed our king and all because I did not have control over everything like I should have had.'

His expression eased; Mr Stopes knew she was talking about him, and he felt guilty – not for what he had done, but for her pain.

'Eliza, I know I did a careless thing by giving Isla her mother's necklace, the pendant – If I could take it back and do things differently, perhaps I would, or perhaps not. Perhaps without my intervention, she still would have found her way back because no matter how hard we tried to keep her from it, it is where she belongs. No matter what we feel, maybe it was time for the truth to come out, to face it and get our home back for us all. I am not asking you to trust me; I am just asking you to let me in, but we both want the same thing, and we both want to find Isla. So please let me help and then after that we will face whatever it is we have to face together.'

Miss Sparrow sighed – not the fed-up kind of sigh, but the kind of sigh that suggested she had exhausted all her options. Mr Stopes thought she looked fragile, trying so hard to keep everything together, which she usually did so well, but the look on her face clearly showed many a sleepless night and lack of appetite.

Despite her inner turmoil Miss Sparrow decided she had kept the secret to herself long enough; she never thought this would ever happen. Therefore, she never thought she would ever have to tell anyone, but she had to, and he was the only one who would understand the gravity of the issue she faced.

'When we decided what we were going to do, it all happened so quickly. Only days after we agreed what we would do if we failed we were doing it.' She stopped, almost choking on her words, as if the memories brought great pain with them. 'Our king had fallen – you, as I know now, were with our lady in her final moments, while I was with Isla and some of the priests of the thirteenth circle. We knew what was going to happen; we knew we would have to leave and never come back. He had gotten too powerful – we couldn't risk him coming straight after us. We charmed the mirror so that no living entity could enter in or out, only their astro self – their spirit form, if you will—'

'I know this, Eliza.' He didn't want to cut her off, but she was telling him what he already knew. 'I know this – I saw you doing it. That's when I decided I was not going to leave you.'

She ignored his last comment. 'Yes, but what you didn't see is what we did before you arrived.'

He looked puzzled and surprised all at the same time.

'What we were doing had never been done before. No one knew for sure if it would work, but what we did need to know was that we could never be found. To enable us to block the path to cut off all traces of our existence, we had to strip our powers – not only did we strip Isla's but we stripped mine.'

Mr Stopes' eyes widened.

'Do you see what that means now? While I am here I cannot use my powers. While I am this side of the mirror I cannot break the spell. While I am this side, Edward, I am useless to her.' She looked at the potions and crystals that lay on her table. 'And Isla has the only thing that could have brought my powers back – Isla has the necklace.'

He understood now why she had been so agitated and stressed with him more than usual; he did not mind that she had kept this from him, but he wished she had told him sooner. He did not want her to carry this burden alone. He dared moving closer to her, wanting so much to put an arm around her, but he stopped tenderly at her side before saying, 'You did what had to be done – there will be a way. *We* will find a way.'

CHAPTER TWENTY-THREE

I sla couldn't breathe; every time she reached for air, she was pulled back under. They had fallen far, right into the depths of icy cold water, and it was freezing the air in her lungs.

'Kallon,' she yelped in between the short breaths she managed to take. 'K-a-aalllon!' But he was nowhere to be seen or heard.

She was caught in a tornado of water, unforgiving and frightening. Isla was a good swimmer, but this would put even the best of swimmers to the test. She had to get out of the water, and soon.

'Isla.' *What was that?* It was hard to tell over the noise of gushing water, but she could have sworn she heard something. '*Isla.*' Yes, she had definitely heard her name.

'Ka-a-allo-o-n. I can't see you.'

'Don't fight the current – let it take you. Just keep your head above water.'

She did as she was told. Fighting for breath and fighting to swim against the formidable force was exhausting, so she relaxed – what her body would allow, anyway – but sure enough, the river's flow naturally brought them together. Kallon grabbed her forearm and held tightly.

'I don't know how long I can keep this up.' They had a tight grip, but it didn't stop them from both being thrashed around.

'There's a tree coming up, just over there.' He pointed, but Isla could barely see through the mist and the stinging in her eyes. 'Just keep hold of me.' Kallon moved her round so that her arms were around his neck and kept his eyes firmly locked on to where he wanted to go – which was the fallen tree not far from the water's edge, its branches breaching the surface like tentacles. They were rapidly approaching their mark.

'Get ready to jump.'

'What?' she shouted, but too late. With an almighty thrust, which sent him underwater, Kallon threw her up. Isla hadn't been prepared, and the next thing she knew, she was scrambling at the crumbling bark above her. She managed to wrap two arms around the robust trunk, while the rest of her body was dragged by the current; she clung on for dear life.

What am I going to do? Her arms were slipping already. *Get a grip!* she told herself. *Literally get a grip!* With strength she never knew she had, her fingernails bleeding, she refused to let go. Sure enough, one leg was out of the water, then the other. The trunk was too big for her to get a good enough grip to swing herself around; she had to shuffle herself along to where it grew narrower. The muscles in her arms and legs burned, though she fought on through the discomfort; she couldn't fail, not now. A couple more inches, one last heave and she had done it: she had managed to lift herself up. It was not quite solid ground, but it was safety for now.

'Kallon. Where are you?' She was suddenly very aware of her heart beating faster. Was this for fear for herself, or fear of losing Kallon? Dawn was just breaking, yet it didn't make it much easier to see. She was a good three feet above the water, but below her was still a dark maze of branches weaving their way through a foamy water top, making it impossible to see.

Then she saw him. Relief filled her body, followed by anxiety, as his head was barely popping out of the water. He was caught between reeds and branches, taking the full force of the river head on; he fought relentlessly to no avail.

Isla had to act fast, but how? He was too far away – at least five feet lay between her and the next big branch strong enough to take her weight. She looked for another way round to him; there was none – not one that would get her there quick enough. He was losing strength, she could tell. There was nothing else for it: she had to jump. Their eyes locked. She knew that he knew what she was about to do, and she knew through his eyes, his intense grey eyes, that he was trying to say *don't*! She looked away; they might have had their differences, but she was not about to let him drown.

Isla steadied herself into a standing position; her feet slipped a little underneath. Her heart jumped, but she focused. One deep breath and she leapt; she closed her eyes momentarily but opened them at the last second – she had actually made the jump. She pulled herself around so that she was lying flat on her belly and shuffled herself along to where Kallon was. Just as she reached him, she felt a tug on her leg. It was her necklace: it had fallen out and was now caught between her clothes and the bark – one move, and it would fall.

She looked between Kallon and the necklace – he didn't have long left, but she couldn't risk losing it. She slowly moved her arm down her side, keeping her body as still as possible. So far so good: it hadn't budged, but it still hung precariously. *Don't move, don't move*, she quietly told herself. She stretched her fingers, trying to gain that extra couple of centimetres. Then the inevitable happened: in slow motion, Isla watched as it became detached and began to fall to the icy waters below.

'*Stop!*' she bellowed, arm outstretched. Her words echoed,

followed by silence, dead silence. The necklace had stopped in mid-air just as she had commanded it to and the river along with it. Where there had been gushing rapids, there was now a calm pool of complete stillness. Kallon's head was way above water, and he was fine, though slowly getting his breath back. Isla was so transfixed watching the necklace float mindlessly that she couldn't hear him calling her.

Somewhere from the back of her mind, she slowly began to notice his muffled voice. 'Isla, Isla, quick, let's get out.' She was back in the moment and suddenly comprehended what he'd said. 'Grab it, and let's go.' She took the necklace, jumped back into the water and was surprised to see it wasn't as deep as she thought it was. At chest height they waded their way through, ducking under and pushing their way through branches. Slowly but surely the rocks began to shrink until finally the sounds of pebbles crunched under their feet. Then sure enough, as soon as they were out, the waves started to crash and the roaring of the water was heard once again.

Dripping wet, they sat in silence, slowly inhaling and exhaling, neither of them daring to speak at first. The sun was rising, and a true picture of what lay before them started to unfold. It didn't look as half as threatening in the daylight, yet they had both almost lost their lives. Amongst a deep descent of limestone and rocks a beautiful turquoise river about half a kilometre wide majestically cascaded in various formations. High above them longleaf pine trees stood like guards overlooking the proceedings below and the sky, now clear of all clouds, perfectly mirrored the water.

Kallon, who really was lucky to be alive after almost having the life choked out of him, seemed more concerned about Isla than he was for himself. He didn't mention anything about what had just happened; in fact, he acted as if it hadn't happened at all. Isla, however, felt completely different; it seemed quite a big thing to her that somehow she or something had just managed to stop a full-blown river in its tracks, but it appeared to have not alarmed Kallon, which unsettled her – did he know something that she didn't?

'Let me have a look at you,' he said.

'Why?' Isla replied, beating his hand away.

'You are bleeding, Isla.' Kallon motioned to the congealed blood at the back of her head; she subconsciously raised a hand to it and winced in pain. She had not noticed the pain before, though it was all coming back to her that she had fallen and hit her head – quite hard, as she now recalled. She reluctantly let him have a look and closed her eyes as he lifted her long, wet, soon-to-be-wavy hair to inspect the damage. As he did, it sent a shiver down her spine – this was becoming a nuisance, the effect he had on her.

'There's quite a sizeable bump. You will be in some pain for a while and will have to take it easy; however, the bleeding has stopped at least.' He delicately let her hair fall back in place, his hands warm despite being soaking wet.

It had not gone unnoticed to Isla his sudden concern for her; then again, he seemed to continually be surprising her. *Perhaps I've read him all wrong?*

Kallon looked deep into her eyes; he was sure they had been green a moment ago, but now they were back to her usual hazel. He didn't alert her to the fact and continued. 'Do you think you will be okay to walk?' He helped pull her to her feet. 'We can't stay here – they will carry on searching for us.'

Isla straightened herself. 'Yes, I guess so.' She wasn't sure if she was convinced by her own answer, but Kallon seemed to accept it and led the way downriver. They walked much of it in relative silence, with Kallon occasionally checking that Isla was keeping up. He was oddly quiet, but she was increasingly finding it harder to stay on her feet, so no talking suited her just fine.

It got to about midday before Kallon came to a stop.

'I think we are far enough away from them for now – for tonight, anyway.' He looked troubled. 'We should rest.' Isla knew that he was only stopping because of her; she felt terrible but grateful at the same time. She had really struggled to keep up the last mile or so, and the dull ache in the back of her head was making it hard to focus.

They stopped where the trees had grown thick, their trunks as big as houses and their branches as long as the eye could see.

'I'll be back in a moment.'

Isla was left on her own, though she could still see Kallon down by the river looking at something. She kicked at the dirt on the ground, already dreading the thought of having to spend the night there.

'What have you gotten yourself into, Isla?' she questioned herself under a muttered breath. She took out the necklace and twiddled it around her fingers. Since arriving here, she had only been left with more questions than answers. So what if everything they had said was true? That she was the prophecy, the beginning of the end, the one to save them all – it still didn't answer the question: why? Why was she chosen? Why not someone else, someone like Will? She could understand that; he was kind, generous, sweet and strong. *Why had they not picked him?*

'I know what you are thinking.' Isla jumped. 'It doesn't take a genius to see that you doubt yourself – us, even?' Kallon raised an eyebrow. 'But I would have thought what happened on the river was proof enough that you are someone special, Isla.' He smiled sincerely.

'But how do you know? How can you be sure it's me?'

'Because I do, I sense it, and it appears your necklace does too.'

She looked guiltily down at it, knowing that she had not revealed this before. Unlike with the dagger when she had first arrived, Kallon didn't seem to question her about this.

'It was a gift.' She held it close to her. 'On my birthday – it was given to me on my birthday.'

'Well, I would say that was no accident.'

'What do you mean?'

'That's not an ordinary necklace, Isla. It holds a purpose – it is unique, just as you are.'

'Unique?'

'What do you think happened on the river? Do you think that was the necklace alone?'

'Well, I'm not actually sure what happened – it was quite a miracle, really.'

'Is that what you believe that it was – just a miracle, a coincidence?' All the time he had been talking to her, he had been creating a little camp for them, chatting as if this was any ordinary conversation.

'Yes… No, but I don't know how to explain it.'

'Well, I can tell you for sure that you know it was no coincidence. You just won't admit it because then you might just have to believe me.' Isla tried to interject, but he was right – she wanted answers but also didn't want to believe what they were saying, as that would make it real, and if it was real that meant that she would have to do the hardest thing she had ever had to do in her life: believe in herself.

He moved close to her; he was so close that she could feel his breath, so warm, so smooth it made her feel dizzy. He held her hands to look at the necklace but didn't touch it directly. 'It looks Valeyan, there's no doubt about that.' It fitted perfectly in her palm; he cupped her hands and moved them around so that he could see it from different angles. 'But there's also something else. I'm not sure what it is, but there's something else about it makes me think this isn't from the Valayen line alone.' He let her hands go. 'Either way, you are connected now. It trusts you, and it's about time you started to trust it back.'

Isla was about to respond, but he didn't acknowledge her

reproach. 'I need to find us some food.' She was about to say that she would help – Mr Stopes had taught them a thing or two about foraging, so she felt confident she could – until he added in conclusion, 'I suggest you rest up. Don't worry – I won't go far.'

She did feel queasy so didn't argue; she watched him disappear into the woods, clipping the necklace around her neck for the first time since she had left the Manor. She exhaled one long lengthy breath as she settled herself onto the ground to rest her aching legs. They were relatively sheltered where they were; looking out only onto the river, nestled within a group of boulders, which helped disguise any fire they would make unless you were looking from the other side of the river, which wasn't easy to cross, as they had experienced.

Isla didn't realise how exhausted she was until she sat down; any last remaining energy she had quickly evaporated, and against her will she found herself falling asleep.

She wasn't sure how long she had been asleep, but it was still daylight so she guessed she couldn't have dozed off for that long. She thought she had heard her name being called, which was the reason she had awoken. However, it was quiet, other than the sounds of the twigs and leaves cracking underneath her feet.

Snap!

That was more than just something breaking underneath her feet. *Wait, what's that?* Isla thought she saw something. *Kallon, it must be Kallon.* She followed the sound and saw it again; she couldn't make him out exactly, but it could only be Kallon.

'Kallon,' she called out. She wasn't sure if it was wise to be shouting, but it was too late now. *There it is again.*

Isla heard the rustle of branches once more and the shadow of someone shoot out in front of her, and before she knew it, she was out and into a run. *Why doesn't he just let me catch up?*

Isla thought to herself. *Typical Kallon.* She began to perspire, her head still causing her pain. She stopped to catch her breath and get her bearings. She looked around but had no clue where she was now or how far she had gone.

'Great, you've gone and got yourself lost.' Isla was about to try and make tracks back to where she had started and wait for Kallon to come back until she heard her name.

'Now he shows up.' She started to walk into the direction where she had heard the voice come from, but as she did it dawned on her that it was not Kallon's, but if not Kallon *then who was it?* She paused, hesitating as to whether to take another step. Her eyes investigated what she could see, but despite the eerie silence, there was nothing that caused her any alarm.

'Come on!'

She turned her head and saw a familiar figure. 'Lexi?' she questioned, squinting in the light. Surely it couldn't be? But the sun was hazy, and she couldn't quite see. Isla held a hand to her eyes to help shade them from the brightness.

'Lexi, is that you?' She didn't get a reply, but there was no mistaking the blonde wavy hair running off into the distance. 'Lexi, come back, *Lexi!*'

Isla scrambled up the last remaining part of the hill until she was in a clearing; it wasn't big but offered views of the valleys, so she must have climbed quite high.

'Lexi, come out. Now is not a time for hide and seek.' She saw nothing. 'I'm serious.'

'Oh, you're serious? Well, I must obey then.'

What? Who? Isla spun around and was faced with a tall, slender figure approaching her. 'Who are you?' Her eyes narrowed, as she gripped hold of her dagger that rested inside her cloak.

'You won't need that. I assure you I mean you no harm.' He held his hands up, his fingers as long and slender as his body. 'I am surprised that you do not know who I am. I did summon you here, after all, and as I can see you were a clever girl to get here unnoticed, until now.'

There was something about the way he spoke that made Isla feel uneasy. 'What do you mean, summon me? No one summoned me.' She tried to say this as fiercely as possible to show that she was not afraid, which was the opposite of how she felt inside.

'But, my dear, how do you think you got here?'

'It's nothing that is of concern to you.' She tried to hold her own but secretly questioned how and why she had arrived in this place.

The man laughed to himself. 'I can see the resemblance.' He was only a few feet away now. He was pale with long white hair neatly tied back into a plait that ran down the length of his spine, and despite being of a slender build, he looked strong. Isla could tell by his upright posture. He had high cheekbones and a strong jawline; his nose was angular yet perfectly proportioned. In fact, he looked perfect in every way – not one part of him was out of place. He wore a dark blue robe that complemented his skin and a silver snake-like patterned neckline.

Isla stepped back as he came closer; again a small grin escaped him. 'Your necklace did not guide you then?' She instinctively pulled her hand to her chest and felt the familiar shape underneath her clothes. 'Someone had to point you in the right direction.' He raised an eyebrow.

'You?'

The man had a smug look on his face. 'No one else has the ability to do that, my child.'

Isla started to feel the same unease as she had done the same day in the attic. Something was not quite right about this man; she didn't know what he wanted with her, and she was not quite sure she wanted to stay to find out. *Where is Kallon?*

'But why? What do you want?'

'Nothing that wasn't mine to begin with; it doesn't belong to you.' He was so calm, so poised, but there was nothing calm about the way he was coming towards her.

'What belongs to you? I haven't taken anything from you. I have never met you before.'

'*You* took it from me from the day you were born, and now you are back I shall see that I have what is rightfully mine.'

Isla stumbled, trying to increase the distance between them. 'You said you meant me no harm.'

The man said nothing and continued to move towards her; Isla fumbled for her dagger, not sure what she was going to do with it but feeling safer with it in her hand. 'Please, don't come any closer.'

'I shall have what *is mine!*' His voice was fierce; he didn't stop coming towards her. Isla continued to yell at him to leave her alone, to go away, but it was too late: he didn't even give her time to move, he ran right into her, right into the dagger.

Isla gasped; she hadn't meant to stab him. She let the dagger go and stepped back. She didn't like the man, but she didn't want to hurt him either. He had his hands wrapped around it, not moving, his eyes glazed – then, to Isla's surprise, he started to laugh, and it was a laugh she had heard before, it was a face she had seen before, in Arnaurd.

'Stop it!' she shouted. '*Stop it!*'

But he kept on laughing and repeating the same thing over and over again. Isla covered her ears, closed her eyes and screamed to block it out, but she could still hear those words, the words that filled her with dread.

He grabbed her arm; he was strong – it hurt. 'Come to me, Isla, come to me.' He pulled her down; his eyes had changed. They were no longer blue but a fierce green instead. He squeezed his hand tighter and pulled her down to her knees. '*I see you now.*'

❖

Isla woke in a sweat, breathing heavily, patting herself down to make sure she was real. That dream was real; it had felt real, that's for sure, yet here she was back where she had dozed off. The sun was warm against her skin, and Kallon was stood over her, wet and topless, holding a pile of fish.

'What's wrong? You were talking in your sleep.'

'I-I just had a bad dream, that's all. It was only a dream – I'm fine now.'

He put the fish down next to the fire that he was still yet to light. 'How's your head? Do you feel any better?'

'Yes,' Isla lied, for she felt awful, but she was not sure if that was because of the bump on her head or the fact that her dream had felt so real that it had scared the living daylights out of her. 'Yes, I will be fine.'

She didn't share what had just happened with Kallon; she didn't want to worry him, and what could he do anyway? Whoever or whatever that was wasn't here now; there was no point putting any more stress on him. He was already keeping himself together for her. She could see the hand-sized bruise starting to form around his neck – he must have been in quite a bit of pain himself. However, if he was, he was doing an excellent job of hiding it.

'I hope you like fish. It was all I was able to catch.'

'Yes, it's okay,' Isla replied, but she really didn't have an appetite.

'I found a few herbs. Once I've taken out their insides, stuffed them and cooked them, you won't notice the difference. It will be just like my mother makes them, and she's a pretty good cook, with what we have available to us anyway.'

'I'm sure she is,' Isla replied absentmindedly. 'I just need to go stretch my legs.' Isla walked down to the river; she needed to be on her own and didn't want Kallon to notice she was out of sorts, or the hand-sized mark that had appeared on her arm. She had noticed it soon after she had woken up; there was no explaining how it got there. *It's not possible.* The man was gone now, the only one who could explain it, the only one who knew whose hand it belonged to. It felt like she had been cursed. *What did he want?* What did Isla have that he so desperately wanted? The whole scenario troubled her; it also troubled her that she'd kept it from Kallon, but either way, she didn't want to think about it anymore. She pulled her sleeve back over her arm. *Out of sight, out of mind. That's better.*

She continued walking and stopped at the turquoise waters, watching the fish swim mindlessly, wondering if they knew what life was like above water – if they too had the same problems, the same fears as she did. She looked at her own reflection. Was it her or had the fifteen-year-old girl disappeared? Oh, how she missed the comforts of the Manor: the warmth, a bed, running water, friends, just the normal, everyday routine. She wondered what they were all doing now: did they even realise she'd gone? Did they also miss her? Surely Will did; of course he did. She held on to the stone that he had given to her, remembering his promise – surely he wouldn't give up on her?

CHAPTER TWENTY-FOUR

'I have a surprise for you!'

Entering the only way in or out, he instructed the guards to lock the door behind him and made himself at home. The presence of chains and locked doors would imply that he had entered a prison cell, which in effect it was, except that this cell was pleasantly furnished, housing a large wooden four-poster bed, a warming fire, fresh water and plenty of food. For all intents and purposes, were it not for the chains bound to her feet, one could easily have been forgiven for mistaking this as the occupant's home.

However, despite the lavish decor, the woman appeared to not care for such things, for though she was beautiful, fair-skinned and equally fair-haired, she was dishevelled and definitely wearisome. She was pale, for not having seen many a summer, and were it not for the only window she would not have seen natural light at all. The chains bound to her feet were not your normal chains either – well, as far as normal can be expected in these circumstances. They did not drag in a heavy metal on the floor; they were something quite unusual: wisps of smoke ran around her ankles trailing off into nothing, and occasionally as she moved a sliver of silver sparked where the chains should be. She moved almost gracefully despite the heavyweight that bore upon her, both in body and mind.

As he entered, she had refused to acknowledge his arrival, preferring to look out the small window. Surprise or not, she had come to learn over time that no visit from him was a good one. He had not visited her in a while and she wondered what mind tricks he had come to play today, something which he had been so fond of doing at the beginning. She wondered why he still kept her, but then, he could never let her go – no, that wasn't an option for him, but it was for her, and sometimes in her darkest moments it was the kinder option, though she tried not to think like that, as even now, even after all this time, she still had hope.

Nevertheless he did look particularly smug with himself today; perhaps he had come for a different agenda.

'Okay, let's play a game.' He took a seat by the enormous fire place, letting his long legs fall out in front of him, and picked at the grapes resting on the table. 'Hmmm, not bad. Remind me, I must tell my servants not to give you such nice things in the future as you clearly do not appreciate them.'

'Get to the point of your visit, or have you come here just to torment me?'

He looked hurt but soon broke out into a patronising smile. 'Now now, is that any way to speak to your guests?'

'I do not recall inviting you?' she replied curtly.

'Well, well, well, aren't we in particularly high spirits today.' He let the half-eaten grape fall out of his hand, crossed his legs and poised himself for his next delivery. 'Okay, as you wish. What's about five foot four, has long brown hair and, let's say, the personality of a sewer rat?'

She looked at him but refused to answer.

'Oh, come on now, don't be shy. Have a guess?'

'I don't know,' she said indignantly.

'I think you do. What if I said…' he pretended to think a moment, 'that after all these years, your years of silence and betrayal, your insolence and lies…' he paused for dramatic effect, 'that she still became enlightened.' He said this with a tone of pleasure.

The woman's eyes grew bigger.

'Oh, I do appear to have caught your attention.' He got up out of his seat and continued. 'Despite all your efforts, despite everything you have done, the shame you have brought upon us, she *still* became enlightened, albeit the connection is weak for now, but that will grow.' He was enjoying himself, giving a dramatic speech.

'You are here, she is here – ironic, don't you think?' He goaded her some more, prodding her, just waiting for her to burst, waiting for that reaction.

'*Don't!*' The woman lunged at him, but the man, with just a small wave of his hand, tightened the chains around her ankles.

'Don't what?' He got into her face. 'Take back what is mine?' He circled her. 'What should have always been mine.'

'It was never done to hurt you; it was to protect you. You have to stop punishing everyone.' She spoke with purpose.

'Punishing everyone? It was them who made me who I am; it was them who refused to see me as I was, who pushed me into the darkness. They should have been proud of me! They should have watched me grow, but instead, I was shunned.' The bitterness in his voice rose with each spoken word.

'This has gone on for far too long now.' The woman's eyes were round, ablaze with emotion.

'It is not I that has caused this, don't you forget that. And now you shall have to suffer the consequences.'

'I swear, if you hurt one hair on her head.' He was just out of her reach, but it didn't stop her from wanting to show him that he could not intimidate her.

'*Don't you threaten me!*' The patronising, egotistical man that had been there before was now overshadowed by a darkening evil.

She tried to turn her back on him, but a burning swarm of gold rings swam around her neck, stopping her ability to move.

He came up behind her and with venomous spite whispered into her ear, 'I shall do what I was born to do. For too many years they tried to suppress me, refused to see me for who I was, to accept me for who I am.' The burning rings tightened around her neck. 'Make no mistake of what I am capable of: I will find her, and I *will* end this.' His eyes were red with anger; he gritted his teeth and let the rings around her neck squeeze tighter and tighter. He took pleasure in watching the life slowly drain out her body, but suddenly he let her go, and she fell to the floor.

'But why?' she chocked. 'She has done nothing to you. She is, was but a child – it is me you have your grievance with and only me.'

'You do not tell me who my grievances are with; it is not I that has done wrong. I think you are all too quick to forget that I am only reversing what should have never happened.'

'If there is any part of you left in there, I am begging you, *please*, do not do this. It is not too late. You can stop this, all of this. We can go back to the way we were.'

'*Things can never go back to the way they were.*' His dark presence filled the room once more. 'It is time for a new dawn, and I shall have it, all of it, and nothing *or* no one will stand in my way.' He made his way to the door. 'But until then, I need you alive, but make no mistake, once I have no more use for you, I will be done with you.'

The woman was a crumpled heap on the floor.

'*Guards!*' He demanded for the door to be opened; the man that had arrived was now the one leaving. 'I suggest you figure out where your allegiance lies before it is too late.'

'Don't do this, pleeease, I am begging you.'
He walked away without another word.
'Akos, please! *Akossssss.*'

CHAPTER TWENTY-FIVE

They woke the next morning surprisingly rested. After Isla's incident with the unknown man and her dream, nothing else strange had occurred, other than Kallon's cooking, which, true to his word, actually tasted quite pleasant.

'What are you doing?' Isla asked, bemused.

'I'm hiding our tracks – if they come this way I would rather they not know that we were here.'

Where would she have been without Kallon? He seemed to think of all the things she did not. Though she was capable of making a fire herself, she would never have thought to have destroyed the evidence after, but then again, this was his world, and maybe he wouldn't fare so greatly in hers either. As she watched him, she found herself thinking about how much he had changed in the short few days that she had known him. Despite the somewhat turbulent start, they seemed to have ironed out their kinks. Dare she say it, she quite enjoyed his company, even if there were parts of his personality that still annoyed her.

'Come on, that will do. You ready to go? We will stop and find some breakfast on the way.' He stood up and met her eyes with a grin; he seemed to be doing a lot more of that now.

The day's walk had seemed easier on them both. Kallon was chattier than he'd been the previous day, and Isla's head was slowly starting to heal. For a brief time, things actually felt normal. If Isla had not known better, she could just as well have been walking in the woods surrounding the Manor with Kallon being a new arrival, though she guessed that he was probably near past the age where he would have been accepted there now.

As they walked speaking back and forth, she told him about the Manor, about her world and the other orphaned children. It was not like her to be so openly sentimental. It's not that she wasn't – there were many things she cherished, but she just preferred to keep them to herself in her own little box, metaphorically speaking. Today, however, she opened that box. While at first recalling these memories made her feel comforted, it did not take long for that feeling to change, and she wanted to close it again, though the reason for it was one that surprised her. While the Manor was a big part of who she was, who she is, she couldn't help but notice that she felt strangely at home where she was now. And she came to the conclusion that it was the feeling of the unknown, the possibilities of the life that she had missed out on, the memories she never had the chance to make. *Is Kallon right – is this where I belong?*

They had stopped only briefly in the morning when Kallon had found some berries and assured Isla they were safe to eat. Now it was well and truly into late afternoon, they were searching again for somewhere to rest before nightfall. If Kallon had been on his own, he would have trekked further; as a single person it was far easier to climb a tree, tie yourself to it and get some sleep. However, having lost most of their supplies in the river, he had no rope and wasn't travelling with someone that was used to the environment. The path they were travelling was going to be a long and arduous one. He wanted to make sure Isla was sufficiently rested for a full day's hike each day;

he couldn't afford for her to become ill or tired if they were to make it to Lestoris before the change of season.

Much like the previous night, they found a place that offered the most shelter. This time it was in the base of a mountainous tree, its roots offering human-sized pockets to sleep in. With the hood of her cloak over her head to help keep her warm and the not-so-comfortable leaves that they had both laid beneath them, she prayed she would be able to sleep at least enough so that she wouldn't slow Kallon down the next day. She was not used to this way of living and was quickly realising what a luxury it was to have a bed each night.

With Isla to help this time, they caught double the fish, though she didn't actually do anything other than sit and watch from the bank. Kallon insisted that she didn't get her clothes wet and that she could help by collecting firewood instead. When she had collected what she thought would be enough, she sat and watched how he caught the fish. He had found himself a large stick that he sharpened at one end to create a spear; he then made multiple dives underwater. Sometimes he came up quickly, other times he was gone so long that Isla thought that he had been swept away with the current. But every time she really started to panic, he would resurface and show his head again. The first time he threw a fish at her he watched in amusement as she chased the flapping thing down the bank as it tried to make its way back to freedom. He had then laughed so much that she wanted to get that stupid fish and slap it right around his smug face.

When they decided they had caught enough, they wasted no time; all they had eaten was a handful of berries, and funny noises were definitely coming out from their bellies. Kallon used the same herbs as he had the day before and cooked them in much the same way, except these were different fish and not as tasty as the ones they'd had before. Still, after three fish each, she couldn't complain.

Laying down, enjoying the feeling of a full stomach, Isla asked the question that had played on her mind all day: 'Do you think they would have given up looking for us? Do you think we are safe now?'

'We will never be safe, Isla, a war is coming. I don't know when, but we will have to fight when it does. I have waited a long time for it.' He was very honest, Isla was coming to learn, sometimes too honest.

'But how can I fight when I don't even know how to protect myself, Kallon?' she blurted out before she had even thought about what she was saying; she didn't want to appear weak or frightened and cursed herself for even saying anything in the first place.

Kallon jumped to his feet. 'You know what? You are right, and we are going to change that, starting from now. I can't be expected to babysit you all the time.' She knew he was joking about the last bit because the grin she had become to recognise when he was playing with her was present. 'Right, come on, get on your feet.'

'Why?'

'I am going to teach you how to defend yourself.' He picked up two sticks that were approximately the same length from their pile of firewood.

'What, now?'

'Yes, now. You have a dagger you seem reluctant to use, yet you might be more inclined to if you actually knew how to yield it. Don't expect miracles, I'm a good teacher but...' he joked, 'we'll see what you have in you.'

Isla felt rather silly at first: one, for fighting with sticks like little kids, and two, because she felt completely out of her depth. Still, she wasn't about to let him see that she was intimidated.

It went much as Kallon had expected: he disarmed her at almost every opportunity, blocking her approach. He was not about to go easy on her just because of who she was; if anything, he wanted to push her harder because of who she was, and his actions made that quite clear. Though what he would not have admitted was that she showed determination and grit. Time after time she got back up again, sporting a few more bruises than she had before, and he was silently impressed.

'This is quite fun,' he said, swiping her advance away once again.

'For you, maybe!' Isla hissed, brushing dirt off herself.

'I don't know what you are talking about,' he replied, the corners of his mouth arching as he wiped away strands of loose hair.

She went in for another strike, but this time he grabbed her, spun her around and held the pretend sword to her neck. 'Your stance is all wrong,' he said, reaching into her clothes and pulling out the dagger. 'You must even out the weight on your feet.' He placed it into her hand, wrapping his around hers. 'You must let it become an extension of your arm.' Standing behind her, his arm following the length of hers, he lunged forward slowly and mirrored a few simple defensive moves. 'Face your enemies head on – do not let them see you are afraid. It is you against them, the strong against the weak.' They continued to fluidly change from one move to another, Kallon's head locked in next to hers.

'Okay, I can do this, this doesn't seem so bad.' They smiled at one another, Isla feeling more and more confident with every move.

'It's all about trust,' Kallon said, starting forward.

It most certainly is, Isla thought to herself. She had strangely trusted Kallon from day one, though she knew he was talking about something different to what she was thinking, to Isla it was all about people, letting her guard down and letting them in, trusting trust itself.

She felt relaxed, euphoric; it was all coming together, all making sense. A vibration began to shoot up through her arm, a tingle, this time it was not from Kallon but from the dagger. She grabbed it tighter – yes, it was definitely the dagger. Through the gaps of their fingers, she could see it, Kallon could see it, the light that penetrated them, the light that escaped, making its presence known, and this could only mean one thing. She was finally starting to believe; she was finally starting to trust.

CHAPTER TWENTY-SIX

The change of season was signified by the arrival of autumnal colours and darker mornings. Isla had been gone for over three months, and the children were starting to believe that she was never going to come back.

Will had tried his upmost to maintain the usual order of things; however, though he was there in the physical form, he was never truly present. He spent more and more time with Mr Stopes learning more about Isla's past, where she was from and how she had ended up in a children's home in Lancashire. Mr Stopes had been reserved at first, but when it was evident that Isla wasn't coming back and Will began asking more questions, he decided to tell him everything. Will was a good lad in his eyes and had been an even better friend to Isla, and he felt that loyalty deserved to know the truth.

He also saw a lot of himself in Will and he sympathised with him. So he allowed him to visit him of an evening, which had become more frequent over time. Sometimes they would discuss what had happened, where she could be, no news being good news, all those sorts of things; but then other times it was just to sit in the company of someone who understood, with no need to talk.

This was one of those evenings, and after spending most of it in silence, he said his goodbyes and took himself back off towards the Manor. He decided to enter through the back entrance as he was a little past curfew, and while a part of him was beyond caring for rules, he also didn't have the energy for confrontation. He entered through the kitchen, careful not to make a noise, when he was suddenly faced with Elizabeth.

'Will, what a surprise,' she said.

'Oh, hello, Elizabeth, I didn't mean to make you jump.'

'Oh, no, you didn't, I think it was more the other way round.'

She looked him up and down, noticing the hunched shoulders and vacant expression; he was quite different from the enthusiastic boy he had been just a few short months ago.

'I was just making myself some tea – would you like to join me?' she said, motioning towards the kettle reaching its whistling point on the stove.

'I think I should head back upstairs before anyone notices I'm not there,' he said, scratching his head. He didn't want to get caught up in a conversation; being Isla's closest friend, everyone questioned him about her whereabouts and when she would be returning home. He wasn't a particularly good liar, nor did he like to do so; therefore, he did his best to avoid those types of conversations when he felt they were coming his way.

'Please, I would be happy for the company.'

'Ah, really, if the sisters see me out, they won't be too happy,' he said, edging towards the door.

'Well, I'm technically one of the sisters now, and really, Will, you're not much younger than me – it won't be long before you get the same privileges. I won't tell if you don't.' It was unlike Elizabeth to encourage breaking house rules, but she was worried about Will and wanted to use this opportunity to chat with him. She felt there had been something not quite right about Isla's disappearance – family or not, she never would have left without saying goodbye, and if her sixth sense told her anything it was that Will knew more than he cared to say.

'I've made you one, so you can't go now,' she said, her rosy cheeks glowing a little more from her deviant ploy.

They sat opposite each other at the rectangular table that took up at least one third of the kitchen. Will deliberately kept the conversation light, but when their teas were nearing their end, Elizabeth knew if she didn't ask him now, she most likely wouldn't get another chance like this when he was on his own and there was no one else to listen.

She pulled her hair to one side then poked it behind her ear, a sign that usually meant she had something important to say.

'Will, I know it is not my place, but I am worried about you.'

Here we go, he thought. *It's starting.*

'I barely see you eat nowadays, and as for getting involved with any kind of activity, we barely see you either.' She paused. 'Are you in some kind of trouble?'

Relieved that she had not asked him anything to do about Isla, he let out a nervous laugh. 'Oh, God, no, I'm not in any trouble.'

'Is someone threatening you?' she added.

'No.'

'Are you sick?' she continued.

He really did start to laugh now. 'No, Elizabeth, I'm not in trouble, no one is threatening me and I'm not sick.'

'Good, I didn't think so – that just leaves Isla then.'

His facial expression changed, and he couldn't hide it.

'Do you know something the rest of us don't?'

He tried to deny her accusation, but not very well, by the way she carried on with her questions.

'There's something Isla said to Lexi the day before she left that has been playing on my mind.'

'What is it?' Will, in fact, did want to know – had Isla said something to the others about what was going on?

'She wanted Lexi to know that she loved her and would never forget her. Now, why would she say that? It implies that she knew she was going somewhere, yet if she had known this why didn't she say a proper goodbye? I don't believe she would have left without saying goodbye to all of us.'

'Honestly, Elizabeth, I don't know.' Will did think it was strange that she had said that; she must have known she was going to go through that mirror, though when he had seen her that night it didn't seem like she had planned it – she was too frantic for that.

'Where did they say she has gone again?'

'She is staying with some relatives.'

'Yes, but what relatives?' Elizabeth was turning into quite a skilled investigator.

'Her aunt and uncle, I believe.' Will was becoming uncomfortable at the line of questioning.

'But why would they show up now? Of course, if she has family out there I am pleased for her, but why, after all these years, would they suddenly turn up?'

'I couldn't say.'

Elizabeth wide-eyed him; she found it hard to believe that he of all people would not know. 'Did you say that you have heard from her?'

'No.' Damn, he said that too quickly. 'I mean, yes – yes, I have heard from her.'

Elizabeth raised an eyebrow.

'But not in a while,' he deliberately added.

'How?'

'How what?'

'How did you hear from her? By letter, phone?'

'Letter.' Will so wanted to leave, but he also wanted to tell her everything. Elizabeth was the kindest, gentlest person he knew, and she also cared for Isla. He didn't want to lie to her, but this was quite the opposite of her usual character. It actually reminded him of Isla – she wouldn't have taken no for an answer either.

'Elizabeth,' he sighed. 'I wish I could tell you, but I've been sworn to secrecy.'

'So she's not staying with her aunt and uncle?'

'Not that I believe, but they are trying to get her back.'

'Get her back? Why?' Elizabeth was not happy that her suspicions had been confirmed; Lexi would be distraught if anything had happened to her.

'Please, Elizabeth, I have told you too much already.' He got up from the table.

'Will, wait.' She reached out to him.

'You just have to trust me that there is nothing that you can do, nothing that anyone can do for now, but you can't say anything to *anyone*, definitely not Mr Stopes or Miss Sparrow. Don't tell Lexi, Sissie – they must still think that she is with her aunt and uncle.'

'Will, you are scaring me now.' Elizabeth's assertiveness had all but disappeared and been replaced with a vulnerability. She hadn't expected her suspicions to lead to this; she didn't know what to think.

Will placed two comforting hands on her shoulders. 'The best thing you can do for Isla right now is carry on as normal.' Seeing someone else in front of him as a reflection of the way he had been the past few months made him realise that he had to get a grip; he had to pick himself up and be stronger for Isla.

'This has to stay between us, okay?' He looked her deep in the eyes. 'You have to promise me you won't say anything,' he pleaded. She nodded, but he wanted to hear her say it. When she told him she swore not to say anything he added, 'But you will see her again, okay. I promise you that.'

❖

Meanwhile, on the other side of the Manor, Miss Sparrow heard a knock at her door.

'Just a moment.'

'It's only me.' With the sound of the familiar voice she gave them permission to enter without making any attempt to hide what she was doing; she stayed at her desk, where she had all sorts of crystals, scrolls, herbs and potions spread out.

'Forgive the intrusion.'

She waved her hand in a gesture that implied she wasn't getting anywhere anyway. It was quite unlike her to be so flippant.

'I thought perhaps you might like some company.' And from under his arm he produced a little bottle of red liquid.

'Where did you get that from?'

'I brought it with me. I've not opened it for all these years – they say it gets better with age. And I guessed now, considering what's going on, it may be a good time for a well-earned drink.'

'Yes, well, you know I don't drink.'

'As I recall, you drank on special occasions.' He smiled and uncorked the bottle. 'This is the finest in Westoria – you cannot let me drink it alone.'

'Well, Mr Stopes, you are out of luck then because today is not a special occasion.' She tried to busy herself with notes on potions and spells; ones that she hoped might just find them a way back.

He ignored her comment and continued to pour two small glasses. 'Well, for me, it is a special occasion.'

As she recalled, it was the finest thing she had ever tasted, and a memory of home was certainly not unwelcome right now, but she hadn't earned the right to relax – things had to be done; she had to make up for her mistakes.

'Just ten minutes, that's all I'm asking, then I promise I will leave you alone so you can concentrate on your charms – unless you think I can help, of course.'

'I most certainly do not think that you can help.' And she meant every word. 'I am tired, Mr Stopes, and want to finish where I am at before I go to bed.'

'Well, this will send you off nicely then.' He passed her one of the glasses.

'I'll give you five minutes,' she said affirmatively.

'Ten?'

'Five!'

'Eight?'

'*Five*,' she repeated with finality.

'Okay, five it is.'

They both took a sip, and Mr Stopes let a long, drawn-out breath escape him. 'Brings back good memories, doesn't it?'

'If you say so, but the memory of drunken hooligans in the great hall drinking far more than what is necessary and making a mockery of themselves is not my idea of pleasant,' she bit back.

'That's not what I was thinking of, and really, Miss Sparrow,' he raised his eyebrows to point out that he had addressed her correctly, 'it was never as bad as that – yes, sometimes they got a bit carried away, but no harm was ever done. However, I was thinking of a different one.'

He took another sip and savoured the taste before he spoke again. 'It was a night much like this – calm, the stars were out, but it was summer, of course. I was walking home from the inn; in fact, it was myself and our lord, before he was king and could afford the odd night of debauchery. We were young, determined, both starting out at the king's guard. We'd trained hard, so when we had a night off I guess we would take advantage of that.'

Now it was Miss Sparrow's turn to raise an eyebrow; she remembered all too well his wild ways.

'Yes, I admit I had my moments, but I still took my responsibilities seriously, I made sure he got back to his room that night then decided the fresh air was agreeing with me, so

I took a walk and stumbled upon a courtyard, the one with the water fountain and a stone sculpture of a lady bearing a child – do you remember it?'

'Yes, I remember it.'

'Well, I must not have been the only one who fancied a midnight walk, as when I got there a woman was sat on the bench – my gosh, she was beautiful. She took my breath away. I would normally have approached her, but something stopped me. She looked far too peaceful to be disturbed and deep in concentration. If I could have guessed I would have said she was a morphar by the way she was moving her hands around, but her back was mostly to me so I couldn't see what she was doing. I watched her for a while and then left her in peace, but I never forgot that feeling she gave me. I felt so alive – all of a sudden my life had meaning. I can't explain why, but there was just something about this woman that made me want to be a better man, so from that day I've done all I could to show I could be that better man, the kind of man who deserved a woman such as that.'

'That's quite a story, Mr Stopes,' she said, taking another sip from her glass.

'Yes, well, that was twenty-eight years ago today – my special occasion, of course, and thanks for celebrating it with me.' He lifted his glass up towards her and gulped down the rest of his drink.

'I only wished I had told her how remarkable she was when I had the chance, and if she ever doubted herself I would have told her she shouldn't, for there was never a stronger, more resourceful, more beautiful woman than she.' He uncrossed his legs, put his glass down and stood up. 'Anyway, that's my nostalgia for one night – you have work to do so I will not disturb you any longer. Goodnight, Miss Sparrow.'

She couldn't bring herself to say goodbye; she wasn't sure if it was the wine going to her head or what Mr Stopes had just said that had made her feel suddenly light-headed, but her hand could no longer hold her glass and she had to put it down, staring at it in disbelief.

Lilypads, she said to herself. *Lilypads.* If she didn't fear it so much she would have told him the woman had been materialising LilyPads. She had always wondered who the man was that she had seen that night, and now she knew.

CHAPTER TWENTY-SEVEN

D ays had passed, perhaps weeks, months even. There was no way to know for sure as she had lost the concept of time, but Isla's clothes were looser than she remembered; she'd forgotten what a proper home-cooked meal tasted like and what a warm comfy bed felt like. She yearned to feel something different other than the sensation of dirt and twigs against her skin and fish and berries in her stomach. She had her good days, and she had her off days when her thoughts would wander to memories of the Manor and all her friends she dearly missed, but that life was gone now, a life that she was realising she was never going to get back. If she was to move forward, she had to try her best to forget them, much like she had done with her parents; it was better to forget.

Kallon, on the other hand, was consistent as ever, never letting the lack of sleep or food get to him. There were times, however, when he seemed preoccupied, and in those moments when his mind was somewhere else, Isla wondered what it was that he thought about. Did he think of home? His family? Did he think of her? She felt silly for even thinking the last part, but sometimes when he didn't think she was looking or thought that she was resting, she would catch a glimpse of him staring at her.

That aside, their relationship had greatly improved since its rocky beginnings, and though perhaps there were times when their personalities still clashed, for the most part, they chatted and conversed like they could be friends. Was that what was happening? *Are we becoming friends?*

Over the last few days, they had moved away from the river and the shelter that it offered onto higher ground up into the mountains, where the bare necessities such as eating and sleeping had proved a challenge.

Kallon had debated with himself whether to risk the mountainous path or to continue following the river's route, which would take them longer but was ultimately safer. In the end he had this decision made for him, when the bridge they needed to cross had been burnt down. He had inspected the scorch marks left behind, and from the concern on his face, it was clear that they were recent. Though he tried his best not to show it, Isla could tell his nerves were on edge.

Again retracing the same steps, they added another day's journey on top, making it three days in total before they arrived at the foot of the mountain path. Despite the unexpected detour, Isla had quickly adjusted and found that she quite liked being up in the mountains. Maybe not the steep climb or precarious drops – heights were something of a challenge for her. But at the end of the day when they stopped and watched the sun's slow turn from yellow, to orange, to red, then to just a mere glow in the distance, it was all worth it to feel a moment of peace; for the rest of the time she battled with an unwanted feeling.

Somewhere in the back of her mind, teetering on the edge of her subconscious, she was waiting for something to happen, for the ominous man to return and for her dreams to be invaded once again, but so far nothing had. What it meant, Isla didn't quite know – all she knew was the voice in the back of her head saying that they were not going to make it to Lestoris. She never told Kallon about her concerns, about the man or the feeling in the pit of her stomach; she just kept it to herself, another secret for another day.

'Are you alright down there?' he yelled.

They were not particularly high in that moment, but they were high enough for the landscape to have changed from dirt to rocks, from trees to stone, and it was proving hard work – for Isla, anyway.

'You know, I may be getting fitter, but I could do with a break, and you could tell me exactly what it is that you keep looking at?'

He held out his hand so she could use it to pull herself up. 'What do you see?' he said once she was firmly on her feet.

Isla slipped him a sideways glance; this wasn't answering her question, but she had spent long enough with Kallon to know that he liked her to figure things out for herself.

'Um, trees, birds, sky, mountains.' She gave him a look as if to say, do you really want me to continue?

'Okay, now focus – what looks different?'

'I don't know, Kallon, it all looks pretty much the same.' Isla wasn't trying to purposely be short with him, but she was out of breath and just wanted a quick answer to a simple question.

'Come on, you can do better than that.' Kallon smiled; he wasn't annoyed with her – on the contrary, he seemed to almost find it amusing that she couldn't see what he so obviously could.

'Look.' He stood behind her, hands on her shoulders, and adjusted her position. 'Close your eyes.'

Damn! There it was again – that electric feeling. *Ignore it, Isla, ignore it.*

'Now open them, tell me what you see?'

She looked out into the landscape and could see nothing different to what they had seen over the past few days. Her eyes focused firstly on the blue of the river then the mountain edge they were following. The birds were dipping and diving into a forest she had come to know; the fluffy cloud formations were all beautiful, all familiar and none were somewhat different. Kallon sensed her impatience and gave her a gentle squeeze, encouraging her to look closer. She really was not in the mood for this, but Isla took another deep breath and tried again; she shaded her eyes so that she could see better and, sure enough, there it was. It was tiny, of course, and no wonder she had missed it, but now she'd seen it; she couldn't unsee it: the tall, angular shapes, the flags.

'It's still another five to six days' walk, though. That's providing we don't get into any trouble – it's going to get even harder to navigate from here.'

'I was starting to think this place didn't exist,' Isla said, feeling that little sinking feeling in the pit of her stomach, for she knew soon she would have to go through it all again. Her story, more people she would have to convince, more questions and quizzical looks she'd have to endure.

'Did you ever really doubt me?' Kallon replied. 'In fact, don't answer that.' He pretended to look offended then smiled; he was in a particularly good mood – maybe because the end was in sight, meaning a good meal and a good night's sleep. Or that he would soon be able to share the burden of her, as that was what she felt like, a burden – not because of anything he had ever said, but because of the way she felt.

They continued on for a further few hours until they decided to rest earlier than previous days, due to the need to hit lower ground and replenish their food supply before dark.

'Hey, what's this?' Isla called out to Kallon.

'We need to keep going,' he yelled back, focused on the deep descent in front of him, conscious that they needed to reach the bottom soon.

'Yes, but Kallon.' She tried to get his attention.

'The river's this way.' He carried on talking, and when he could no longer hear her, he turned around, but she was nowhere to be seen.

'Isla, *Isla*,' he called out.

Nothing!

Oh, she hasn't. Frustrated, Kallon retraced his steps and saw what must have caught her attention: an overgrown opening that looked as if it had once been a path. He pushed his way through, using his arms to protect his eyes from the thorns, and called out to her again.

'Kallon,' he heard her yell back. 'Come on,' she called excitedly.

'Isla, just stay where you are, I can't see—' He finally made it out.

'Come on, let's take a look around.' Isla suddenly appeared in front of him with a smile so full, so happy – the dimples were out, and she didn't even care.

'Isla, you can't just disappear like—'

She cut him off. 'But take a look around.' She walked backwards, revealing more for him to see. She was giddy, excited.

'This can't be real.'

'It sure is.' Isla took a bite of fruit and threw one to Kallon; he caught it and did the same.

'This is amazing. How can this still be here?' Kallon was awestruck. He had not seen anything like this since before the great battle; fruit did not grow like this anymore – at least anywhere he had been or known.

'What's this?' Isla asked, pointing to a large, green oval shape with tiny little yellow and black spikes.

'Oh, a Buffafin opal, because the little spikes look like the fin of a Buffafin fish.'

'Cool. And this?' She picked off a large blue one, the size of her fist.

'A Teardrop fruit, because of the colour and shape of it – you see this part here? The light blue ring around the top that means they're ripe and ready to eat.'

'Amazing, we'll take this one.' She added it to her pockets.

'What about this one?'

Kallon caught Isla's hand and pulled it away. 'I wouldn't touch that one – looks pretty, I know, but don't be fooled. That's redwood, and the smell is enough to wipe out a small village.'

'A village?'

'Don't worry, they don't actually harm you. They are really quite nice, but you see these little red flowers on top? If you knock the pollen off, it releases a wretched smell, one that you won't be able to get rid of for days. It's near impossible to peel the fruit without knocking it, so it's not worth it. Though they are brilliant for masking other smells, so depending on what you need it for they can be handy to have around.'

'Wow, okay, yeah, we can leave that one.'

'Are you sure?' Kallon pretended to throw one in Isla's direction, and she ran off as fast as she could; there was no way she was going to be left smelling like a skunk for the next few days.

'I was only joking, Isla, come back.' He ran after her through the labyrinth of trees, weaving in and out, trying to catch her up. They were playing a game now, innocent, laughing, somewhat a reprieve from the seriousness of everything that was going on. They stopped abruptly as they came out from under the canopy of the fruit garden and out into a richly green meadow.

'This place looks like it has been left untouched for years. Kelina would love this.'

Isla was quite surprised to hear him mention his sister's name; Kallon rarely talked about his family, which made her think of something that had more than once crossed her mind.

Isla walked out into the open. The grass felt like velvet as the blades brushed past her knees; Kallon joined her to feel the warm, gentle breeze and fresh mountainous air caress their skin. This really was a hidden gem, and they both felt it – even the clouds had parted for their arrival.

'I'm sure your mother and Kelina would love this place too.' Isla plunked herself onto the ground, the grass parting to wrap itself around her body. 'Kallon, can I ask you something?'

'You can ask me anything,' he said, lying down beside her, raising his hands under his head.

'I'm not sure you will like what I'm going to ask.'

He laughed. 'Isla, I am sure there is nothing you can say to me that I wouldn't openly say to you, so go ahead.'

'Where's your father?'

When she said she had wanted to ask him something, he hadn't figured out it was going to be that.

'I'm sorry, I knew I shouldn't have asked. I can see you are upset.'

'No, I'm not upset, just surprised, that's all. I've not spoken about my father in a long time.'

'You don't need to answer that question. I'm sorry, it's none of my business.' This was unlike Isla; she didn't say she was sorry all too often, and here she was saying it twice in the space of thirty seconds.

'It's okay.' He paused momentarily. 'The truth is, I don't know where he is.'

She turned on her side to face him. 'What do you mean? How can you not know?'

'He was one of the many that fought in the great battle; he wanted to fight for his family, for his home, to ensure our safety. When it was over, we were informed that he was okay, that he was coming home.' He paused again, still not looking at her, choosing to stare at the sky instead.

'And?'

'But he never made it; he just never came home.'

Isla gasped. 'Oh, Kallon.' She went to approach him, to give him a comforting arm, but he didn't appear to need comforting;

it was all just words to him. 'I just assumed – I mean, you are so capable – with all the things that you can do, that you had a man around the house to teach you.'

'Arnaurd.' This time he turned to face her. 'My father couldn't be around all the time, in fact he really wasn't around that much, so when I was young, he moved my mother and me back to Branstown where he was born. My father's father had been close friends with Arnaurd, and when he passed quite young, he took care of my father, the same thing he did for me.'

'What about Kelina – I thought she was your sister?' Isla shouldn't have blurted this out so easily, but she was far too young to have possibly had that same father.

'She is, well, she is my half-sister. When my father didn't return my mother met someone new – he was good to her. I liked him, but unfortunately he died when Kelina was just a baby. So you see why I am so protective of her – without me or Mother she would have no one.'

'She would have Arnaurd.'

A look of sadness crossed his face. 'He is getting far too old now. He cannot be tasked with such things anymore.'

'I am sorry about Arnaurd.' Isla felt responsible for what had happened to him. 'I hope he is okay.' This time she did place a reassuring hand on his arm; it felt quite comfortable to be lying there with him.

'Thank you. Alexis would have done what she could – she is much stronger than she appears.'

Isla took her hand away. 'Alexis is special to you, isn't she?' she stated bluntly.

'She is like a sister to me; we both lost people close to us.'

Isla didn't know why, but she felt a little better hearing that.

'And what about you? You are always looking at that – someone special?'

He was referring to the stone that Will had given her that day under the tree.

'Oh, this.' She felt awkward now; half the time she never even knew she was playing with it. 'It was a present – it's meant to remind me that I'm not alone.' She tucked it back into her pocket. 'But it's silly, I know.'

'I don't think it's silly, I think it shows you have people that care about you – you're lucky.'

'I guess.' She looked up at the sky, wanting to think about anything else other than Will or the Manor. It was so surreal to be where she was, somewhere so beautiful, so peaceful, yet be walking towards an uncertain future. Was it possible to feel blessed yet cursed at the same time?

'Do you think that it's my fault?'

'That what's your fault?'

'All this, everyone's suffering.' It was something that weighed heavily on her, that she questioned every day, that somehow all the suffering everyone had had to endure was her fault.

'No, I don't. Don't ever think that – no one is suffering because of you.'

Isla sat up, ignoring what Kallon had to say.

'*Hey*, do you understand me? You did not create the darkness, you did not make him do this – we all make our own choices,' Kallon said firmly.

'And what's your choice?' Isla asked.

'To see this to the end. You're not alone, Isla, you are never going to be alone.'

Isla smiled meekly back at him. She knew he meant it – he had stood by his word, had done everything he could for her – but could he do this? Could he really see whatever it was she had to do out to the end?

'Kallon, look!' She pointed to where the sun sliced through the clouds, instantly forgetting their current conversation. 'Kallon, look, there's a horse.'

'Isla, don't.' He quickly reacted and tried to pull her back.

'Why not?' She shook his arm away and approached without hesitation, and as she did, she could see it was bigger than any horse that she had ever seen before. The purest of white with the mildest hint of pearl in her coat, she was a picture of beauty and innocence, and Isla was mesmerised.

'Where did you come from, girl?' She let her stroke her without hesitance. 'You are a beauty, aren't you?'

Kallon watched in awe from a distance at what he was witnessing. Only once had he seen one of these horses, and even then it was in a flash that he hadn't known was real or not.

'You know they are a rare breed.' Isla turned to face Kallon, who still kept his distance. 'She's an Equinox.'

'An Equinox?'

'Yes, they get their name because they don't show themselves too often; they are very untrusting animals, and for good reason.' He took another step closer. 'People used to poach them due to their belief in their magical powers. You can tell it's an Equinox by the way they have that pearly presence in their coat. It is believed to be a kiss from God; therefore, they are seen as givers of life, and old folk believed that their blood could extend a person's life. So they were hunted by many, their coats skinned to make cloaks and their blood drained to be drunk; it is even said that Ilandrya had them hunted in their masses in her bid for eternal life so that she could bathe in their blood and keep her skin youthful, and now sadly only a few remain.'

'Who could do such a thing to something so beautiful?'

'They are very intelligent too, more so than any other. They're not your average horse – they can hear your call from miles away; they can sense danger from a mile away – this is why they are very rarely ever seen. They avoid people.'

'I wouldn't let anyone hurt you.' Isla insisted Kallon join her. He hesitated; he had always dreamt of seeing one, but he also knew how dangerous they could be due to their untrusting nature, and this made them unpredictable.

'I promise she won't hurt you.' Isla took his hand to stroke her mane; she huffed and puffed a little, but when Isla insisted she soon obliged. 'See? You just have to show respect, and she will respect you back.'

He couldn't believe it; this really was a sight he would remember for the rest of his life.

'I'm going to call her Serenity – suits her, don't you think?'

He gave the horse a good look; he couldn't think of a better-fitting name himself.

'Though you know you can't keep her, right?'

'Of course not, but all horses deserve a name. I shall know if I see her again.'

'Well, Serenity, nice to meet you,' he said, running a hand through her mane, but she became agitated. 'What, you don't like the name?'

'No, it's not that – it's something else,' Isla answered, trying to calm her down. 'Something's wrong, Kallon.'

Kallon shot into alert mode, eyes darting from corner to corner, but the space was too large and too camouflaged to be able to focus on any one point. He couldn't see anything, but if the Equinox sensed something then they were in danger all right.

'I think we need to get moving – quick, climb up.' He gave Isla a lift.

WHOOSH! Something shot straight past them.

'What was that?' Isla lay flat down against Serenity back.

'Quick.' Kallon led them into the bush. 'Hunters – we must get her somewhere safe.' He ran along beside them. *WHOOSH!* There was another one; this time, an arrow landed in a tree right in front of them, quickly followed by another.

'Where are they coming from, Kallon?' Isla was struggling to keep Serenity still. 'She won't calm – she's nervous. I can't control her.'

'You've got to ride her, and fast. You've got to get her away from here.'

'What? No, not without you.' Another one just missed Isla's head.

'I'm sorry.' He hit the back of Serenity and urged her to go; she shot up on her hind legs. *I will find you!* Kallon shouted after them.

Isla couldn't believe that he had just done what he did; he could have got on. There was time – he could have ridden with them as well. *Why didn't he just get on?* But she couldn't get off now – Serenity's speed was too fast. She dodged, jumped and flew through the forest; Isla was lucky she was an experienced rider, but riding bareback at this speed was difficult even for her.

Kallon hadn't wanted to let them go, but she hadn't noticed what he had: while the arrows were flying, men with chains were closing in, ready to pin down their prey. It was a distraction method served to disorientate her, and within seconds of Isla leaving three of them had already closed in, and they were not happy. He had thought on impulse, and he knew she would never have forgiven herself if anything had happened to Serenity. Plus he couldn't let them discover who Isla was either: they were both precious and rare, both worth a pretty penny and these hunters would not care what they did for money. They were both safer together and as far away as possible in that moment. He only hoped he could find them, but he couldn't think about that now; he was outnumbered, and they were not about to let him go without a fight!

'Slow, girl, slooooow.' They had gone so fast Isla had no clue in which direction they'd gone or how far. Nothing looked familiar to her anymore – the forest was decidedly more ominous-looking, and as if it had died long ago. 'Here, girl, come.' Isla led Serenity to a stream that she only hoped would be clean enough to drink.

Isla was angry, so angry with Kallon; she still couldn't understand why he had done what he did. Now what was she meant to do – wait for him? Or find her own way to Lestoris? But if she made her own way, how? She had no idea where she was or how to get there; this was one of the stupidest plans Kallon had ever had.

She walked around in circles hoping the answer would come to her, that someone or something would lead the way, that she wouldn't actually be in the mess that she was in, or that Kallon would turn up despite how angry she was with him.

'Think, Isla, think. What would Will do? What would Kallon do? More importantly, what are *you* going to do?' It was somewhat therapeutic to speak out loud, but in doing so, she hadn't noticed that Serenity was gone.

'Serenity! Serenity!' she called out in a panic. She knew the horse did not belong to her, but she'd felt comfort knowing that she was not utterly alone, and now she was. More alone than she had ever felt.

She heard something snap and ran to investigate. '*Serenity!*' she shouted, feeling relieved. She spun around, saying the only thing she could think of.

'*You!*'

CHAPTER TWENTY-EIGHT

'Oh, am I glad to see you.' Without thinking, she flung her arms around the dark, manful figure. He let her embrace him and let go when she was ready.

'Henri, you have no idea how happy I am to see you. What are you doing here?'

'I may have asked you the same thing. We are on our way to Lestoris. We had every hope that we would meet you there, but fate, as it seems, has thought of an alternative path.'

She wondered perhaps if he had come across anyone else, eyes wild with anticipation. 'Kallon, have you seen him?' she asked urgently.

'I'm afraid not, should I have?' Henri didn't look alarmed that Kallon and Isla were no longer together; he was somewhat indifferent.

'He said he would find us; he was supposed to find us.'

The last thing that Kallon had indeed said was that he would find her, but how was that possible? Had he known where Serenity would take her? Had he somehow known that Henri would find her like he had done when the grey hoods were chasing them? But what if he hadn't? What if he needed help? What if he was hurt and she was wasting time? Arrows had been flying from all directions – one of them could have easily hit him. He could be injured, or worse.

Henri sensed Isla's agitation. 'Why don't you come with us and you can tell me what circumstances have come to pass to lead you here?' he said in his even tone.

'But what about Kallon? I cannot just leave him,' she shot back defiantly.

'I think he would rather know that you were in the company of friends.' He let his words sink in. 'Don't you think?'

Isla thought it over: the sky had almost darkened; she had no food, no shelter and no way of knowing where she had come from. She did not like the idea of delaying her search, but she did need help, and perhaps Henri could give it to her. However, it was clear that he would be in no rush to do so right then.

Isla relented. 'Only for tonight, then I will leave to find Kallon.'

Henri's beard was slightly longer than she recalled, his hair wilder, his skin tougher. However, his presence was every bit as calm as she remembered, and she found it reassuring.

'If tomorrow you still feel the same I will not stop you; I will even let you take some of my men. All I ask is that you eat and rest for tonight – tomorrow will bring a new perspective.'

In silent agreement, she followed him and the rest of his crew, who made camp quickly and efficiently. Isla sat herself down around the low burning fire, but something felt different to her. 'There are considerably far less of you than I would have expected – where are the others?' Following the stares she received, she immediately regretted asking the question. It was foolish of her to point out something so obvious to all the eyes around her, yet was not so to her.

'You do not need to look so worried, Isla. We have separated into smaller groups; we bring less attention to ourselves this way. Though we are close, what separates us from the borders of Lestoris is the Fen.'

'The Fen?' she repeated, awaiting further clarification.

'The Fen is a dark path to travel, Isla. Many creatures live here, creatures you do not want to disturb.' He took a bite of his food. 'Men would be the kinder option to come across here.'

'So why come through here at all?'

'It is the quickest, most direct route and, at times, valuable.' He pulled apart at his bread, dipped it in his broth then popped it into his mouth. 'We all know the risks we face being here, but it is not I who I am concerned for.' He raised an eyebrow, pursed his lips then carried on eating his food as if his comment was just a passing one.

Henri was not trying to frighten Isla, but he did know what was out there – some of it, anyway; he had many a scar as a reminder. But he also knew Isla's character; he'd known it from the moment he saw her. She was not easily swayed, and if she had an idea in her head, she was going to do it.

'Oh.' Her eyes met with the floor. 'I hope we do not disturb what's out there then.'

'Hope would be a good place to start.' And he let her think about that.

Isla would usually have enquired further, wanted to know more of what he spoke of. She could see what Henri was trying to do – discourage her from continuing on her own – but right now she could not take on any more, and if she could not persuade him to help her search for Kallon, then the unknown or not, she would have to do it on her own.

They continued the rest of their meal in silence, her mind replaying the last scene with Kallon over and over again. *What have I missed? What did I not see?* Kallon wouldn't have deliberately left her, she knew that much, yet he had. *But why?*

When the others had taken themselves away to sleep, and there was nothing but the flames of a fire burning between them, Isla felt more comfortable explaining what had happened. She told Henri everything, right from the point where they had parted ways, leaving nothing out; she even told him about the necklace. She couldn't explain why, but Isla trusted Henri, maybe even more so than Kallon.

At first, he said nothing, but he ran his coarse fingers through the bristles of his beard. Isla knew better than to demand answers this time; she knew Henri was thinking, taking in every word and absorbing it. So she waited until he was ready.

'I cannot speak for Kallon or his actions – a person's actions are no one's but their own – but what I can speak for is his character.' He lifted himself to a taller position. 'He was but a boy when he first came to us, too young to be of any use but too smart to shake off. Time and time again he would find us, and time and time again we sent him away. No one wanted the life of a young boy on their conscience. However, he was persistent: at first, his father would come and find him, take him back and pray that his boy would never have to see a day's fight. Over the years as he grew up, his father no longer came in search for him, and over time I began to see past the young boy and see the determination and grit of a young soul who just wanted to do right. So one day I took him aside; I explained he could not keep coming to us, that he needed to be back home to protect his family – however, when he turned fourteen, if he still felt the same way, to come and find me.'

The lines on his face did not give away any emotion, but his eyes told her what was coming next. 'Sure enough, on the day he turned fourteen, I had been waiting, and in the distance walking over the hills I saw a figure – I knew who it was immediately. Three times the size, his features had changed, but his passion had not.'

'He never told me this.'

'And why would he? Would it change your opinion of him? Would you trust him any differently?'

No was the answer to all of these questions, yet still she felt there was so much about him that she did not know.

'I trained him, worked him hard; he was a stubborn lad. He had some skill about him, I'll give him that, but he acted too quickly and often in haste or anger. In fact, he reminds me of someone else I know.'

Isla shifted under his gaze.

'I can certainly understand why you two got off on the wrong foot – more alike than you probably see. Determined, loyal and honest, I have known Kai to be nothing but that in all the years I have known him, and sometimes to a fault. I do not believe he would have purposely left you or put you in greater danger; he must have seen something that your eyes could not.'

'But what do I do? I cannot just leave him – what if he is hurt?' Her voice wavered; she was angry and worried, but most of all she was scared, scared to continue on without him by her side. All the strength, she had realised, came from him. She did not feel she could do what it was that everyone was expecting of her without him. And it took them losing one another for her to realise that.

'Isla, we cannot change what has happened, only what will come. It is not your fault, and you must stop blaming yourself.'

Was that what she was feeling, guilt? Perhaps they would not be in this situation if it was not for her. If she had just got the food and found somewhere to rest like Kallon had wanted; if she had not encouraged him to go out into the open, she would not have found Serenity. They would not have been attacked by hunters, but Serenity would have, and Isla hated to think what could have happened if they hadn't been there.

'Then tell me, what should I do?'

'I cannot tell you what to do, Isla. You must make your own choice.'

'You will not help me then?'

Henri knelt down beside her. 'My word still stands: tomorrow, if you feel the same, I will not stop you. I will let you leave with three of my best men. They will take you to wherever it is you want to go, but I cannot change my course; we will journey for Lestoris tomorrow and reach there in three days, but the dawn is yet to break. Sleep on your thoughts and tomorrow you will have your answers.'

And so she did; she did not get as much sleep as she had hoped for, but come morning she had her answer.

CHAPTER TWENTY-NINE

'Wake up.' She stirred to the sound of a familiar voice.

'I'm sleeping, go away.' She waved a hand in the air, dismissing the voice that was trying to disturb her from her slumber.

'Isla, it's time to get up.'

'Will, leave me alone.' She paused; her eyes sprung open. 'Will?'

Alert, she shot up, searching for some sign that she really had just heard what she thought she had, but the only thing she saw was the empty imprints of Henri's men.

'Will!' She stumbled to her feet, still feeling the effects of sleep. 'Why are you not answering me?' She had heard his voice; she knew one hundred per cent she had.

SPLASH!

She looked down – her feet were ankle-deep in water; she wasn't in the forest anymore but on the edge of a lake. *How did I…?* It didn't matter.

She called out to him again. *Wiiill,* it echoed.

But what was that? There was another voice trying to break into her thoughts. *Go away*. That's not Will; she was looking for Will.

'You need to *wake up*, Isla!'

She blinked; the next thing Isla knew two hands were clasped around the tops of her shoulders, and she was once again back around the campfire.

'You were talking in your sleep,' Henri informed her.

'I was? Sorry,' she mumbled.

'You do not need to apologise, but you can understand why I had to wake you – a voice can carry in a place like this at night.'

'Oh, right, yes. I hope… What was I saying?'

Henri didn't respond.

Isla looked around; no one else seemed to be awake or disturbed by her midnight talking.

She hugged herself, thinking about what she had just seen; it had felt so real. A part of her wanted to believe it was, but that was impossible, surely? Dreams weren't real; they were just that – dreams, your imagination playing tricks on you.

'I suppose you think I'm mad, talking in my sleep,' Isla said, more defensively than intended.

'I think you are warier of what you talk of in your sleep than I am.'

'What do you mean?'

'This is probably not the first time you have experienced a vision.'

'You think this has happened before?'

Henri shrugged, in a "you tell me" kind of way. She thought about it; was this like the dream she had had with the strange man?

'I think I have had a dream like this before – maybe, I can't remember clearly – but not like this; this felt different.'

'Probably because it was.' He came and sat down next to her. 'Recent changes to your life have caused a series of effects, ones that have weighed greatly on you, I know.'

'You mean Kallon?'

'Yes.'

'Kallon was not who I saw.' She wanted to make that very clear.

'Maybe not, but think of it as a stone. You drop it into the water. First, you see one ripple, that's expected, but then you see another that creates another and so on and so on. Your starting ripple may not be your end result; however, they are all connected.'

Henri had a way of explaining things in a way that made sense to her; she had felt guilty about Kallon, leaving him behind. She had abandoned him, just like she abandoned Will, but to Will, she'd done it in the worst possible way. With Kallon he had made the choice, but with Will, she had chosen – she had chosen to leave him.

'I can see you thinking. What's troubling you?'

'I don't think it is Kallon that is troubling me.' Her cheeks pinked speaking his name out loud. 'I think it is someone else. It felt as if someone was, I dunno, was trying to communicate with me, though this person, it would be impossible for them to do so.'

'Isla, the fact that you are here – does that not tell you that the impossible is very much possible?'

'But I don't think this is. He is not one of us, or whoever I am meant to be.'

'But you are. What does your vision show you?'

She noted how for the second time, he had opted to use the word vision instead of dream, implying a form of reality to it. 'I had a friend back home, at the Manor, he is…' she corrected herself, 'was my closest friend – that's who I could hear. That's who I thought I saw.'

'Isla, tell me, has anything ever happened to you when you have been around sources of light or things that reflect? Have you ever felt a strange feeling, or empowerment in those moments?'

'I'm not sure what you mean?'

'Take your time, recall your memories,' he advised her gently.

She thought about it; there was the time in the attic when all the light bulbs smashed. But she had definitely not felt empowered then and there was definitely no sources of light – if anything she had felt afraid. The reminder of the voice sent chills down her spine. Now the mirror, she had felt empowered around that, or perhaps more inquisitive rather than empowered. *Is this what he means?*

Henri saw a vague recollection that she had indeed experienced something. 'Valeyans' have a certain set of abilities, things that they can do that no one else can. I've never seen it, only heard of it. If you are a descendent of the Vale, then I can only guess that you too could do the same.'

'What kind of things?' Isla pushed, eager to know what he meant.

'It is said they can manipulate sources of light, anything that reflects. The moon is particularly sacred to them. If this vision of yours is sending you to water, maybe there is something for you to learn there.'

'What could I possibly learn?'

'That is not for me to discover, but something I think is time for you.'

'How?'

'It is a clear night, the moon is out, there is a stream nearby – maybe you'll finally learn what comes next.' He walked with her to the stream.

'What am I meant to do?' anxiety prickled at her extremities.

'Just listen, start there.'

'Henri?' She turned round in a panic; she didn't want to be left alone but didn't want to say it.

'I won't be far,' he reassured her.

She didn't like it, but she had no choice.

'Listen – that's all you have to do, Isla, just sit here and listen.'

She closed her eyes and waited; she listened, and she waited, but nothing happened. *This is silly.* What was she expecting? Frustrated, she chucked a stone into the water, diluting some of her anxiety. She felt better but was nowhere closer to figuring out what it was that she was meant to discover. 'Maybe you can help me?' she said to the necklace, pulling it out from under her clothes. 'Do you know?' *Nothing.* 'Of course you don't.' Isla let it drop to her chest, tilted her head and looked up at the moon.

It's a ripple effect, she suddenly thought, then picked up another stone and threw it in the water; this time she concentrated on the ripples it created and began to feel sleepy, relaxed.

She replayed the words over and over in her head. *Wake up, Isla, it's time to wake up!* What did they mean?

But they were fading; she couldn't hear them anymore. She felt like she was underwater – no, not underwater, floating, drifting; she couldn't be sure. But wherever her mind had taken her, she liked it; wherever she was, she did not feel; wherever she was, she...

CHAPTER THIRTY

He was starting to feel useless, that he was wasting his time. He was so sure that he had seen something, but no matter how many times he kept coming back, he never saw it again. It was the starting of winter now: the flowers having given way to the cold a while ago, wilted for another season, and soon the snow would follow.

He knew he had not achieved anything in all these months, but he needed to feel like he was doing something, that he had not just given up, because friends don't give up on one another; he had to believe there was hope.

'Will, come on, it's freezing. You've been down here for hours – your lips are turning blue.'

Will turned around to face Elizabeth standing in a long, pale blue coat; it was only now, looking at her, that he realised how cold it actually was, for she resembled a frozen sculpture. He looked past her towards the Manor, every window brimming with Christmas lights and decorations, he couldn't believe it was December already; this should have been such a happy time. Of course, he would have already brought Isla her present – Isla no doubt would have left hers to the last minute as usual, but he didn't care what he got; it was all about the giving for him.

'You can't keep coming down here like this,' Elizabeth expressed, concerned.

Will felt her hand gently press against his shoulder as he stood staring into the water on the jetty where he had found Isla hiding all those months ago.

'Will.'

'You know I saw her, on the other side of the pond? You believe me, Elizabeth, don't you?' Was he trying to convince her or himself? He didn't know the difference anymore.

'That was months ago, Will.'

'You don't believe me, it's alright. I don't expect you to.'

Elizabeth didn't confirm whether she believed him or not, just encouraged him to come back into the warmth. It was hard to believe something you hadn't seen with your own eyes, and he didn't blame her.

'I'm coming, just give me a couple of minutes.' He turned around and tried to give her a reassuring smile, but she knew better than to think he was okay.

'I'll put the kettle on – don't be long.'

He watched her leave before turning around facing his own reflection. *What have you become?* he said to himself. He was no longer the happy Will that people enjoyed being around. Instead, they now avoided him, and he didn't blame them; he didn't like this version of himself either.

Back in the autumn, he had sworn he had seen her, Isla, on the other side of the pond in the very spot he stood now. It was not long after he had spoken to Elizabeth confirming that Isla wasn't really with family, and it had given him hope. It had only been a split second, but he knew what he saw; she was trying to contact him, as weird as it sounded – but that was then and now was now; his belief was wavering.

'Ah, this is ridiculous,' he shouted, sending the nearest rock plunging into the water, and walked away.

'Will.' It was faint, but it was enough to make him stop.

'Hello?' he said, looking into the bushes ahead of him; perhaps Elizabeth had been waiting for him until he was ready.

'Will, turn around.'

He did, but no one was there.

'It's me.'

'No, it's not.' There was disbelief in his voice. He was hearing things – maybe the cold had got to his head.

'Will, it's me, I can see you.'

'Whoever is doing this, it's not funny. Go back to the Manor.'

'No, Will, it's me – look down.'

Panic and excitement coursed through every part of his body. *Surely I'm not hearing this?*

'*Look down.*'

'I don't understand.' Dumbfounded was an understatement.

'Neither do I, but you can see me, right?'

Did his eyes deceive him, or was he looking at…? *No, this is impossible.*

'Will, tell me you can see me?'

'I can see you, or I am going mad and I am talking to myself.' But he wasn't, unless his face was that of a brown-haired, hazel-eyed, pale-skinned girl. Unless his name was Isla.

'Are you okay?' They had not seen or spoken for months; she was the one that had disappeared yet she was the one asking if he was okay. 'Will, it is so good to see you.' He was speechless. 'I am so sorry.'

Will found his voice. 'What for?'

'For leaving the way I did, for shouting at you, for even walking through that mirror, for not finding a way to contact you sooner, for everything.'

'That doesn't matter – Isla, where are you? I can't believe this is even happening.'

'It's hard to explain.'

'Try me.' He wanted to get answers out of her as quickly as possible before whatever was making this happen stopped.

'Will, this is not what I want to talk about.'

'Well, it is what I want to talk about.'

She wasn't used to this side of Will: demanding, authoritative. 'It's a different world here, Will – people are different; they live differently to us.'

'What do you mean?' He was impatient; he needed answers.

'They need my help – things are not good for them. Bad things are happening, Will, and I'm the only one that can help them.'

'That doesn't make sense – what kind of things? Are you in danger, Isla? Just tell me how to get to you, and I will come for you.'

'You can't, Will. There's no way for you to get here.'

'Well, then come back.'

'You are not listening to me, Will.'

'I am listening to you – bad things are happening, you are in danger and, whatever it is, you are going to do it by yourself. But you can't, Isla. You can't do it on your own – just let me know where you are, and I will help you.'

'*I'm not coming back!*' she blurted out to even her own surprise, and as expected, it was met with silence. 'I mean, there's no way for me to come back, Will. That's what I am trying to say.'

'But there must be?'

'Will, please believe me when I say there is no way for me to come back.' What she didn't say was that she had stopped looking for answers, that a part of her wanted to stay, that no matter how strange things felt, despite not having her friends, she felt that she belonged there.

'I'm just glad I got to see you one last time.'

'Don't talk like that, Isla, we can fix this.'

'It's too late, Will. Please do not make this any harder. You will always be my best friend.' It pained her to see him looking so abandoned, and now she almost wished she hadn't seen his face at all. He never could hide his emotions very well, but she needed to do this, and if he knew what was happening she knew he would understand.

'I don't believe you, Isla – there must be something we can do. It is not like you to give up.' Then it dawned on him. 'Unless you are choosing to.'

'Will, they need my help. I can't just leave them.'

'Who? Who needs your help? Tell me.'

'Stop making this difficult, Will.'

He knew he could not convince her; when she had made up her mind that was it – just like the time when she arrived at the Manor and she didn't want to talk to anyone. That took weeks of convincing; only he didn't have weeks – seconds, maybe. The image of her in the water was starting to fade, and he was about to lose her forever.

'At least tell me where you are – tell me something,' he pleaded. It was faint, but he was sure he heard it, right before the clouds burst open and the rain broke the surface.

CHAPTER THIRTY-ONE

'I know where she is!'

Will did not stop running until he had reached Mr Stopes' cottage, bursting through the door like a tornado. 'I know where she is – she told me,' he said breathlessly.

Nothing had changed in the time that Isla had been away, except for the chair that used to sit by the window, the chair that Will frequently used, now sat opposite, adjacent to the fireplace. He took his seat, panting, wanting to get the words out as quickly as possible.

'I spoke to Isla. I actually spoke to her.'

The tiny hairs on the back of Mr Stopes' neck prickled.

'I know this sounds crazy, but just hear me out. I said it before that I saw her – no one believed me, but I knew it, I knew she would come back, and she did.'

'She's back?'

'No, not exactly. We spoke, though.'

'What? Where is she now?'

'Gone.'

'What did she say?'

Will thought about that: the pang of hurt he'd felt when she told him she was not coming home, that she had no intention of ever coming back to him. He refused to believe it, though. *She wouldn't?*

'She said she was sorry for leaving the way she did, but there are people that need her help and that she couldn't come back.'

Mr Stopes cursed to himself; he knew that she could only be talking about one thing, the very thing that they had spent the last ten years protecting her from.

'She's talking about him, isn't she?' Mr Stopes had eventually told Will what he knew, but seeing it was completely different to hearing it – until now Isla had just been missing, but now she was missing and the rest.

Mr Stopes ignored him. 'What else did she say? Did she say where she was?'

Ten minutes later and they were banging on Miss Sparrow's door.

'Eliza, its Ed. Open up.'

She opened the door, ready to question his behaviour.

'We don't have time for this – we have something to tell you.'

Will followed closely behind him. 'I spoke to her, Isla.' He was no longer afraid when talking to her anymore – so much had changed, so much had shifted that she no longer intimidated him.

'She's back?'

'No, but I spoke to her.'

Miss Sparrow waved him off as if this was another one of his false claims.

'You need to listen to this, Eliza,' Mr Stopes pressed.

'I don't *need* to do anything you tell me to.'

'I'm telling the truth. I thought it was just my own reflection at first, but it wasn't – I spoke to her in the water. It was if I was looking into a mirror, only not at my own face.'

This got Miss Sparrow's attention. 'Through the water?'

'Yes.'

'Manipulation,' she murmured to herself. She knew it was a skill of a Valeyan. Isla's mother and Miss Sparrow had done as much when they were teenagers. If she had learnt to do this already, who knew what else she had discovered about herself, or who had discovered her?

'We know where she is, Eliza.'

Her amber eyes sparked.

They were silent for a moment. After all these months, did they really have a lead, some hope that they could find her, bring her back safe?

Miss Sparrow was the first to break it, jumping into action. 'I must arrange for an emergency council meeting straight away. They must know – they must find her.' She stopped and looked at Mr Stopes, then at Will. 'You may leave now.'

'What? I'm not leaving. If you are going to find her, I'm staying.'

Mr Stopes took her arm gently; she froze. 'Let him stay – he needs to see this.'

Miss Sparrow walked away from his touch; she knew he was right. Still, it did not stop her from wanting to keep the two worlds apart. Isla or no Isla, she still had a house full of children in her care, and it was her responsibility to keep them safe as well.

'You may stay, but nothing will happen for a few hours yet. I will send for you both when it is time.'

'I'm not—'

Mr Stopes placed a hand on his chest to cut him off and whispered into his ear, 'Learn when you have won the battle. Don't push to win the war.'

'She won't let me back in now,' he growled as soon as they were outside the door.

'She will. I know her; she only says things she means.'

'I hope you are right,' Will said, more calmly this time. It was not natural for him to have such a temper and he felt ashamed, though he sensed Mr Stopes understood. 'I just want to find her.'

'I know, we all do, and we will,' Mr Stopes replied reassuringly. 'But you better prepare yourself for tonight – a new world is opening up to you.'

CHAPTER THIRTY-TWO

The doors to the grand hall opened, sending an echo bouncing off every wall like a pinball machine. Two lone figures walked its length in scurried steps; lost within the grandeur of architecture, they did not speak, for they knew better than to speak out of turn and waited until they had reached their master.

Even in its current state, it was a sight to behold but also a sad one. The grand hall in its day could house over one thousand guests and even more if you counted the three observation levels and private boxes. The high ceiling was supported by vast pillars, all of which were strategically placed so that they didn't block the grandiose windows. The decorative pieces of the kings and queens before were no longer there, the house flags that used to hang with pride had been torn down long ago and any memory of the house of Blackbourne having inhabited these walls for hundreds of years had faded; only the walls themselves would know now.

'We have news, my king,' the first one said with pleasure.

The slender figure poised himself. 'Come closer.'

The second man, who was only halfway through his life but

was already displaying signs of a hunched back from years of not being able to look his lord in the eye, did as he was instructed. He hated calling him king, for he was not his king, but he had a family and a family that would be no more unless he did just that.

'Speak!' he ordered, sitting up in his throne. 'I'm waiting.'

The second man, who was clearly more frightened than the first, spoke. 'Yes, sorry. There's been some unusual activity.'

'She's been sensed,' butted in the other man with glee.

'Why wasn't I told sooner?' the lord bellowed with an almighty roar to the second man.

He cowed back, unable to disguise his fear. 'I... we weren't sure. We sent Raverings to follow; we've only just had confirmation. You said not to disturb you unless I was sure.' The man was trembling, he had held off for as long as he could, but he couldn't delay it any longer; the others would grow suspicious.

'Never mind what I said – where is she?' When the man replied, his face grew even angrier. 'Take me to the tower.'

She quickly hid everything when she heard the door open and did her best to compose herself.

'*Show me your hands,*' he growled.

Her eyes averted to his companion, who did not dare look her way. 'My hands, why?'

'You know why. Now show me.'

'I'm not sure this is necessary. These are my chambers, and you come barging in here making demands for no reason.'

'You know I can make you,' he said in a much lower, spine-chilling tone. 'You can make this as hard or as easy as you like, but give me your hands.'

'This is absurd.'

'Give them here.'

'No.'

They fought, but Akos's strength undoubtedly was stronger than hers; he turned them over with little effort and on the palm of her hands was what he had suspected. Silver lines spread across them and up her forearms; they were fading, but the proof was there, evidence that his suspicions were correct.

'How long?'

She didn't say anything.

'How long have you been trying to block my sight?'

'I had to do something.' There was no hiding now what she had been doing; all she could try and do was to plead with him.

'Did you really think you could stop me? You foolish woman.'

She glanced at the man cowering even further by the doorway and Akos saw the slight exchange. 'But you weren't doing this alone, were you?' He walked closer to her and whispered, 'Someone would have had to bring you Solumanite – someone who has access to the grounds,' he leaned in even closer, 'and your chambers.'

She was quick to jump to his defence. 'No one helped me; it was all me. The proof is on my hands – I acted alone.'

He almost found it amusing; she was no match for him – he knew this and she knew this. He would have found out what she was doing eventually. He knew something was not right when he could no longer sense the girl, her enlightenment, but he didn't think she would be the cause behind it. It was both brave and foolish of her – he almost admired her for it, for having the guts to go up against him. He missed a challenge; perhaps when this was over he would keep her around a little bit longer – he did love a game.

'Akos, did you hear me? No one else had anything to do with this.'

He shrugged her off his arm. 'Oh, please do not insult my intelligence. You know me better than that.' They looked at each other; he peered down at her, while she tried to hide the terror in her face, for she knew something bad was about to happen.

'*Guards!*' Four big, menacing men entered the room, all in full armour; their faces could not be seen for they were covered by helmets bearing the shape of a wolf. The only thing you could see was the misty whites of their eyes swirling in a hypnotic motion. They waited for further instructions.

'Seize her!'

'What! No, where are you taking me?'

'Why, I am taking you nowhere, my dear.'

She fought as hard as she could, trying to shake off the two sets of hands, but the more she tried, the stronger they became.

'Hold out her arm,' he ordered.

They forced her into the chair, one keeping a firm grip on her shoulder, the other pulling her arm out straight on the table in front of her.

'Akos, what are you doing?'

'You have put me in a predicament.' He pretended to ponder over his words as his long legs paced the length of her room. 'You have deliberately disobeyed me, plotted against me – do you have any idea how hurtful that is?' The irony was not lost on the woman at all, for years kept locked in this tower.

'Word of this will get out if I don't show some sort of punishment. Others will think they too can do the same, and, well, I just can't have that.' He knelt down next to her and lightly brushed the side of her cheek; she looked away, her long fair hair covering her eyes. He quickly clasped his hand around her jaw, jerked it back and spoke very softly. 'Every crime must be punished, and seeing as you used your hands to harm me, I must stop that from ever happening again, but don't worry, I shall leave you with one. Now, please hold her tight, I don't want to take more than is needed.'

Akos rose to his feet and slowly pulled his hands apart. Electric currents sparked from his fingertips until they had formed a sword that looked like an almighty lightning bolt.

'You can't be serious, Akos.' As hard as she tried she couldn't break free; her arm tensed, her veins fighting to break free from the grip. He brought his sword high above his head, sparks flying ferociously, his eyes growing wilder. Then he let his arms drop like a pendulum.

Swoosh!

He stopped, just short of the hairs on her arm. It was quiet at first, but then he heard the man repeat it again.

'It was me – it was I who brought her the Solumanite.'

Akos locked eyes with the woman, not giving anything away but knowing his sadistic plan had worked. He had no intention of removing her hand, or any part of her body, for that matter. His plan was to flush out the perpetrator, but he would have gone through with it all the same if his instincts had been wrong.

'No, he knows not what he says,' she responded immediately then waited with bated breath.

Akos let his hands fall to his side, still not taking his eyes off her. All were still apart from the man quivering from his admission.

'You have done the right thing,' Akos said. 'I respect your bravery.' Then he turned around; however, something on the look of his face said that he did not respect him. 'Come now.'

'Akos, it wasn't his fault.' She ran to the door, trying to reach it before it was locked. 'What are you going to do to him, Akos? He's done nothing wrong. You can't punish him for something he did not do.' She was still trying to save his life. He had been a loyal companion to her for years; he hadn't wanted to do what she had asked of him, but in the end, he had relented. And in the end that was the last she ever saw of her dear friend and loyal servant.

CHAPTER THIRTY-THREE

*W*as *that a dream?* No, it wasn't; it was as real as anything she could imagine. She had just spoken to Will, of all the things that she thought might have been possible, that was certainly not one of them. And now she was more confused than ever; she had managed to keep her longing for the Manor buried deep down inside her, or so she thought. She had a job to do, she knew that, and the first job was to find Kallon, but could Isla really leave all that she knew behind so easily? It had seemed more manageable the longer she was away, but seeing Will, how distraught he was, she missed him more than he would ever know.

She felt a presence behind her; Henri had returned. 'Did you find what you were looking for?'

'Yes, no – I mean, kind of.' She looked up at him. 'Did you know that would happen?'

'Well, considering I do not know what just happened, I would have to say no.'

'Do you always have to speak in riddles?'

He laughed. 'It is not my intention to confuse you, Isla. Contrary to what you think, I don't know everything. I only have an idea of the possibilities that lie before you, but that does not make them true.'

'Well, I wish there was someone around here who had a better idea than you or I.'

'You may be confused now, but you are one step closer than you were a moment ago, you have more information at hand and that can only be a good thing. What you choose to do or not do with it is your choice, but these things are there to guide you, not deter you, so don't think as such.'

Henri didn't want to know what had happened down by the stream; he was a complex soul, and, as he explained, there are some things in life we must face on our own, to have someone else's input might not always encourage the best result.

So she kept it to herself: the feeling of weightlessness as if she was floating, how when she looked into the pool of water it was like looking through a mirror. At first, she was stunned to see the fields of the Manor, the secret garden that, by the looks of it, was not so secret anymore. Then she had seen Elizabeth, the way in which she had touched Will so tenderly. It had sent a jolt of jealousy through her; she could not hear what they were saying, but they looked to be rather close. *Have I been replaced?* She could not blame him if she had; she did tell him she was never coming back, so maybe it was for the best he had someone else who cared about him. Elizabeth was kind, sweet and honest; they were one and the same, really. He had said all the right things when they'd spoken, and she believed him. But he did not look like her Will anymore – perhaps he was better off without her; maybe he was better off living a life without her in it to complicate it. She would do anything for him to be happy. She so desperately wanted him to be so. It was just a shame that had she heard the conversation she would have realised the only person that could make him happy was she.

❖

After the remaining hours of darkness passed, they made an early start to make the most of the day and get to their much-awaited destination. Henri had filled her in on what to expect when they arrived and that he was sure that if Kallon was to be anywhere, it would be there, though he would live up to his promise if she still wished to go ahead with her search for him. She decided against it.

After her chat with Will, it made Isla realise that she had lost focus on who she really was; the prophecy had made her forget her past, where she had come from, and she no longer wanted to forget that. Yes, she had agreed to help Kallon, and as the weeks went by she couldn't deny that she was able to do things that others couldn't, but did that mean she should deny the life she had had before now, the only life she had ever known? The people she had left behind knew her, loved her, had been there her whole life, and now she felt guilty that she was so easily swayed to give that all up, for a place she didn't even know. So Isla made the decision she would do as she had promised, she was sure about that, but as soon as whatever had to be done was done, she would find a way back to the Manor, to her home, her real home.

'Something troubling you?' Henri enquired as they walked side by side in silence.

'Am I that readable?' She used to be so much better at hiding her thoughts, her emotions, but Henri somehow saw right through it.

'Well, it doesn't take a genius,' he said, breaking out into a broad smile that instantly put her at ease. He didn't smile often, or rather didn't allow himself to, which made her sad. No one could fault him for his diligence, and if Kallon had spent a lot of time with him, Isla now understood where his seriousness came from. It had taken a while to see past that with Kallon, but with Henri, it was a different kettle of fish, far more complex in many ways than Kallon. She liked him a lot, but she also wondered where all his pain came from; she was not the only one that could be read.

'You can ask me,' he said to her.

'Ask what?'

'Whatever question is on your mind – you may ask it.'

Was this really the place to ask such questions, in the middle of the Fen, the middle of a forest so dead that even the sun avoided it?

'You know, my daughter was much like you.'

'Really?' This took Isla by surprise; he had never spoken about a family before.

'Yes, she took after her mother more than me. Though her mother would have said otherwise – Thalia, my wife.' He stopped as if a deep pain was reaching the surface and swallowed hard. 'Well, she was an incredible woman in every way.'

'Was?' Isla repeated, wanting to know the answer but not daring to enquire further.

'She died, along with our daughter.' Again there was a longer pause.

'Oh, Henri, I had no idea.' The truth was she had some idea that he had suffered some loss, Kallon had said so himself in the cave, but he had not said what and Isla had never asked.

'It was a long time ago. She would be a little younger than you now – Thaya was her name.'

Isla didn't know what to say; she awkwardly listened and waited for the silence to pass until he spoke again.

'Her mother and I met when we were very young; we lived in nearby villages and, like most kids that age, had a harmless rivalry. Oh, she knew her mind, and I admired her for it. You see, I was a little soft back then.'

Isla gave him a look that questioned this statement.

'Okay, okay, I was soft on her.' He was talking with a smile on his face; this was obviously a fond memory for him. 'She was, inquisitive, outspoken, insatiable – everything I respected. Our paths were to end, though, when my family left for better land to grow crops, but I never forgot about her. So when I was older and had grown into a man, I came back. I wasn't sure what I was going to find, or if even she was still there, but my heart would not have rested if I did not try. It must have been fate's will, though, for she recognised me straight away, and she was exactly as I remembered, only more beautiful. I will not bore you with the rest, but when Thaya came along we decided that she could no longer come with me. It was her choice, actually – motherhood changed her. She didn't want her daughter to be brought up around violence and slaughter, so she protected her from it instead and it worked for a while. We found the perfect spot for our family home, out of reach of any main towns or roads, and every few weeks or months I would come back. Each time Thaya was twice the size from when I'd left her, and more and more like her mother each day.'

Henri's face grew dark; Isla could tell he was going through it methodically, reliving the pain. 'One day, unbeknown to me, I had been followed, and my perfect little pocket of happiness was destroyed. Before I had even reached them, men, followers of Akos, came out of nowhere. I could see what was happening right before my eyes, yet there was nothing I could do. They didn't stand a chance or see it coming themselves, and that is the only comfort that I can take, that they never knew their lives were coming to an end. I buried them that night, and I have never returned.'

'I would have liked to have met them,' Isla said. She felt that was the right thing to say; he was not a man who would want sympathy.

'I would have liked that too,' he simply replied.

They walked only a few more steps when Henri's lookout, by the name of Armatis, brought them to a halt. He made a signal, and all eyes looked to where he was pointing. Isla couldn't see what they all so evidently could, but the way Henri held on tightly to her informed her that the turn of events were not positive.

'They've seen us!' Armatis shouted.

'Who?' Isla asked.

'Patrollers,' Henri growled under his breath. 'Quick, stay with me. *Do not* leave my side.'

Isla could feel her heart race and felt that all-too-daunting familiar feeling that she was yet again going to have to run from something, an unknown enemy in an unknown place. Henri's men scattered, but they were all keeping close enough so that they could still see each other, if that was even possible.

'Who are they, Henri?' Isla asked again as they came to a stop at a tree that looked like it had been struck by lightning.

'They are lowlifes, men with darkened hearts. These are men who had evil in them long before the darkness, but with him on the throne, there is no one to stop them. They quite happily do his work for him in return to live their life as they please.'

'But they are just men, human – they can be beaten right?'

'They are not to be messed with, Isla, do you understand me? I will not let you see the same fate as Thalia and Thaya.' His eyes were intense; sadness and anger overwhelmed them.

'*Do not move!*' Henri said slowly.

'What?'

'Do not move,' he repeated, quieter.

'Henri, what's wrong?'

'Just be still.'

'Henri, please tell me?'

'Silver Tongue.'

'Silver what?'

His eyes moved to her feet, where a silverish-looking vine had started wrapping its way around her leg. Isla went to shake it off, but Henri grabbed her. 'Stop! It will only move quicker if you move. You need to remain completely still – do not move until I tell you.'

Isla gently nodded her head and whispered okay, her heart beating a thousand times per minute. She could hardly feel the silver tongue, but now, thanks to Henri, she knew that it was there and it was hard to fight the urge not to shake it off.

Isla tried her best to see what was happening but dared not move her head. She could feel Henri, however, gently place his arm against her leg, his face full of concentration. As it worked its way up her leg, Henri coaxed it with his fingers ever so slightly, much like you would do with a snake. It began to wrap itself around Henri's arm and loosen its hold on Isla's leg; with his free hand keeping his movements as still as possible, he gripped his sword and raised it above his head.

'Now,' he whispered.

But Isla did not move; her brain was having trouble connecting with her body.

Henri nodded for her to go again. 'Quickly,' he said, and this time she didn't think; she just acted. She jumped out of its hold and leapt as far as she could. The Silver Tongue seemed to sense that something had moved and within inches of where Isla's leg had been it squeezed so tight that it surely would have squeezed the life out of her had she still been within its grasp.

It continued to make its way up Henri's arm, inching closer towards his neck; feeling that it had been duped out of its prey, it looked like it was not going to make the same mistake twice. Henri was full of concentration, the rest of his body like a statue while his other arm found its strike point. Prepared, he swung his blade, and just as the Silver Tongue was about to meet with its death Henri's arm was brought to a sudden halt.

'What do we have here? Trespassers.'

Within seconds their situation had changed once again. Isla was caught in the clutches of a wild-looking man, with beady eyes, long, piercing nails that dug into her skin and sharpened teeth that he used to repeatedly hiss at her.

'What would bring an unlikely pair like yourself to a place like this?'

'We are *not* trespassing,' Henri spat. The Silver Tongue carried on, making its way up his arm, getting closer and closer to his neck. The man had Henri in a predicament, and he knew it. If he moved, he lost; if he stayed, he lost.

'Now, come on, no need to be touchy now. We're merely enquiring why you would be here; this is no place for a lady. Shame on you to bring such a pretty thing here.' He approached Isla and stroked her hair; he tried to smile reassuringly, but there was nothing remotely reassuring about him, and from the look of fear and disgust in Henri's eyes, she knew she should not be fooled.

He approached Henri, getting as close as he dared, and spoke quietly so that no one else could hear. 'I reckon I'd get a pretty penny for her, but then again, what kind of gentleman would I be if I gave her away?'

Henri was trying his best to keep his composure; he knew that he was trying to say anything that would rile him up, but he also didn't put it past him to mean what he said.

The man walked back to Isla. 'Don't worry, we will look after you. This is no place for a lady – you shouldn't have been brought here in the first place.' He stroked her hair again, which made her feel sick.

'I was *not* brought here. I came here on my own free will, and I shall be leaving on my own free will.' This time she managed to shake off the gangly, disgusting man as he had not been expecting it, but the larger one caught her; he was powerful and looked as if he was enjoying himself.

'I can see why you kept this one now – she shall be fun,' he said, laughing, then threw Isla back to her original capturer. 'We'll take her with us. We'll find a use for her.'

'*No, no!*' Isla cried; she kicked and screamed as hard as she could.

'What about him?'

'Leave him. Let him remember these last few moments.'

There was nothing Henri could do other than to watch them drag Isla away. He could not alert them to who she was; he had to let them think that she was just an ordinary girl. If they thought that they would keep her around – the only question was, how long for?

CHAPTER THIRTY-FOUR

S he landed on the floor with a thud, and before she'd even had the chance to get to her feet, the heavy bolt was pulled across with an almighty bang.

'I'll be back for you later,' said the man with teeth as sharp as his nails.

Isla ran to the door. 'You can't keep me in here – hey, come back! I said you can't keep me in here.' She pulled at the wrought iron bars in anger; there was no way they were coming off, but it didn't stop her from trying. 'He'll come for me, you know, Henri will come back for me.' *Oh no!* Should she have said his name? Now they knew who he was. *Too late now.* But it didn't seem to have made a difference; she heard him say something and laugh, though he was too far away for to catch what it was.

Isla dropped herself against the door and slid down into a ball. 'He will come for me, I know it. He won't just leave me,' she said feebly to herself.

'No one is coming for you.' A hollow voice cut through the wall.

'Who said that?' Isla's ears pricked at the hope that she wasn't alone. 'Who's there?' she asked again. 'Can you tell me where I am?' She waited for a response, but again, nothing. '*Fine!* If that's the way you want to be.'

Why does this keep happening? For every one step forward, it felt like she took two steps back. She had already lost Kallon and now Henri; she felt so weak and defenceless, but she wasn't, was she? She had risen up against obstacles; she had overcome difficulties, so why not this time? She felt like she had let all the men in her life down, starting with Will, then Kallon and now Henri. That seed of doubt was beginning to creep its way back in again – surely if she was the prophecy, all of this wouldn't be happening? *This wouldn't happen to the person who was meant to be the beginning of the end.*

'This kind of thinking is not going to help you, Isla,' she told herself. 'Now think, there has got to be a way out of here.' She got to her feet, shook herself out and inspected her meagre accommodation. It was literally four stone walls, stone upon stone, nothing else inside it, not even a bed. She noticed markings etched into the walls and realised the previous occupant must have had some kind of sharp object to do it with, though if they did it was not there now.

A few hours passed – maybe more, maybe less, she didn't know, but already it felt like she'd spent a lifetime in the claustrophobic cell. She found herself mindlessly trying to chip away at the wall with her handcuffs. If she kept this up maybe she would be able to produce a hole big enough to fit through in fifty years.

'Humph! This is useless.' She leant against the wall and decided she would try one more time to make contact with the unknown voice.

'You know, it would really help me if you could tell me where we are, or what I am doing here at the very least.' Unsurprisingly there was no response, so she mocked a fake reply to herself. 'I know you can hear me, so you may as well talk to me. I'm hardly a threat – I mean, what can I do from in here? I've done nothing wrong.' She waited another minute, hoping they would have a change of heart, but whoever it was, it appeared they were not going to. 'Well, I'm Isla, by the way – it's nice to meet you.'

CRASH! Something had fallen over, but what? She couldn't tell.

'*Fine!* At least I tried to be nice.' Before she had the chance to choose between giving up or trying yet another approach, she heard the faint sound of footsteps. Perching herself up against the door, she listened as they got closer and closer until they stopped right in front of her.

'I'm not going anywhere until you tell me where I am,' Isla said defiantly. She had not seen this man before; he wore an apron, which she assumed used to be white, had a shiny bald head and a big wobbly belly that bulged out the sides.

'Don't make this any harder than what it is. Please, it will be better for both of us if you just comply. Keep your head down and you might just get out of here.'

'So there is a way out of here?'

'That's not what I meant.' He was finding every word an effort. 'I mean, maybe you'll get out of this cell, to a nicer part of the castle, but you'll be punished if you keep them waiting. Now come on, I've spoken too much already.'

Isla still refused to move, so he was forced to enter and pull her out, but he did so with a far gentler hand than any of the others.

Before leaving the cell he attached a chain to her handcuffs and then to himself; there was no way she would be able to run away unless she could carry the weight of an eighteen-stone fully grown man with her. He closed the door and pointed Isla in the direction he wanted her to go; they had barely walked a few steps when, out of nowhere, two frail arms shot out and grabbed her. For the first time, she saw who she presumed was the owner of the mystery voice, which was not much, for his face was covered in mottled hair that made him look wild.

'Get off!' the big-bellied man said to him, and he let go, immediately disappearing back into the darkness. 'Come on, we're taking too long already.' He gently manoeuvred her down the stairs and picked up a lantern to light his way.

'Where are you taking me?' Isla asked, peering up to the man whom she had mentally named sausage fingers, due to his short and chubby hands. He chose to ignore her, keeping his gaze facing forward. Although the sheer size of him could threaten any small child, Isla didn't feel threatened by him at all. He didn't seem like he had it in him to hurt so much as a fly, yet here he was, following orders, probably because he was too scared to say no.

After what had felt like navigating their way through a rabbit burrow they eventually came to a halt; the stench of stale food instantaneously making her feel nauseous.

He uncuffed her hands and popped the chains on the table. 'I wouldn't suggest running if I were you; they have guards on every door, and it wouldn't be worth your trouble to do so.'

Isla rubbed at her wrists, massaging them after their long-awaited release. She looked around at the hazardous place he had brought her to, a badly maintained kitchen piled high with dirty pots and pans and animal carcases that were most likely the source of the stench.

'Here.' He held an apron out to her. 'I suggest you wear this.' He had to thrust it forward twice before she took it.

'What's this for?'

'What do you think? Look around you.'

She did, but still didn't understand; Isla was expecting to be taken somewhere else. She didn't quite know where, but she wasn't expecting this.

'You best get started – they'll be hungry soon.' When she didn't move, sausage fingers explained further. 'You can start by peeling the potatoes, and once they are done, you can make a start on the washing-up.'

'They want me to be a maid?' Isla replied, surprised.

'Count yourself lucky that's all they want you for. I had to do some serious talking to get them to agree to have you in here to help.'

'Why would you do that?' Her surprise grew.

Clearly a bit frustrated now, he turned away from the meat that he had proceeded to carve. 'This is no place for a young girl; in fact, this is no place for anyone other than the inebriates that have decided to take residence here. I needed help, I've said that for a long time, you came along and I saw my opportunity. Does that answer your question? Now please, if you wouldn't mind.' He pointed to the large sack of potatoes that lay on the other side of the room, half-peeled, with a bigger half waiting.

Isla diligently did as she was told; she didn't see any point in arguing or causing sausage fingers any further grievance. He seemed quite nice in comparison to the others, and she didn't want her actions to change the course of anyone else's fate.

She had been peeling potatoes for what felt like hours; her hands were sore from holding the knife in the same position and had left indents on her fingers.

'You'll be here all night if you don't get a move on, missy,' said sausage fingers; he had finished carving up the meat and was busy making some brown slop that was to accompany it.

'Surely you can't expect me to do all this by myself?' she replied, wiping a sweaty strand of hair away from her face, leaving a smudgy potato fingerprint in its place.

'Well, I don't see anyone else, do you?'

'Yes,' she quickly replied, 'I see you.'

Sausage fingers chuckled to himself in an oddly high-pitched tone that didn't suit his appearance. 'I'm having a well-earned break – I've not gone to bed before midnight for the past six years. It won't hurt you to get your hands dirty.'

Isla held up her hands in response to say that they already were.

'A bit of hard work is not going to cause you any harm, and if you don't want to get bothered around here, you're best keeping your head down and not drawing any attention to yourself.'

'You are under the impression that I am staying, which I have no intention of doing.'

He dropped what he was doing and faced her. 'Look, the quicker you get this idea out of your head that you are somehow getting out of here the better it'll be for all of us; it is not worth the consequence for your trouble.' He picked up his spoon and carried on stirring mindlessly.

Isla replied, without thinking, 'Well, not all of us just do as we are told, or think it is okay to be treated like that. I'm not going to be kept here.'

This time he threw his spoon and slammed his hands down on the table, which made Isla jump. '*It can't be done!*'

'Why not?'

'Because I've tried!' He took a deep breath before he spoke again. 'I've tried, okay?' he said, calmer. 'And it's not something I am prepared to do again. If it was not for the fact that they are too lazy to cook, they would have had my throat without a second's thought. I don't like being here any more than you, but I don't want to die either.'

Isla felt sorry for sausage fingers – could he have been one of the people on Henri's map, stuck with no way out? She wondered how many others there were out there just like him. She empathised with him, his sadness, and decided that now was not the right time to pick a battle.

'I think there are enough potatoes. I'll get started on the pans.'

They didn't speak any further and continued to work in silence – that was until sausage fingers was summoned and Isla learnt his real name, which was Alfled.

'Don't stop, I'll be back in a moment.'

She watched him leave the room and carried on with her chores, wondering what they may have been calling him for; she felt uneasy being in there on her own and now that he was gone she realised she found his company soothing, but when he returned he looked forlorn and was carrying something with him.

'Missy, come here, would you?' He paused. 'Please.'

She shook out her hands, dried them and joined him where he was stood. 'Are you okay?' Isla asked, for he looked a little white.

'They want you to wear this.' In his arms, he held out a red and gold dress with a tight bodice.

'Why?' Isla asked, confused.

'Umm, you are their guest and guests should dress more appropriately,' Alfled/sausage fingers said sheepishly.

'Guest?' Isla choked. 'They took me against my will and locked me in a cell – I'm not wearing that.' Despite not being much of a dress girl, she didn't see the need or reason why she should have to change.

'Please,' Alfled pleaded. He couldn't look her in the eye; he didn't want her to be forced to wear it and be paraded around like some trophy, but he also knew there were consequences to disobeying them. Either outcome would not be a pleasant one.

'Do you really think I should wear this?' Isla questioned.

'Yes, yes, I do.' He hated saying the words. He didn't want her to wear it, but he didn't like the thought of what they might do to her and he just couldn't think of an alternative.

'Okay, I'll do it.' She took the dress off him, and Alfled showed her where she could get changed.

'It's not quite a changing room, but I promise I won't look.' He was right – it wasn't a changing room; it was a little alcove in the wall that was slightly covered by barrels. However, he did turn his back and did not turn around until Isla had said she was ready.

Though it was a bit short, the dress fit surprisingly well. She had never worn anything quite like or as tight as it before, therefore she wasn't sure if she had done it right, but when she reappeared Alfled smiled.

'Well, don't you look a picture.' He meant what he said, but his facial expression did not match his words.

'I feel like an idiot.' She winced.

'You look lovely.'

'Alfled.' He looked surprised that she had called him by his name. 'I heard them call you it earlier,' she confirmed. 'What are they going to do to me?'

'*Nothing* – they will want you to serve them their food, I suspect. Just keep your head down and you will be fine.'

'I thought I was meant to be a guest?' Isla retorted.

'Well, our ideas of a guest is very different to theirs – just do as you're told and whatever they say or do, don't bite back.' He smiled, already knowing in the short time he had got to know her that this would be somewhat impossible.

'*Food!*' They heard shouting through the vents; Isla noted there was no "please", or "is it ready", just a demand.

'I will be with you now,' Alfled called out, on edge. 'Come on. We best go. They get impatient.'

Isla followed him, carrying a big tray of potatoes, and put them down in the middle of a large table that twenty men sat around.

'Where are the others?' she whispered to Alfled.

'These are all the men favoured at present. The others are either on guard or still seeing to other jobs and will eat later,' Alfled replied, then rushed off to retrieve more food.

The dining hall had a very distinct smell of sweat and other unpleasant odours that didn't agree with Isla, it was nauseating just being in there. The poachers (as she recalled Henri had called them) had already helped themselves to tankards of beer, which, judging by their crude remarks and ghastly manner, was not their first one. They laughed and joked about who was the strongest, the scariest, the deadliest, and Isla was relieved that she had been left alone. That was until the man at the head of the table called her over, the same man that had left Henri to his death, which she prayed to an inch of her being was not true.

'*You!*' he growled. 'Come here.'

Isla looked at Alfled, who gave her a reassuring smile. She straightened her back and held her head high; despite what Alfled said, she didn't want them to think they could intimidate her as well.

'Refill my drink,' he ordered. He watched as she picked up the jug that was right in front of him and began to pour it. All the men were hushed as they watched the man with the dark eyes ogle her. Isla forced a smile once she had refilled his drink and, upon placing the jug back down, went to walk away, but he caught her wrist and stopped her from going any further.

'I didn't say go,' he snarled. 'I think we *all* need our drinks replenished,' he said, leaning back in his chair, not taking his eyes off her.

Alfled tensed watching the scene unfold, unsure whether intervening would make it worse or not.

'You show her who's in charge, Broc.' One of the men from across the table laughed.

So that's his name. This disgusting man was called Broc.

Isla picked up the jug a bit too hastily; it sent drops splattering onto the table. She refilled each drink for every one of them, offering a putrid smile in return. By the time she had made her way around the table, Broc had finished his and held out his tankard for more.

'There's none left,' Isla confirmed.

'So, go get some more,' he replied patronisingly.

'I thought I was a guest?' Isla mumbled under her breath as she walked away.

He grabbed her arm and pulled her back. 'What did you say?'

'Nothing,' she replied.

'Oh, I think you did.' Then he raised his voice. 'Men, wouldn't you like to hear what she has to say?'

They all roared in unison and Isla was struggling to keep her cool. They were not the kind of men she should be upsetting, Alfled clearly thought not, and Henri had not been a fan of them either. *What had he referred to them as? Men with darkened hearts.*

One of the men closest to her, who had a thick ginger beard with pieces of food stuck in it, pulled at her dress. Isla quickly kicked him away and glared at him coldly.

'That's okay, I prefer my woman quiet...' he put a hand up to her face, 'sometimes,' he added, and they all laughed, which infuriated her more.

'Get your hands *off* me,' Isla yelled back at him.

Alfled winced watching the scene play out; the very thing he hadn't wanted to happen was happening, and he didn't know how to stop it.

This time the man laughed a nervous laugh, as if to say "you are embarrassing me" and "do as you are told", then proceeded to pull her down onto his lap. Isla yelped, grabbed the first drink that she could see and splattered it right across his face, then watched it drip from his wiry ginger beard.

Alfled quickly stepped in. 'You have to excuse her – she's not used to so much work and she's tired. After a good night's sleep and perhaps some warming accommodation I am sure she will be more forthcoming.'

Isla went to interrupt to say that she wouldn't, but he stopped her and waited for a response from Broc, who all the while had remained quite happily back in his seat laughing at what was happening.

'Take her away. She is no good to us with a mouth like that,' he finally said.

'Thank you,' Alfled said, relieved, pulling Isla with him.

'She has one chance, and only because this food is better than anything you have produced in the last twelve months so I should like to keep her around, *but* if she continues to insult my men…' He stopped speaking and stood up so fast that Isla hardly believed her eyes had witnessed what they had done before he was comfortably back in his seat. Right at the end of the table, firmly in the middle of the pig's head was the end of a knife that only seconds ago had been in Broc's hand.

'And her accommodation will not change – perhaps it will make her grateful for what we have given her already.'

'As you wish,' Alfled remarked.

'And send the others in.' Instantly about six women entered the room who were immediately grabbed to sit on several laps, with Broc at the head of the table seemingly no longer concerned with Isla.

Alfled scurried Isla away as quickly as possible, and once back in the safety of the kitchen, he burst, as if he had been holding his breath the whole time.

'I'm sorry, I tried, but—'

'Yes, I know,' he quickly cut in, 'but you must really be more resilient next time.'

The noise grew louder, as it sounded like more women had entered the room, their giggles and screams carrying down the stairs.

'I don't want their hands anywhere near me,' Isla bit back.

'Yes, well, let's not worry about that for tonight; they are occupied now. We best get a move on with all off this.' He pointed to the room that was now filled with more dirty dishes.

Despite what he had initially said, he stayed with Isla until every last pot, pan and dish was washed and the place was looking a bit more like a functioning kitchen, much like what she imagined they would have had many, many years ago at the Manor.

When the last plate had been put away, they sat down for something to eat themselves; the noise of the rowdy men had slowly dwindled, and only a few gruffly sounds remained. With a ravished appetite, Isla didn't need to be told twice to delve in; it was the first proper meal she had had in days and regardless of where it came from, she needed to eat. They'd finished it off with a warm drink when Isla finally broke the silence.

'Alfled.' He looked tired but gave her his attention. 'What happened here? To the people, I mean, the ones that were here before?'

'I'm not sure it's a story for you to know just before going to sleep.'

'But I want to know. I think I deserve to know.'

Clearly not having the energy to argue, he relented. He may have missed out some of the gruesome bits, but Isla understood that some time ago they'd commandeered the castle, slaughtering the lord and lady and anyone else who'd stood in their way. Alfled was the last remaining original occupant; everyone else had either escaped when they'd had the chance or had been killed over the years for trying to do so.

'They can't keep you here, Alfled. They can't keep me either – they shouldn't be allowed.'

'What else can I do? You have seen what they are like, and this is them on a good night.'

Isla paused, thinking about whether she should ask her next question or not. 'Alfled, do you believe in the prophecy?'

His eyes widened then relaxed again. 'Why do you ask?'

'I just wondered, that's all.'

'I used to,' he said in response, 'but now, after all this time, I don't know. We seemed doomed to this life and perhaps it's better just to accept what is.'

'Well, I don't think we should. I don't think we should at all.'

He cast that warming smile at her, admiring her spirit but knowing full well that she too would end up like him one day, defeated.

'Do you know who the prophecy is meant to be?' She wondered if there was any more to the story than what she had been told.

'I don't think anyone does, do they?'

'But what do you think?'

He hesitated, wondering why she was asking so many questions but decided to humour her. 'Well, there is one theory.'

'Yes.'

'That it is the king and queen's daughter. No one knows where she is – in hiding, most likely – but she is the rightful heir to the throne, so one would think, well, it would make sense that she would be the prophecy, after all, but then again, she could have died along with her mother and father.'

'But what if she was still alive? What if we found her?'

'Someone's been filling your head with too many stories, young lady.' He laughed, then got up and took their plates to the sink. She followed him, ignoring his comment.

'But it's possible.'

'Nycolas Blackbourne was the last good man to come out of this kingdom. I would love to see nothing more than a Blackbourne sitting on that throne again. If you are asking me if it is possible, I'd say yes, but if you are asking me if it is probable, I'd say no. Now come on, it's time to get you back. I will find you a blanket at least for tonight, but you will need to get your sleep – we will be up early.'

'But you didn't say?'

'Say what?'

'Their daughter, what was her name?'

'Ilarya, Ilarya Blackbourne.'

CHAPTER THIRTY-FIVE

Henri unravelled the Silver Tongue from around his neck, the part that had been sliced off by Armatis, and threw it to the ground, squishing it under his foot.

'Henri, are you okay?' Armatis asked, alarmed. Had it not been for his timely arrival, the Silver Tongue would have constricted his last breath out of him by now.

'Yes, I owe you a debt,' he replied, seemingly unaffected by what had just happened but rather more preoccupied by what he saw. He walked towards a bush, leaving Armatis somewhat bemused, knelt down and when he returned, Isla's dagger was firmly within his grasp. *What a clever girl*, he thought to himself. Henri had seen her drop it. He knew she understood the complications its discovery could cause, the wrong hands it could end up in. Their eyes had made contact, only for a few short seconds, but seconds was all he'd needed to understand the words they would have spoken, and he felt honoured that she would entrust something so important to him.

'I saw them take her. What do you want to do?' Armatis eventually asked.

Henri did not need time to think; he already knew what

they had to do, and that was to stick to the plan. He had fought his immediate urge, which was to chase them down. The man that had spoken, he had seen his face before; it had been younger then, but even now, with a beard, there was no mistaking it was the same man. He could never forget the face that haunted his sleep. But going into battle when emotions were high was risky – detachment was the way forward. He needed numbers, and there was only one place he was going to find that.

'We make way for Lestoris.' Armatis wide-eyed, but did not question. 'Call for the others. We leave as soon as we are all together.' Armatis nodded, leaving his leader alone.

Henri took one last look at the dagger then placed it inside his coat patting it down as he did; he swore to himself the next person to set eyes on it was to be one person and one person only. He then looked up and called out to Armatis just before he was out of earshot.

'And tell them we do not stop until we get there.'

CHAPTER THIRTY-SIX

'Lord Lestrone, I thank you for being able to meet with me. As you can see, you are the only one that is with us, which I will explain the reasons for in just a moment, but first I would like to introduce you to Will. This is Isla's closest friend.'

Both Lestrone and Will looked just as puzzled as one another. Will had not expected to be introduced, especially with how guarded Miss Sparrow always was, and for Lestrone this was the first time he had seen anyone other than Miss Sparrow and Mr Stopes within their new world, which was unexpected to say the least.

'Will has come into some information that is very significant and we felt it important for you to know. Will, if you please?'

'I'm sorry?' He was uncertain if he had understood correctly.

'If you would inform Lord Lestrone of your encounter.'

'You want me to speak?' This surprised both him and Mr Stopes.

'Yes, I think this is best coming from the person who actually had the encounter, so if you please.' Despite the quizzical expressions she received there was a reason behind

Miss Sparrow's request; Lord Lestrone, contrary to his outer shell, was an emotional man at heart, and she hoped Will's more personal version of events would have the desired effect, more so than if she told it herself.

Will cleared his throat and introduced himself again; there was no need for it, but his nerves got the better of him – after all, this was the first time he had seen an apparition and on the same encounter he was having to speak to one. The man he was talking to, despite the fact that Will could actually see right through him, looked important; with his sword at his side, large weighted jewellery and long fur coat, Will felt he was in the presence of royalty – for all he knew the man could be.

He swallowed the lump in his throat away and found once he got started the rest flowed easily. '…Then that's when she said she was heading to Lestoris, just as her image disappeared.' Will waited for a response and turned to Miss Sparrow for reassurance.

'So you see now why I only called for you.' Miss Sparrow let Will take a seat and she took over.

Lestrone scratched at his chin as if he was deep in thought. 'Yes, yes, I do. I guess this is a good sign.'

'I'm glad you see it as that. We were hoping now that we know where she is and her intentions that you would send your men in search of her.'

'But you *don't* know where she is. If I send my men out I am leaving my people unguarded,' he replied pragmatically.

Another voice entered the conversation, one of a man who could no longer bite his tongue. '*Oh, come on!* All this was said last time. We've had contact; we know she's alive and where she is heading. That cuts your search area down by half if not more – she must be close.'

'*Mr Stopes!*' Miss Sparrow cut in. 'You forget your place. Lord Lestrone knows what is at risk here. I'm sure he just needs some time to process the information.'

'With all due respect, Miss Sparrow, I don't. Ever since Isla's return there's been a change in the air: raids are more frequent, people are being attacked, their crops burned, their houses destroyed; they are scared and all retreating behind city walls. I do not have enough space for them all, let alone resources to feed them, but that's another issue altogether. Without her definitive whereabouts, I cannot afford to leave my people without protection. I will send a rider out to the mountains and inform my men that are already there; they will search all useable paths leading to Lestoris, but I cannot deploy the little I have left protecting my city walls. I have women and children to think about.'

Miss Sparrow looked just as exasperated as Mr Stopes, but it was Will's voice that spoke up next.

'I cannot imagine what life is like for you, to be honest. My imagination never even thought something like this was possible. Yet here we all are. I know we have no right to ask you to sacrifice the safety of thousands of people's lives for the safety of one, but I would never forgive myself if I didn't try. Isla is the only real family I have; all I want is for her to come home, to know that she is safe, but if the stories I've heard are true then safe she is not. Please if you can help, just, please.' Will delivered his speech with just enough emotion that Lestrone's hardened exterior softened.

Lestrone and Will were worlds apart in every sense of the word, but there was something in this young boy that reminded him of himself, and he too would not have taken no for an answer if it was the other way round.

'You speak very well for someone so young – perhaps you are the wisest of us all.' He stepped closer and raised a hand to his shoulder, though Will could not actually feel it, the gesture was enough to show that he understood him. 'You speak your truth, and from the heart, I respect that.'

'So you'll send men out, as soon as you get back?' Mr Stopes piped in abruptly.

'As soon as I can and no sooner,' replied Lestrone, still firm on his word.

That was the last straw for Mr Stopes; he erupted, bringing the two men to a showdown.

'*I will not* be bullied into doing so,' bellowed Lestrone.

'You can't refuse the will of the king or refuse to do what has been asked of you – *no*, what has been demanded of you. It is your duty to do so,' retorted Mr Stopes.

'With all due respect, the king is no longer with us, and I *do not* have to do anything; the quarters have disbanded. I have stayed loyal for all these years because I believed it was the right thing to do, but it's a different time we live in now, and I can no longer stretch my men and endanger my people further. I am a city in my own right.'

'*But—*' Mr Stopes went to push his point further; however, Miss Sparrow silenced him.

'As I have said, I will send a rider, one rider, to inform my men who are already on the ridge and they will spare who they can to go in search for her, but I will *not* leave countless of innocent lives ready for the taking once my city is left unarmed and I should *not* be asked to do so. I cannot be any fairer than that.'

Miss Sparrow stepped in, sensing it was time to finish the conversation; it was clear that they were not going to convince him otherwise.

'Thank you, Lord Lestrone. I obviously cannot hide my disappointment that you will not send more riders, seeing as we have a strong indication of her whereabouts, and furthermore it disappoints me that you no longer recognise your king. However, we do still value your alliance; after all, if the unthinkable happens, this will affect everyone. Isla's safe return is in the interest of everyone, even your own people.'

Lestrone looked slightly ashamed; he had every respect for his king and had spoken in anger, but times had changed and no longer did a king – a true king, anyhow – sit on the throne. It was hard to maintain loyalty to something that had gone.

'I suspect my rider will return in three days.'

'Three days?' snapped back Mr Stopes.

'The strike of ten in three days and I expect you to have done at least what you have confirmed that you will do here today,' declared Miss Sparrow, whose voice carried an undertone of a threat.

'On that, you have my word.' Lestrone bowed, then he disappeared.

CHAPTER THIRTY-SEVEN

I sla struggled to sleep that night; it felt like hours that she had been staring at the ceiling until the first signs of dawn crept in, and shortly after Alfled had come to collect her for morning prep.

The reasons for her lack of sleep were not down to the fact that the floor beneath her was hard and cold or that the room was damp and chilly, but rather down to something that Alfled had said.

The king and queen had had a daughter! Kallon had not mentioned this before; in fact, no one had mentioned this. Why had they all led her to believe that she could be the only one? That she *was* the one? Isla's thoughts had gone around and around in her head all night, ignoring the most likely answer, the one that stared her straight in the face, but she didn't dare think it. She didn't want to believe it; she didn't want to allow herself to believe it could be true, because if it was then everything that she had ever known, her whole life before now, it would all have been a lie…

Isla managed to get through the day relatively undisturbed, which she later learned was because Broc and his men were going night poaching and had slept for most the day. She didn't enquire as to what that was, because it sounded far from pleasant from what she had overheard, and she was happy to be kept in the dark of what it fully entailed. Now that evening was upon them, once again, Alfled was taking her back to her cell.

'I'm sorry, I don't want to do this, but Broc, after last night, he's insisted. I promise I will try to get you transferred to somewhere more preferable, but until he knows you're not going to be trouble, he will keep you here. I have found you more bedding, though, which should help see to a better night's sleep at least.'

She took the extra bedding from him, one being the fur from an animal and indeed felt she was in store for a far comfier night.

'It's okay, Alfled. In a way I feel safer up here – at least I know I am as far away from them as possible.'

'Aye, that is true, but no one will be troubling you tonight – you have my word.' He went to walk away, but Isla called him back.

'Alfled.'

'Yes?'

'Thank you.'

'What for?'

'For being nice to me.'

He froze. He wasn't sure how nice he was being; he had just locked up a young lady in a cell for the night – not his finest hour. How she could show him gratitude in a situation like this, he did not know. He was ashamed of himself, and he wouldn't have blamed her if she was too. He placed his chubby fingers on her hand, giving them a squeeze, not able to speak. He had the beginnings of a tear in the corner of his eye and he wanted to leave before the floodgates released themselves. As he closed the door, he accidentally let a barely audible, high-pitched squeak escape and walked off as quickly as possible, not even acknowledging the face pressed up against the bars watching him leave.

'I would not trust him if I were you.' It was the man from the cell, whose only encounter with Isla until now had been the one from the previous day, and she didn't react too kindly to his comment.

'Who do you think you are, telling me who I should and shouldn't trust?'

'If it was your life or his, I guarantee you he would save his own skin every time.'

'How would you know? You don't even know him,' Isla snapped back; this man had kept silent all this time, and now he wanted to badmouth the only friend she had in this place.

'I know enough.'

'Humph, you don't know what he has been through.'

'You don't know what I have been through.'

Isla knew what the man was getting at. Still, she didn't want to agree with him. A part of her trusted Alfled; anytime he'd wanted to, he could have made life more difficult for her, yet he hadn't. He may not be breaking her out, but he was doing his best to keep her protected, and that, he didn't have to do.

'Well, I don't know what you have done – for all I know you deserve to be here.' Isla knew it was a little too harsh the moment the words left her mouth, but he had gotten under her skin; he had not reached out to her when she had needed help, and now all of a sudden he was providing "advice", and unwanted advice at that.

'Do you deserve to be in here?' he replied.

That was her answer: she knew he could not have done anything that warranted being locked up – she knew that she hadn't. In fact, other than being in the wrong place at the wrong time, she had not done anything wrong at all. However, it did not mean that she should trust him any more; he had still chosen to remain silent when he should have spoken out, and that unnerved her somewhat.

'Well, who's to say that I should trust you either?'

'I'm not asking you to. I am merely passing on something to think about.' He spoke well, with a firm yet even tone. He sounded educated, unlike the others she had come across, who would not have known any manners, let alone have a vocabulary.

'Thank you, but I am sure you will understand if I do not take your advice right now.'

He laughed. 'I guess I should not be offended.'

Isla wondered why he felt it necessary to laugh was he laughing at her? She had certainly not said anything funny, so was he mocking her?

After the sound of his deep laugh trailed off, he continued. 'I do not mean to offend you. I suppose we have rather got off on the wrong foot, haven't we?' he offered, opening up the conversation.

Isla half-smiled to herself; she knew she could be stubborn. 'I guess we have.'

'I have been here for quite some time. My manners have somewhat escaped me. It may take me a while to remember how one should interact with another.'

'Well, you could start by introducing yourself – that is where most people start.' He didn't respond, so Isla prompted him again.

'Elston.' He coughed. 'My name is Elston.'

'Well, it's nice to finally put a name to the face, Elston.'

He remembered the day before and knew what she was referring to. 'I'm sorry, I should have never invaded your space like that. Please accept my apologies.'

Isla noticed that he didn't give a reason for his actions, why he had not just spoken to her like he was doing now, but she guessed solitary confinement could do strange things to a person, so she accepted his apology.

'Do they ever let you out, like they have done with me?'

'No, and I don't want them to, not if it is to be a slave to their needs and to be treated with disrespect.' He realised the words that he spoke, for in essence, this was exactly what was happening to her, so he quickly added, 'Though I am an old man now, too stuck in my ways to be of any use to them. To be honest, I think they have forgotten I am up here.'

'Why did they bring you here in the first place?'

'Why do they do much of anything? Because they can.'

Isla could sympathise with that statement. She had undoubtedly been at the receiving end of their actions.

'I get some food when they remember, but pretty much no one comes up here – that was, until you arrived.'

'Yes, well, I don't plan on staying here long.' She thought of Henri and hoped he was okay, but with or without him, she was finding a way out.

'You don't, do you? And how do you propose on doing that?' Asked Elston, bemused.

'I'm not sure yet.'

'Well, no time like the present.' He encouraged her, for he was curious to know what she had come up with.

So Isla ran through every possible way she could think of, but with every idea she had he shot her back; he seemed to know a lot about tactics, and it was very evident she did not.

'I don't mean to knock your spirit, young one. Actually, I admire it – you are the most sensible person I have come across in years. Don't give up.'

'That's easy for you to say – you already have.' Isla apologised immediately; of course he was not there by choice. As she had already discovered, it was not as easy to escape as she thought.

'No, you are right, I have, or rather, I had. I was like you – I thought I would escape this place, God knows I've tried, and somewhere along the line I gave up. But promise me one thing:

if you see a moment, an opportunity that you can get out of this place, you take it. You don't look back – you just go.'

It felt oddly comforting that he was rooting for her, being supportive, offering encouragement, but equally, she didn't quite understand why. Until today neither of them had known the other one existed, and therefore what did they owe each other? Still, she supposed he was just trying to be nice. Either way, she didn't want to think too much about it. She knew once she started, she would never stop, and she was tired, exhausted and needed to rest.

'I am going to get some sleep now – no doubt I will be summoned for my slave duties in a few hours,' she said, peeling her numb body away from the iron bars; it was a cheap shot, she knew, but his earlier remark had actually got to her and on some level she wanted him to know it.

Elston sighed, regretting his previous choice of words. He didn't reply because truth be told he worried about making it worse; instead, he stared out at the night sky, where he remained, just thinking, until morning.

CHAPTER THIRTY-EIGHT

'Not now!'

'My lord, there is someone here to see you.'

Lord Lestrone did not look up; instead, he kept his gaze firmly set on the table in front of him.

'I'm sorry, but they said it was important,' voiced the young messenger.

'This is important,' he growled.

He was in his private office; the place he liked to go when he wanted to think or be left alone. His mind was troubling him, and it was the king's daughter that was the cause of it. True to his word, Lestrone had sent a rider out as soon as he had concluded his conversation with Miss Sparrow, but a restless night and an uneasy conscience had seen him overlooking a miniature map of Westoria since sunrise and his conscience was still not any lighter.

He thought hard about what direction Isla could be coming from with the little information he had been provided. With all four corners covered, it was a treacherous journey for anyone, let alone someone of her significance. There would be many obstacles standing in her way. The mountains were a dangerous choice to travel through, especially for those who did not know them; the darkness was creeping further south by the day, and if she were to enter the Fen, he feared she would not leave. Without knowing exactly where she was coming from, it was a difficult task to move his men accordingly, not to mention a risky one too. His army (what he had left of it) was strategically placed to stop unwanted guests as well as carrying out the will of the council; he was already spread too thin – was it wise to spread them even further? Yes, it appeared Isla's intention was indeed to head his way, but the lands still spanned for hundreds of miles. There were many different paths she could take, and he could not cover all of them.

'My lord.' The man came closer. 'I do not think they will be convinced to wait.'

He slammed his fists down on the table. '*What part of I am busy do you not understand?*' he shouted at the startled messenger.

Suddenly a piece of parchment fell from the shelf and landed at his feet, an action that was symbolic only to Lestrone. Looking down at what stared back at him, he gently picked up the piece of parchment, a painting of the view from the room he currently stood in and apologised for his outburst. His late wife Neressa would have reminded him of his temper; she was also the subsequent painter of this particular picture.

He recalled a time when she would have spoken to him in person, but now it was through a series of signs – that did not make it any easier for him to accept. He yearned for the days when he would be at his table thinking of battle strategies or seeing to other important work, and she would sit in silence in her chair, content with painting. And though she kept quiet, she listened to every single word spoken, and if she ever felt the need to give her opinion, she gave it in such a way that it did not undermine her husband or those that advised him. She was quite often his voice of reason, and he loved her for that; her unwavering support and confidence in him had been what kept him going for years, but her years had come to an end. Her illness was sudden, and he had not had time to prepare himself, though one can never prepare themselves to lose the love of their life. The only comfort he took was that she didn't suffer long, not like he had done every day since.

Lestrone rose to his feet. 'I will be down shortly. Please make my apologies to our guests for keeping them.'

'Of course,' the messenger replied. 'I will have them meet you in the grand hall.'

Lord Lestrone waited until he had left then lovingly replaced his dearly beloved's picture back where it had been. It was the one thing he had kept after she had passed, and it meant a great deal to him. At first, he couldn't bear to have anything out that reminded him of her. He had to be strong for his people; they were and still are all going through tough times. He couldn't grieve for his wife, for that meant he would be vulnerable, but over time he'd allowed himself to feel the loss, and her painting, one that he had been so fond of, had found itself brought to the light and had been where it was sat ever since.

Ten minutes later and Lestrone had made his entrance to the grand hall known; they all turned and waited patiently while he took his seat in the overly large wooden chair at the head of the room.

'My lord, this is—'

'I know who he is – please save the introductions. What I want to know is why you are here, Henri. This is a long way from home for you.'

Lord Lestrone and Henri had met on a few occasions before; they had mutual respect for one another but had not always seen eye to eye.

'I believe you suspect the reasons that bring me here today.' Henri approached while his men remained seated; Lestrone's guards moved closer to block Henri from stepping any further, wearing their shiny, pristine helmets even inside.

'Stand down. He is of no threat to me.'

Henri returned his gratitude, then furthered his approach. 'I speak plainly to you when I say we need your help. The one has returned to us, which I already believe you know, and I know where she is.'

'*Leave us*,' he said with authority, ordering everyone to leave bar his trusted advisors. Henri's company did not like taking orders from someone else, but once Henri assured them it was okay, they left.

'Tell me, what do you know?' Lestrone asked.

Henri filled him in on all the events that had passed – the parts that involved him, anyway – and also where he believed Isla had been taken. Lestrone appeared to have soaked it all in but was yet to pass comment.

'My lord, if I may?' came the voice of one of his advisors.

'Yes.'

'Forgive me, I didn't know its importance until now, but I believe there is something else you should know…'

'And where is he now?' he said through gritted teeth.

'We let him go, my lord. A mistake, as I now see.'

'Find him and bring him back. You better pray that he has not left Lestoris – if he starts talking it will be your head and not his.' Of course, Lestrone did not mean this, but if there was anything he despised, it was people thinking for him and trying to protect him in the process. He was strong enough to still make his own decisions, and he did not need to be made to feel patronised.

The advisor embarrassingly left as quickly as he could with a promise that he would not return empty-handed. But they needn't have worried, as perhaps little over an hour passed before he had returned.

'Henri!' Kallon shouted, and tried to make his way to him, but he was held by two guards.

'Let him go,' Lestrone demanded.

'Isla,' Kallon choked out.

'I know, I know what happened,' Henri returned calmly.

'What, you've seen her? Where is she? Tell me she is with you?'

'No, she is not with me, but she was.'

'What? That doesn't make sense. I don't understand.'

'She's been taken.'

Kallon lunged for Henri, who merely held him back until he had calmed down so he could tell him what had happened.

'I'm sorry,' Kallon said. 'It's just I've had no idea if she was safe. If what I did had caused her...' His words petered out, with him not wanting to say what he had been thinking.

'What's done is done. We must move forward, not dwell on the things that have passed,' Henri reassured him.

'Well, we must go now then, surely. What are we waiting for?' Kallon was eager to fix what he had done and felt more time talking was more time wasted.

'Sit down, young man, you *do not* get to go around making orders. I have brought you back here because I realise your significance, but you are still in *my* walls and under my graciousness.'

Kallon tried to protest; however, Henri cut him off. 'You have to forgive him. He has not kept well these last few days, as you can see. However, he does have a point. We do need to move quickly. There is no telling how long they will keep her there for, or if you know who, realises – they are, after all, men of the darkness – we cannot take the risk of waiting another day.'

'That may be, Henri, but you said you *think* you know where they have taken her. How can I send all the men I have to somewhere I cannot be sure she is and subsequently bring attention to ourselves and most likely induce an attack on my city walls? It is not myself I am thinking of here.'

Again Kallon tried to speak, but Henri held up an arm to stop him from approaching. 'Then just give us a few men. We are strategic, you know this, but I cannot go only with what I have – I need twenty more. We will go quietly, check out the place, and if we need more we will send for them; it is only a day's ride, so your walls will not be undefended, but we have a chance at finding her.'

Everyone's eyes were fixated on Lestrone, waiting for his verdict. The room was so silent that you could hear a pin drop; Kallon was about ready to burst until Lestrone rose to his feet.

'Prepare my horse!' he declared, then he left the room.

'Are you sure you want to go, my lord? You know there are plenty of men rested that can go in your place,' said Elrich, the closest of all his advisors.

'Yes, I am sure. Now please stop questioning my decisions.'

'Of course,' Elrich replied, tightening up the leather strap on his belt.

Lestrone knew what Elrich was doing; it had been known for some time that his health was deteriorating, but it had not been voiced by anyone. Lestrone tried to go about his day-to-day tasks just as normal, and everyone else tried to shelter him from it. It was getting quite tiresome. He knew his time was coming to an end and quite frankly he welcomed it, but until then he was determined to do what was within his responsibilities.

'The men are ready when you are,' said Elrich while clipping Lestrone's black fur cloak to one side and handing him his sword.

Lestrone gripped it and could feel his hands tremble; he quickly placed his other hand on top before Elrich noticed. It had been a while since he had seen any action himself and now, with sword in hand, he too worried whether his health could live up to it.

'I'm ready.' He holstered his sword and kept a stern face. No matter what, he would have to be up for it; this was not a task he wanted to be seen done without him.

Lestrone joined the others in the courtyard. Henri had twenty-five men and women, plus himself and Kallon, and Lestrone's more than doubled that. He stared out at them all from his mounted horse. How different they all were, yet they'd all come together for the same cause. Lestrone's men were expertly trained, uniformed in their armour and they thought as one, whereas Henri's were individuals from different backgrounds. They had each other's back, yes, but also their own unique style, most not opting for any armour at all, preferring the agility of not having such restrictions.

They waited for the go-ahead, for the march out of Lestoris and on through the lands of Westoria.

'I know some of you do not know why we ride today, but I shall tell you.' Lestrone didn't see any reason keeping it a secret from his men; he felt it imperative that they know what they are fighting for. 'The *king*,' he paused, 'and the *queen's* daughter – she is back! And she is in the wrong hands, the ones that wish to do us *all* harm, harm to your children, your wives, your brothers, mothers, sisters, and it is up to us to save her from these heathens. There is no option of failure here: today we shall fight as brothers, today we shall fight as one, today we will see the rise of a new dawn, today we will welcome back a Blackbourne!'

It was slow at first, but the men began to beat, the sounds of sticks reverberating on the ground, picking up speed as Lestrone's speech reached its climax. A roar erupted: all were energised, all with a hunger to do what was right.

Henri jumped on his horse next to Lestrone; Kallon followed. Three unlikely souls, spanning three generations, all brought together for the same purpose, and that was to bring Isla home.

CHAPTER THIRTY-NINE

T he sun was high in the sky by the time they left the safety of Lestoris's walls behind them. Autumnal shades of red and orange burned fiercely in the surrounding woodland, somewhat symbolically connected to their spirit as they marched. However, as beautiful as the lands that surrounded Lestoris were, it was overshadowed by the uncertainty of what lay within them.

Since Isla's return, there had been a shift in the darkness and his lingering presence; the rise in activity from his followers had increased, seemingly caring less about their opposition, almost as if they knew something the rest of them didn't. Increased sightings of grey hoods had been reported, raids of villages had risen and it was becoming increasingly harder to spot who had and hadn't been infected by the darkness.

All Lestrone and the others of the council could do was try and keep what they could at bay, and that meant never letting leaving their borders unmanned. Though there were pockets of happiness and moments when things felt like they were back to the way they used to be, Akos was always there, in the shadows like a dormant volcano waiting to erupt. Exactly what he was waiting for no one knew, but it was not a matter of "if" it was a matter of "when", and the bubbles of this particular volcano were reaching boiling point.

However, despite the nature of his journey, this was the first time since his wife had died that Lestrone had seen outside of his city walls, and he was reminded of the land's beauty and breathtaking scenery. It had never failed to amaze him every time he returned after battle: the high arches, the colourful blossoms, the open meadows leading right up to the front gates, all against the mountainous backdrop that, year round, was covered in snow.

The mountains, especially these ones, could be quite hard to navigate, though there were no mountains between them, and where they were going now, in fact, it was unnervingly close. What ungodly men lay there he didn't know; he only hoped he was able to see the job done.

'We will be back,' Henri related, sensing Lestrone's sombre mood.

Lestrone ignored his comment. He was too proud a man to show his weakness, especially when a battle was near.

'We will ride as far into the night that is safe; we cannot bring attention to ourselves,' Lestrone told Henri, who in turn agreed. 'But we stop when I say,' he added firmly.

'As you wish,' Henri clarified.

Kallon gave Henri a look that questioned his answer. He knew that Henri was a respectful man, but also not one to take orders that he did not agree with.

Henri could feel Kallon's eyes burning into him. 'Hold your questions,' he directed, then looked back towards Lestrone. 'For now we ride.'

Henri dug the heels of his feet into his horse, which gave the signal to pick up speed; Lestrone did the same. They started as a trot, but after a few more digs and shouts they were soon both galloping at full speed, creating a sight to behold as a sea of horses and men seamlessly moved from the open fields of Lestoris and disappeared into the unknown of the Fen.

They had ridden at full speed until they were forced to slow down to a trot and then eventually a walk. The horses were some of the best breeds in the land – they could go longer than their human counterparts and still have plenty of energy – but the conditions of the Fen became too challenging to navigate, and they had no choice but to succumb to their environment.

'We shall rest here until dawn,' Lestrone commanded. All his men did as they were told while Henri's men remained mounted, eager to continue while there was still light in the day to move.

'But we have plenty of light to continue on,' one of them voiced.

'I do not have to answer to you,' Lestrone replied. 'My orders have been given.'

'There is still daylight left,' Henri confirmed, backing up his companion.

'And you said you would not question my orders. We are perhaps but a few miles away. I will not go barging in without a plan or a full scope-out. We do not know the full extent of what we are up against. Any closer and we will be sure to make our presence known before we intend to. No, we rest and plan.'

Lestrone was not stupid; he knew there was plenty of residual light to keep going for a little while longer. He believed in every word that he had just said, but the part he left out, the part that he would not have wanted to admit, was that he was tired and his failing body was telling him.

'Take your rest while you can,' Henri reiterated. 'For this will be your last chance – eat, drink, sleep. By morning we will be gone.'

Kallon grabbed Henri's arm as he went to take his possessions down off his horse. 'What are you doing? You know we need to keep going. We can't just sit around here – either they'll find us before we find them, or we wait another day, and she could be gone.'

'Ssssh,' Henri whispered to Kallon. 'I said, keep your questions until later.'

Kallon stormed off, increasingly angered by Henri's secretiveness. All he wanted to do was get back to Isla. They'd clashed on many things, and he found her hard work and impetuous, but for some reason, now she was no longer there all he could do was think about her. She was constantly on his mind, and he could not rest until he saw her again.

The next thing Kallon knew, a hand was being placed over his mouth and someone was saying, 'Ssssh. Be quiet.' It was Henri.

Kallon sat up; all was still bar the sounds of a few restless bodies and nocturnal animals moving in the night.

'Bring your sword. Leave the rest of your things.'

Kallon didn't question anything, quietly doing as Henri had instructed.

Lestrone's men were on guard and the two watched for their backs to turn before swiftly making their exit.

'What's this about, Henri?' Kallon demanded to know.

'We're going. We are going to scope them out now.'

'Now? Why not earlier? Why didn't you put Lestrone in his place when you had the chance?'

'Because we need him. It would have been nothing but wasted energy to cause a confrontation – he means well, but to argue with him would have served no purpose.'

'I still say we could have done this without him in the first place, then we wouldn't need to abide by his ridiculous rules.'

'It is not always obvious when you may need a friend, Kai,

and Lestrone *is* our friend. Even if he has a different way of doing things, he deserves your respect.'

Kallon looked like a small child who had just been told off and was finding it hard not to argue.

'We leave now – be back by dawn with a plan. Come, we travel on foot.' They were joined by three of Henri's company, Loic, Alise and Hofter. Five of them in total, five of them to save Isla, but in Kallon's mind there only needed to be one, because he was not going there and coming back without her.

They left as quickly and as quietly as they could, keeping up their pace until they reached their destination. The terrain had proved difficult at some points – the thorny woodland and its many creatures had threatened to slow them down – but they were quick to avoid any traps, finding their way through until they reached their destination, and it naturally paved a way for them.

They stopped at a safe distance, where burning torches could be seen flickering from inside. The castle/lavish stately home was situated on an incline, surrounded by forest on all sides, dead grass span five hundred yards from the edge of the trees to the curtain wall, which was heavily guarded by men.

'Go have a look,' Henri ordered Loic, who left one way, and Alise the other.

'I see twenty men at least, and that's just on the walls. There could be many more on the inside,' Hofter announced in observation.

'Who cares?' cut in Kallon. 'They are sure to lack skill, so we could easily take them.' He was acting irrationally and out of character; Henri was questioning himself now whether it had been a good idea to bring him along.

'Ease your mind. We are just here to observe,' Henri cautioned him.

They watched as the men looked as if they were swapping over and being replaced by fewer men that were there before.

'This is good,' Kallon eagerly declared. 'We can pass them easily.'

'Don't be getting ahead of yourself, Kai. Just because we can see less of them, the others are still there, and countless more we don't know about. Remember what we came here to do.'

'I remember, but do you?' Kallon shot back.

'There's a back entrance. It's small, but there is a door – it's guarded, though,' Alise confirmed, having arrived in the middle of their conversation. 'For a moment, I thought one of them spotted me, but they were just changing over. They must be on a shift pattern.'

'Okay, good, let's note the time and see how long it is until the next one. I want you to go back and watch their movements – anything significant, I want to know.'

Alise, nimble on her feet, was gone again within seconds.

'Hofter, go with her. We will wait for Loic.'

Hofter swiftly followed until it was only Kallon and Henri. 'Speak your mind.'

Kallon was unsure how to take Henri's request; he wanted to yell, hit out, to shake everyone who prolonged their rescue attempt any longer: Lestrone for taking command, Henri for letting him. None of them had been there from the beginning, had they? Only Kallon – he had been there from day one; he had been there from the day she arrived and, until a week ago, every day since. She was not his responsibility; he knew this. She had proven on many occasions that she was capable of standing up for herself, and if he was honest, that was what scared him the most. She never knew when to hold back; if she said or did something, even unknowingly, that could put her in further danger, he felt responsible for it.

'I should have never left her, Henri.' Kallon felt defeated, deflated and angry all at the same time.

'You had your reasons.'

'I know, but I should have found another way.'

'You think fast on your feet, Kai. I believe that had you have seen a different outcome you would have taken it.' He placed a reassuring hand on Kallon's chest.

'Perhaps, but what was I thinking, sending her off on her own in a place she doesn't know? And in the Fen of all places. I can't help think she may have stood a better chance if we had stuck together. We wouldn't be here right now if we had.' Kallon slumped down against the bushes that kept them hidden.

'You're right, perhaps we might not, but I have taught you better than that, Kai. Sometimes things happen not because we want them to but because they have to.'

'Why would this *need* to happen? What possible good could come out of this?'

'I don't know, but something tells me this was somewhere that she needed to go; it may not have been our course, Kai, but for Isla it was. Don't put this upon yourself. You are here now – that is all that matters.'

'Try telling her that. I don't think she will be so pleased to see me again, not after what I did. She won't understand.'

'Well, she might surprise you.' Henri smiled.

CHINK! SCRAPE! CRUNCH! They both lifted their heads at the same time as they heard the drag of heavy chains pull on the concrete floor; the gates were opening and approaching in the night were torches making their way towards the front gate.

'Who's that? What if they've discovered the rest of us?' Kallon sounded concerned as the group of men marched towards the open gate with dead animals and prisoners in tow.

'I don't think so, else there would be more than farmers to show for their efforts. This must have been what Lestrone was saying: they've been raiding. Poachers.' Henri bowed his head and muttered a silent prayer, for he knew what end they were to meet.

Heading up the pack was one clear dominant leader, whose muscles bulged to the point of bursting; they were proudly showed off through his choice of sleeveless attire. He was bold, with an air of self-importance, and had hold of a woman in front of him, who was fear-stricken to the point of obedience, and he knew it, for she was unbound and free to run if she dared to.

Henri did not know this man by name, but it was the same man that had taken Isla and the same one that he had seen many years before that. He watched him and only him as they marched back into the fortress, so transfixed he was that Henri hadn't noticed Kallon slip from their hiding place and make his way out into the open.

'What? No, Kai.' Henri panicked.

'This is our chance; the gate is open. I said I wouldn't make the same mistake again.' And he ran off as fast as he could across the open field towards the backs of the men entering through the gates. Kallon could hear the crank of the chain as it was about to drop; he needed to pick up his speed. He could see it getting lower with each turn of the wheel. It was perhaps only a few metres off the ground now. He had no time to see who was round the corner or what would meet him on the other side; he had to take his chance – he wasn't going to get another one like this. He dropped to the floor, he skidded, he rolled, then *BANG!* The gate was closed.

He patted himself down just to be sure there weren't any holes in him; satisfied he was still alive, Kallon couldn't afford to stay where he was. He needed to keep moving, which at first glance looked like it was going to be impossible. To his right was the iron gate, to his left the front; it looked as if he was stuck, but his focus caught the flicker of a light. It was dim, but sure enough, it led him to a small gap in the wall and a staircase. He shot up, taking two steps at a time, ignoring the suffocating, tight squeeze as it spiralled around and around until it finally reached the top, where he flung unintentionally out onto the curtain wall, for there was no door to break his speed.

Fortunately for Kallon, under the guise of darkness, no one saw his startled body shoot out from the doorway or subsequently jump back in just as quick. Taking better care the second time, he finally stepped out; he had a clear view of everything. He peered over the wall in the direction from which he had left Henri and wondered if he was still there, in the darkness staring back at him. But it didn't matter what Henri thought of him now. If he didn't get Isla back, none of it would matter.

Kallon heard voices chatting, approaching him; he dived back in under the archway, glued himself to the wall until they had past, then stepped out, his senses on heightened alert. They were so close; all they needed to do was turn their head, and they would have seen him following them, gradually trying to find a way in. He saw a passage that looked as if it led right into the hornet's nest – not a place he would have recommend for anyone to go, but Kallon was not anyone.

He descended two levels before looking out onto the courtyard again and up at the men that were guarding it. Had he still gone undetected? It would appear so, for their biggest concern was not an outsider stealing their way through the night, but the prisoners being thrown into a cage one by one, face down into the mud. They didn't even have the kindness to unbind them first so that they could break their own fall. Once that was completed they carried on through a passage, where demands for beer and wine shortly followed. This was a small, internal victory for Kallon, for he now knew where most of them were and their intentions for the evening.

Kallon scoped out the rest of the castle. It looked more like a grand home from the inside, with the rest of the castle features added at a later date. It wasn't overly big, but big enough to house a small army, and had been heavily mistreated by the looks of things. Though he did not care about the interior or what had happened before; he was only looking for one thing, and that was the highest room in the tallest tower.

'What have you seen?' Henri asked breathlessly, with Loic not far behind him.

'Nothing, why? What's happened?' questioned Alise.

'Kai.'

Alise and Hofter were puzzled as to what Henri seemed so anxious about.

'He's gone inside.'

'What? How?' they both asked, shocked.

'When the gates were up,' Henri confirmed.

'What are we going to do?' questioned Loic.

'You're not going to do anything – I am.'

They all looked back at him, expressionless, presuming they must have misheard.

'Alise, that door, where is it?'

She pointed. 'Just over there, behind that dip. It's quite hidden.'

'I'll find it. Now, you two, I want you to head back and inform Lestrone. I don't care what he says. Tell him it's happening tonight, either with or without him. There's no stopping it now.'

Loic and Alise both looked at each other, silently agreeing that they did not think this was a good idea.

'Hofter, I want you to stay out here. You may need to create a diversion, and if not, just keep your eyes peeled.' They went to speak, but he cut them all off before they could raise their concerns. 'The way is written now; I will take my fate, whatever it is. Now go.'

Knowing Henri, they knew when he had his mind made up and now was one of those occasions; therefore it was pointless trying to convince him otherwise, so they wished him luck and left on foot as fast as they could.

Hofter and Henri watched the men on the walls; they weren't very good lookouts, chatting amongst themselves. They were either too lazy or never had any opposition, so they had let complacency get the better of them. Either way, Henri saw his chance. Leaving Hofter behind, like a bird gliding through the sky, with barely a sound, he swooped his way across the open field.

Alise was right: it had been very hard to see, especially with a storm coming their way, but Henri was thankful, for it helped hide his arrival. As Alise had already confirmed, there was one man on guard; however, he appeared to be sleeping with his back against the wall and his chin slumped into his chest. Henri had to move quickly to keep his element of surprise. A few more yards, a jump, a slide, and he hit the ground. Just as the man startled at the sound of Henri's feet meeting with the floor, his fist connected with his face, and before he could regain his balance Henri was on him again. They scuffled, Henri trying to keep the attack as quiet as possible. He squeezed hard at his neck to stop him from moving, to stop the man from breathing, until his lifeless body fell to the floor. He hated causing harm to another human being; he did not enjoy the prospect of taking another man's life, but this was for the greater good, and sides had been taken.

Henri patted the man down, looking for any keys, as there was no way he was getting through this door without them, but he had no such luck. *What to do?* he thought; he didn't have the opportunity to ask Alise how often they changed over, so there was only one thing for it. He took the man's helmet, placed it over his head and rolled his body out the way. Henri then banged on the door and muffled some grunting noises that he needed to come back in. After a minute or so he heard someone come to open it up, moaning what all the fuss was about.

Luckily for Henri, it was only one guy whose reaction was too slow when he realised he had not opened the door to his comrade but to a stranger, a stranger who quickly plunged his sword into his chest and saw to the end of his life.

Henri moved his body, found somewhere to conceal it the best he could and hoped no one would discover it until they had got what they had come for. He was underground, but Henri was only interested in going up; he took a staircase that looked like it led to the surface. His assumptions had proved right when he emerged into the courtyard. It was full of junk and discarded weapons, and evidence of many a good night, and tonight, by the sounds of it, was to be a night like many others. Henri looked at the sky again; from the short time he had been inside it had become completely covered, and he could feel the first signs of rain starting to reveal themselves.

Much the same as Kallon had done, he had a look around for the most likely place Isla would be and for any signs that her presence was still there. He had a good feeling she would be, but he was outnumbered, Kallon was outnumbered and together they were outnumbered. They had the element of surprise, but that would not last them long; they were surely walking into an ambush.

CHAPTER FORTY

'I expect they will be returning soon – we should get you back before they do,' said Alfled, putting down his kitchen knife.

'But I don't want to go back. I hate being locked up.'

Alfled studied Isla. 'They'll be hungry and worse than how you have seen them before – better if you are out of their way. For your own good.' Alfled tried to guide Isla out the kitchen, but she wouldn't move.

'They don't frighten me.'

'I know, and that's what frightens me.' Again he tried to steer her in the direction of the door.

Isla pleaded, 'I don't want to go back just yet. If it makes you feel any better, I promise to stay in here when they return, so I'll be out of their way, plus I can still help you.'

It was a tempting offer; Alfled weighed his options and finally gave in to her. 'Only if you promise to eat. You've barely touched any food all day.' He sighed, sitting her down. 'Now that's not a request – that's an order.' He placed a plate of cold meat down in front of her, then filled up a bowl of stew that had been simmering away on the stove.

'When did you become so assertive? You know if you spoke to them like that, they wouldn't mess around with you half as much as they do.' Isla gave her opinion while forcing down some food; she really wasn't hungry, but she made an effort for him.

Alfled ignored her comment, pushing the bowl closer to her. 'Here, you need something with a bit of meat. You are looking ever so boney.'

Isla gave him a look but didn't respond; she knew what he was doing. *Don't mention things to me I don't like, and I won't say them to you.* Alfled was not far off the truth, though – when she lived at the Manor Isla looked healthy, had a nourished glow, clean clothes, restful sleep and, now that she looked back on it, no worries at all, not like the ones she had now, the ones that kept her up at night.

She looked down at her dress, the same one that she had been given on the first night she arrived; it had only been a matter of days since then, and though it had not magically grown in length, it no longer felt as snug. Isla needed to be taking better care of herself, especially if she intended to escape, which, following her conversation with her fellow captive, didn't seem as possible as she'd originally thought. Though much to her surprise, he still continued to encourage her, and something he said had stuck in her mind.

Nothing is impossible; just don't be afraid to act on the things that others don't. This really hit home with her; she didn't know why. She didn't know the man well enough for his opinion to matter; in fact, she hardly knew much about him at all. He was very evasive whenever she asked him questions about himself. However, there was something soothing about him that made her feel at ease, which was odd considering he really was just the voice from the wall.

Alfled joined Isla with a bowl of hot steaming stew for himself. The sound of it hitting the table prompted her to come out of her daydream, and he basked in his own efforts.

'You know there was a time I used to really enjoy cooking. Yes, the hours are always long, but the lord and lady used to show genuine appreciation and, furthermore, whatever was left over, they were happy to go to poorer families.'

'Really?' Isla looked up from her spoon.

'Oh yes, the lady would often even deliver it herself. You see, it was safe then, for her to leave the castle walls, and when people used to live in the surrounding forest. But of course, when things started to go bad, she couldn't make those kinds of trips anymore; it became unsafe to leave, and many families went without food.'

'They sound like they were very nice people.'

'Oh, that they were. Everyone who worked for them was happy and, not to mention, treated well. It was easy to feel as if we were in our own little world, in the middle of so much woodland, woodland that was beautiful, once upon a time. We welcomed visitors from all over the place, hosted them, gave them a bed for the night, but then we could not do so anymore; it was too risky, people's moods changed and they started to turn on each other – fear can do that to you.'

Isla wondered why he was telling her all this; he didn't tend to talk much of his past, and whenever she tried to ask him about it, he always told her it was best not to ask such questions.

'This kitchen was full of people, with me at the top,' he announced very proudly. 'You know, food control. I wouldn't let anything go out that I didn't think was our best – of course, nothing went to waste, but they got the best of what we could do. I used to be proud of something, I used to take pride in something, I used to belong somewhere.' He stopped abruptly, deciding he didn't want to continue any further down memory lane.

Isla felt sorry for Alfled, his sausage fingers wiping away something that he insisted had got in his eye, but she knew better.

'I don't even know why I am telling you this; I resigned to my fate a long time ago. I guess just having you here has reminded me of what it used to be like, and I suppose they were my family.'

'It's okay, Alfled.' She got up to give his large, cuddly frame a hug; he brought his hand up to reach hers as she nestled her head into his shoulder.

'You have to forgive me.'

'Whatever for?' Isla replied, surprised.

'For the way I have treated you. This is no place for someone as young or as spirited as you are; for selfish reasons I have enjoyed your company.'

'Alfled, you have been the nicest person to me here – in fact, one of the nicest people I have ever met. I want you to take that back right now. You have done nothing wrong; you have done nothing to me.' And, as if on cue, they heard the clang of the front gates open. 'They are the monsters; they are to blame. They have no right keeping me here, keeping *us* here.'

The noise of gruff men grew louder as they approached the dinner hall. 'Food, beer, wine,' they heard bouncing off the walls down into the kitchen. Alfled lifted his deflated lump then something else was heard coming down into the kitchen: footsteps.

'*Alfled!*' boomed the demanding voice before it had even reached the bottom step. 'Where's our food? why is it not set up on the table already?'

Alfled scuttled around like a fly trying to find an exit. 'I was keeping it warm until you returned.'

'Well, hurry up. At least bring beer – it wouldn't take you as half as long to do half the stuff around here if you were half the size you are.'

'Don't talk to him like that.'

Alfled's eyes shot open.

'Oh, it's you. I thought I said to get her under control?' growled Broc.

'I don't need getting under control.' Isla stood up to him boldly.

Alfled tried to step in. 'It's been a long day *and* night. We're all tired – get yourself settled and I'll bring extra ale. She doesn't mean what she says.'

'Oh, I do, I mean every single word. You are a horrible man – in fact, I wouldn't go as far as calling you a man. You are cruel and mean and—'

Broc grabbed Isla by the wrist. 'It looks like I'll have to get her under control, seeing as you are too weak, Alfled,' he spat.

'Let go – you're hurting me.'

'Oh, I'm sorry, am I hurting the little princess, am I?'

Isla tried to shake him off, but he took enjoyment in watching her struggle, and Alfled stood there in shock, not knowing what to do.

'Not so big now, are you?'

He was clearly enjoying acting menacing towards her. He was easily three times the size of Isla; clearly, she would be no match for him, but it didn't stop her from wanting to stand up for what she thought was right. He spun her around and pulled her into his chest, one arm across her body which he could comfortably keep her in place with.

'What do we do to those that disobey us, Alfled?' He pulled out a very long, very sharp-looking knife and gently stroked it down the side of her face. '*Speak up*, Alfled – what do we do with them?' But he couldn't; he couldn't even get out one word. '*Speak!*' Broc roared. 'Perhaps I should refresh your… Whoops, memory.' Broc nicked the tip of his blade on Isla's cheek, releasing a red trickle down the side of her face.

'Ouch.' Instinctively she jerked her head, but Broc pulled it back; she held her breath, not wanting to risk another cut from the shiny blade.

Broc pointed the knife at Alfled then licked the side of Isla's face, the same place where he had just run the cold blade down.

'Ah, she tastes good. So what do you say, a little nip here?' He pointed it to her stomach. 'Or here?' He moved the blade up to the side of her ribs. 'Ah, now that will hurt – you choose,' he said with a terrifying smile on his face. 'Or shall we make it quick?' He held the blade up to her throat; Isla tilted her head back, trying to get away from it, eyes glued to Alfled.

'Broc, put the knife down. I think she understands; you've given her enough of a scare,' pleaded Alfled, every part of him trembling.

'Ha. pleading for the girl's life. What do you say?' He turned to Isla, knife in hand, grabbing her now-mangled hair and tilting her head so that she was looking right up at him. 'Alfled thinks you understand your place now, but I don't think you do. Only a woman would understand, maybe I have to turn you into one!'

'*No!*' shouted Alfled. 'Broc!'

Isla didn't know much about the love between a man and a woman – she had not experienced that in her life – but she didn't like the way he said that.

Out of nowhere and out of character and before he'd even realised what he was doing, with a heavy hand and an almighty swing Alfled had grabbed the nearest thing and hit Broc hard over his head. It sent him flying and his hand went immediately to his head to ease the pain. Alfled stepped back, stunned, holding a big iron saucepan in his hand, and everyone momentarily stopped, shocked at the change of events.

'I knew you had it in you,' Isla cheered, trying to make her way back to Alfled, but Broc grabbed her back with one hand still on one eye, trying to correct his blurry vision.

Before anything else could happen, they all looked in the direction of the steps leading out of the kitchen. Noises were coming from up above: men shouting, things moving – there was quite a commotion.

Broc steadied himself; he was torn between whatever was happening up above and the two that stood in front of him.

Finally, he turned to face them. 'This is *not* over.' He pointed his knife. 'I will be back for you,' he turned to face Alfled, 'and *you*, your end has come.' Then he left, wobbly on his feet.

They waited until he was gone then Isla jumped in the air. 'Alfled, that was brilliant!'

Poor Alfled was still stunned by what he had done; adrenaline coursed through his body and he couldn't string a sentence together. He half-smiled, the other half of him wanting to cry. 'I-I...' he stammered. 'I know.' Then he noticed Isla and the cut on her face. 'But look at you – come, sit down, your face.' Isla appeared to have forgotten about it too. Alfled grabbed a cloth, slightly wetted it and held it against her face to stop the bleeding.

'You did it, Alfled, you stood up for yourself! You really showed him – they won't mess around with you now.'

'No, he will get rid of me now instead.' The realisation of what he had just done was sinking in; the adrenaline was wearing off, replaced by fear, for he knew what was to come, and there was no escaping it.

Isla dropped her head; she didn't want anything to happen to him because he had been defending her and her ability to always speak before she had thought about what she was saying. *Did I bring this upon him?* He looked sad, very sad, and it was all her fault – if only she had gone back to her cell when he'd first said.

The silence that had now fallen between them gave them the chance to listen to what actually was going on above.

'Intruders, intruders, be on your guard.' They heard along with the sounds of footsteps, people running, things moving, men shouting.

'What's going on up there?' Isla asked.

Alfled looked quite concerned. 'I don't know, nothing like this has ever happened before.'

Henri. 'Henri,' Isla said, a hopeful smile forming across her face. 'He came; I knew he would. This has to be Henri – it's got to be.'

'Henri? Who's Henri?' queried Alfled.

The unbelievable smile on Isla's face grew wider. 'My friend, he is my friend.' Isla jumped up. 'Don't you see? This is our way out. You can be free, Alfled.'

Alfled didn't know what to say; he hadn't heard those words in a long time.

'Freedom, Alfled, it can be yours.'

He had not thought about it until now, but the thought of freedom scared him. What would he do? Where would he go? He had not seen the outside world for years, and he still couldn't bring himself to say the words.

They both looked up; it sounded as if something had been spotted.

'It's now, Alfled, we have to go now – this is it.'

'Okay.' He drew a deep breath. 'Okay, are we really going to do this?'

They went to leave, but Isla suddenly stopped. 'I can't.' She turned to face him.

'What do you mean, you can't?' Alfled was puzzled, somewhat surprised now he had just come to terms with the ideas of leaving.

'I can't leave him.'

'Leave who?'

'Elston – I can't leave him there. It's just… I can't.'

'You can't risk going back for him – it's too dangerous if they catch you.'

'What do you expect me to do? We can't just leave him.'

'Yes, you can. You more than I need to get out of here. If you don't leave now, while they are busy, you are not going to get this chance again.'

'I know, but I have to try.' Without another thought, Isla went to run off, but Alfled called her back and held out his hand.

'You are going to need these.' He put his keys in her hand and smiled at her. 'I'm sorry, but—'

Isla smiled back. 'I know, it's okay. Thank you.' She gave him a quick hug, then she was gone.

CHAPTER FORTY-ONE

Kallon stood at the bottom of the staircase, heart pounding. This was it: as soon as he took the first step, there was no going back. He'd managed so far to pass his enemies undetected. How much longer that would last he did not know; his only hope was that they soon would be too drunk to notice that he was ever there.

He was nervous, anxious, not because of where he was or that at any point a sword could be raised against him, but because of Isla and how she would react to seeing him again.

It was ridiculous that he was even thinking like this, that he let it get to him; he hadn't even known who she was a few months ago, yet he cared what she thought. He shook his head as if the action would somehow rid him of his thoughts; it must have worked, for the next thing he knew he was teetering on the top step. He braced himself. *This is it, the final one. Time to face whatever it is that may be there – time to face Isla.*

To his surprise, it was empty – no one was there. He kept his sword steady, though. He did not trust that he was not about to walk into an ambush, but as he soon discovered, other than the cells themselves, there was nowhere else anyone could hide. He whispered Isla's name, checking each cell, but nothing; he heard absolutely nothing. Now he began to panic. *Has she moved on? Is she somewhere else? Is she in the castle?* Or had something he didn't want to even think about happened?

Then from the quietness, a voice spoke. 'She's in the kitchens.'

Kallon immediately raised his sword. Of course, there was nothing a voice locked behind bars could do to him. Still, it was a reflex that he had learned after years of training.

'She's in the kitchens,' he heard again.

Kallon found where the voice was coming from, for a face appeared at one of the cell doors. 'How do I know you are telling the truth?'

'Because I would have no need to lie to you. You've come here to free her, yes? She said someone would come.'

Kallon smiled. She was not angry after all; in fact, she had believed him when he said he would find her. She had never given up on him.

'Henri,' came the words.

'Who?'

'Are you Henri?'

'No.'

'She said someone named Henri would come for her. If you are not him then who are you?'

Was it jealousy or pride that struck him? But Kallon was not happy to hear that it was Henri who had her trust. But Kallon had no time to discuss what else she may have said. 'Where are the kitchens?' he asked quickly.

'You haven't answered my question.'

'What question?' Kallon was getting impatient.

'If you are not Henri, then who are you?' Elston may not have known Isla all that well, but he did want her to be in the best care possible.

'I am a friend of Henri's and a friend of Isla's, or at least I thought I was. I'm here on my own and am her only chance of escape – now, you can either help me or hinder me.' Whatever Kallon said must have been enough, for he got his answer without delay.

'They are below the grand hall – just follow the direction of the noise, and you will find them.'

Before Kallon could ask for any further information, they heard another voice, and this time it was from outside. 'Intruder!' they heard a man shout, then another. 'Intruder! Intruder! Intruders!'

Kallon looked at the stairs; these were his only way out. His element of surprise was lost. Both men thought the same thing and both men felt the same urgency that Kallon had to go.

'It's okay, go!'

Kallon only hesitated momentarily; he would have released the man had he the time – he had not been brought up to leave people behind – but his presence had been discovered, and now he had to try locate Isla with the whole castle looking for him.

The slumped body was found just where Henri had left him and just as he had anticipated, which sent the whole castle into uproar. Broc made his way outside where he could hear the majority of the commotion. He grabbed the nearest man by the cuff of his neck and demanded to know what was going on.

'A body has been found, inside the castle.'

Broc grabbed the man with his other hand and held him close to his face, seething. 'Tell me where,' he spat.

'The cellars, by the back entrance,' he said as quickly as possible.

Broc didn't care about his men – people died; it was a part of life. They were dispensable and replaceable to him. What he cared about was how and why someone had breached his walls. Still feeling light-headed, he moved as quickly as his heavy body would allow, shoving anyone who happened to be in his path out of his way. He needed to see for himself, and he needed to see how they had done it. He found the lifeless body and the now-darkened pool of blood behind the barrels where Henri had left him. He looked for signs of forced entry, for any signs of struggle, but whoever had done this was skilled and had done it quickly.

Broc felt the presence of someone arriving after him.

'What do you want us to do?'

Broc didn't reply at first; he was too angry to speak. Someone had outplayed him, outmanoeuvred him, but why? Then the reason clicked, the understanding behind it.

'The girl, they've come for the girl.'

'Who?' the newcomer enquired.

Broc screamed. '*Goddamn it*, they've come for the girl.' He was seething but also knew that he still had the upper hand. They were alert now, and they had the girl. *She must be someone important for them to risk coming back for her.*

'Tell the men to get to their posts; I want everyone on the walls. If we are expecting more company I want to be prepared for it. I want to be spitting fire from the gates when they arrive.' The man started to leave. 'And find me that girl – if they are coming for her, she is staying with me. *And find whoever killed one of my men and bring me his head!*

CHAPTER FORTY-TWO

So much commotion was unravelling that no one had taken any notice of Isla moving largely through the castle on her own. She had no idea what exactly was happening, just that everyone was preparing for some kind of altercation, a battle of sorts. *It has to be Henri.* She was sure of it.

She huffed and puffed her way through, not stopping to catch her breath or call out his name; she just placed the key into the lock, turned it and swung the door open.

'What are you doing here?' Elston questioned.

'Come on, we've got to go.'

He completely ignored what she said. 'I told him where you were.'

'Come on,' Isla pushed, but again he ignored her.

'I've sent them to the kitchens. You shouldn't be here; you should be there.'

'Elston, we don't ha… Wait, who did you send?'

'A boy – he'd come looking for you.'

Kallon. Her stomach flipped.

'What did he say?'

'Not much, but he knew the friend you spoke of.'

'Which frie—'

'*Find her!*'

Isla had no time to ask any more; they were calling out for her. She was the new prey, and it was about time they got a move on.

'Well, it doesn't matter now. We've got to go.'

'You'll be quicker without me. I will only slow you down.' He discouraged her, but Isla was not going to accept his response, so she purposely walked over to him and heaved him off the floor.

Of course, his muscles were wasted – he had not left his cell for years so he was weak – but she was determined that with her help he would be able to walk and finally gain his freedom.

'Well, I'm not leaving without you, so either we both stay or we both go.'

Isla must have said it with such conviction that he agreed and let her lead the way. She supported him with her arm around his waist and encouraged him to let her take his weight, not that there was much of him to support, but it still proved difficult to manoeuvre them both down the stairs at the same time. However, the more he moved, the more his muscles seemed to remember what to do, and she felt the pressure of him leaning on her lessen.

'Do you know the way out?' Isla asked.

'Not really, but there was a back entrance if I remember rightly.'

'Do you know how to get there?'

'No, sorry, I've not seen anything past those walls for years.'

'Don't worry, we'll find it.'

They slumped against a wall as they reached the bottom. 'Really, you should go without me. I'm too weak for this,' Elston wheezed.

Isla looked him square in the eyes; they were sharp and on point, unlike his body hidden underneath clothes that had outgrown him and hair that betrayed him. 'No one deserves to live like this. We are *both* going to get out of here.' Isla pulled him back up. 'You're the one who told me nothing is impossible. Just one step at a time.'

So much was happening now; it was hard to tell where the core of the commotion was coming from: outside, inside – it was all the same. Still, Isla's ears were able to pick out the voice of someone that had noticed her.

'*There!* There she is.'

Two men were coming straight for them. '*Go!*' she yelled urgently, and they ran around one corner, then another and another. 'We need to make our way down.'

They found some steps that led them out onto the terrace and were hit by the full scale of the uproar. It was chaotic, like a flurry of bees had just broken free from the confines of their home. Weapons were being collected; all points of entry were being further reinforced; women ran half-clothed, screaming, not one person caring for their wellbeing. A single man held out torches as the others ascended the walls, creating a barrier of raging fire between the outside and them.

Isla had a quick look for Kallon, for Henri, but she couldn't see them; she had never felt so far apart, so fearful. Alfled had been right; fear can do funny things to a person, and in Isla's case, it was a motivator.

Elston pulled her away. 'We can't stop here.' And this time it was Isla who followed him.

They jumped into hideaways, they disappeared into doorways, they held their breath, they bided their time, they listened for footsteps. All in the effort to evade their captors, but it was hard to outrun the inevitable and the unlikely duo was soon spotted again.

'Quick, grab her!'

BAM! Isla tripped and hit the floor.

Precious seconds were lost – that was just enough to bridge the gap. *This is it; there's nothing I can do now.* Isla was stuck to the floor. There was nothing she could do to stop it: the hands coming for her.

'Come here, bitc—'

'*I think not.*' Something swung over the top of her head; she felt the swoosh of the blade as it swung again. 'Run, Isla.'

It was Elston, fighting the two men. *How could he possibly…?* But he was, and his skill was undeniable; he disarmed one and used his sword to kill the other, but more men were arriving, and they were arriving quickly.

'I said, *go!*' he yelled at her.

Isla scrambled to her feet; he did not look the kind of man anyone could have reasoned with in that moment. The look of anger and desperation was that of a man that had everything to lose, but what?

'Please, go.'

And just like that she did: she ran as fast as her feet could on the uneven surface. She did not look back; she couldn't, as she knew he was surrounded. She heard the sound of metal swipe against metal and she didn't want to know how it would end. She just had to keep moving, but where to?

Isla tried a series of doors; she was somewhere unfamiliar, a place she had not been until now. She reached the last one. *Will this lead to the outside?* She pulled at the handle – stuck! She twisted and pulled, twisted and pulled; she tried with all her might, but it wouldn't budge. It was useless: she would need to go back, retrace her steps, find another way.

Isla turned around. She should be moving now, she should be halfway back to where she had come from, but she wasn't; something was stopping her, something was in her way, something was blocking her stride. She looked up and up until their eyes met.

'Where do you think you are going?' Broc smiled.

CHAPTER FORTY-THREE

Kallon ran as fast as he could as he jumped, rolled and skidded his way down to the kitchens. He definitely was feeling a little more battered and bruised than before he'd entered the castle, but the adrenaline was keeping him going.

'Isla, *Isla!*' he shouted, jumping three steps at a time. '*Isla! Isla!*'

When he made it to the bottom, his heart sank for the second time. *What is happening?* There was no one there again. Had the imprisoned man deliberately sent him to the wrong place? *Surely not?* Plus Kallon believed he was telling the truth. Either way, whether she had been there or not, whoever had, they had left in a hurry.

It was now, taking a closer look, that Kallon noticed the tiny mark on the floor; he bent down to confirmed that it was what he suspected. 'Blood.'

Tap! Tap! Tap! Someone was coming. *Could it be Isla?* Kallon's senses were heightened. He wasn't about to take any chances: he rose strong to his feet, his sword abreast of him, as the footsteps grew louder. *Tap! Tap! Tap!*

'Henri.'

'Kai.' He came rushing towards him.

'But how did you—'

Henri cut him off. 'We don't have time for that. Isla was not in the tower, I take it?'

Henri hadn't quite made it there himself before the commotion broke out, and he was forced to take cover until he saw his opportunity. However, by that time he'd seen Kallon's retreating body with no Isla in tow.

'No, but there was another person up there. He told me she was down here, but look.' Kallon showed Henri the bloodstain on his fingers, and where it had come from; they both looked concerned, but neither of them wanted to say the words.

'All we can do now is continue to look for her,' Henri finally said.

Together they made their way back to the empty dining hall. Henri stationed himself by the window; he took a moment to take it all in, to absorb every single detail. The sound of rain splattering on the ground, the sharpening of weapons, the beating of feet hitting the floor, where they were congregating, how many doors there were, how many windows, where their weapons were stashed – he needed to know it all; he needed to understand their strengths and weaknesses.

Then he saw his own weakness staring straight back at him. For a moment Henri thought he had been spotted; however, disguised by the rain and the steamed-up glass, it was unlikely he was visible from the outside. Still, their eyes locked, maybe only for a second or two, then Broc smiled and walked away.

'So what now?' Kallon asked.

Henri stepped away from the window. He knew Kallon would do whatever he could to retrieve Isla, that much he was sure of, so he let him lead; he needed to be sure Isla would get out so that her destiny could be fulfilled, and he needed to be free to fulfil his.

'This is your fight now, Kai. I follow you,' Henri replied.

Kallon had not expected this, to lead a leader. *What is Henri doing?*

'What say you?' Henri pushed. He wanted Kallon to take charge; he needed him to, for he couldn't trust himself to face his own weakness.

Kallon had no time to think it through, to understand his request, because time was not on his side, not on Isla's side.

'We search the castle until we find her; we search every room until there are no rooms left to search; we don't stop until something makes us stop.' Kallon was happy to see that Henri agreed with his decision. They were both of the opinion that a path had been started and it must be walked to the end.

Leaving the hall, they moved cautiously, one room at a time, most of Broc's men – or poachers, as they were more commonly known as by now – were up on the walls, waiting to face whatever was coming their way, but there were still a few sprawled within the grounds.

They heard noises approaching and ducked into the nearest hiding place, listening to the footsteps as they passed; they sounded hurried but light. Kallon wedged himself behind a statue while Henri jumped into the nearest vacant room, leaving the door ajar just enough so that he could see whoever was coming their way.

First, he saw a man, old and fragile – he didn't look like a poacher, more likely one of the farmers that he had seen imprisoned earlier who had found his opportunity of escape – then he saw it, the long, wavy, light brown hair swishing from side to side as she ran.

'Isla,' he whispered. 'Isla,' he repeated. 'Kai, it's Isla.'

Kallon immediately pushed himself free, Henri following suit, swinging the door open.

'Which way did she go?'

'That way.' Henri pointed.

They both went to gather up speed, elated that finally there was confirmation she was in the castle and, more importantly, she was alive. The end was near, everything was going to be okay, she was going to be okay, but then that bubble burst.

'*Who* the *hell* are you?'

They both spun around to the sight of three men who did not like the look of them. Both opponents paused, coming to terms with the situation, sussing the opposition out, then, as if in unison or as if they were in a well-rehearsed play, they all raised their swords.

And so it begins.

CHAPTER FORTY-FOUR

'*Come get what you came for.*'
Broc had Isla by the hair and pulled her out into the open; her feet were barely able to keep herself upright.

'I know you are out there.' Broc almost looked excited, as if he was thrilled by what was about to come next. 'I guess I will have the pleasure of killing you myself.'

Kallon's instincts told him to not give away their hiding place, but something else in the pit of his stomach wanted to. He had seen many situations like this before. You could not save everyone. In battle you had to keep a level head for the greater good, Henri had taught him that, but this was different; this was Isla.

'*Don't!* It is me who he is after, it is me who he wants,' Henri said, stopping him.

Kallon was clearly puzzled. 'Why would he want you?'

'Let just say we have some unfinished business.' Henri could not tear his eyes away from him. *The time has finally come.*

'I won't harm your precious little woman, not if you show yourself.' He pulled Isla up to her feet; she was muddied and wet from being dragged along the soaking ground. Her hair was plastered across her face, and her chest rose and dropped heavily.

'Come out, come out, wherever you are,' Broc shouted playfully.

'*Don't! Don*—' Isla screamed. She didn't want anyone to give themselves up for her; enough had already been sacrificed on her behalf.

Broc, with his one free hand, banged at his chest like a gorilla and screamed, '*Come fight me like a man.*' He banged again. 'Come get your *bitch!*' Then he slapped Isla around the face and sent her flying into the mud, waiting for a reaction.

…Which he got from Kallon, who was ready to jump out, but again Henri stopped him. He felt sick; his blood boiled, seeing Isla like that, humiliated and assaulted, but she was strong. She didn't let him break down her wall; she didn't let him see that he had broken her. She kept her stance and refused to be a victim.

'He'll let her go,' Henri reassured Kallon. 'He's using her as bait. They don't know you are here, and they have not figured out who she is either, else none of us would be standing where we are now if they had.'

'Henri, this is suicide. You can't face him on your own – he's a force,' Kallon urged.

'I've faced worse.' Henri stood up, forcing Kallon back down, and stepped out from the shadows.

'We have to stop meeting like this,' said Henri pleasantly.

Broc smiled, revealing a set of healthy, large teeth. 'I knew you would not be able to resist.'

As Henri had anticipated, he forgot all about Isla now that he was fixated on him. Isla was just a girl – insignificant, to say the least, a pawn to draw out his prize. Broc was an animal by nature; he lived for the thrill of the hunt, the excitement of the fight. Henri had rattled his cage; he gave him a challenge, which both excited and nerved him. Single and narrow-minded, Broc was easily predictable, and even though he was twice his size, Henri hoped he was predictable in battle too.

Henri kept Broc talking; this was his plan: he needed to keep him occupied long enough for Isla and Kallon to make their escape. While he had his attention, it appeared he had everyone else's too. No longer concerned about what other dangers may threaten them, they had all stopped to watch the meeting of these two men unfold.

Both Broc and Henri eyed each other fiercely with anticipation, both yet to raise a weapon.

Finally, Henri spoke again. 'I know you know who I am.'

Broc sniggered in agreement, snorted and spat on the floor before speaking. 'You know, at first I didn't, I took you for one of those do-gooders, but as I watched the life drain from your eyes, I knew I had seen them before, the same dying eyes.'

Henri struggled to keep his composure; he could see that Isla still lay where Broc had discarded her. They locked eyes briefly, and in that second Isla's face said it all, that she finally understood. The look of shock, horror and, worst of all, sympathy confirmed it, confirmed that she knew Broc was not just any man or any bad man for that matter – Broc was *the* man! The man that had changed Henri's life forever, the man that had taken lives, the man that had killed Henri's family.

'I will not let you hurt any more people,' Henri declared.

Broc returned a patronising yell, 'did you hear that?' his audience roared in laughter that there was a man foolish enough to think that they could challenge him.

'You have to admire his determination,' Broc said with hunger in his eyes. 'An easy fight is never fun.'

Silence was restored, and the onlookers froze, waiting for that first blow, but to everyone's shock that did not come from Broc's fist or from Henri's sword but from one single arrow. The whole courtyard gasped as they watched the body of a man fall from the walls and plummet to his death. Eyes darted in every direction possible, looking for the assailant, for where the arrow had come from. They did not get much time before they were all running in different directions, holding up whatever they could to block the arrows slicing through the air.

Henri picked one up and looked at the imprint on the blade: it was the emblem of Lestoris, a simple depiction of a mountain.

They came. Henri threw it back to the ground and dodged his way through the crowd and many arrows; he still had to face his fate, but he felt a hand on his shoulder and someone spinning him around.

'Kai?' Henri looked over to where Isla had been and saw that she was no longer there.

'She left with the man we saw her with earlier – come on, we've got to follow them.'

Henri felt torn; he knew he could not leave Isla to end up in the wrong hands again, but he was so close, so close to ending his own nightmares. He could see Broc, not at all daunted by the arrows flying past him. His men ran around in a panic, for they could not see their enemy, but Henri knew where they would be: they were hiding in the trees, picking them off one by one.

Broc could see Henri staring at him. This was not over, for either of them; this was going to be settled one way or another, but today would not be that day.

'Quick, you've got to go now – follow me.'

Isla looked up at the arms pulling her off the ground and willingly allowed them to. Exhausted both physically and emotionally, she couldn't quite articulate the need that she wanted to go back, to support Henri, to be by his side and offer whatever comfort she could. However, before she knew it, she was out of the rain in what looked like a junk room with Elston trying to get some sense out of her.

'Ilarya, Ilarya!'

As if someone had just turned the sound back on, Isla was suddenly fully aware of her all her senses.

'There's no time to explain, your necklace,' pressed Elston.

Isla's thoughts had caught up with her and she registered the words that he'd spoken. *Necklace, Ilarya.* 'Hang on, how do you know about my necklace?'

'I saw it – there's no time to explain.' With that, he hastily pulled down a huge sheet, letting it drop to the floor. Isla immediately stepped back. *Is this a trick?*

'How, you? How, this? Why now?' Isla couldn't quite get the words out that she wanted to say – a mirror, exactly like the one she had used to get there in the first place was in this castle, right under her nose the whole time, and Elston, he seemed to know something about it.

'Ilarya, the necklace.' Elston motioned to her neckline, where he could see just a tiny bit of a silver chain.

'*Stop it!*' Isla pushed him away. 'Who are you? Why do you keep calling me that?'

Elston was anxious; he looked as if he was battling with wanting to pick her up and hold her until it was all over and the pressing matter for whatever it was he was trying to do. He bent down calmly on one knee and placed his palm to the side of her face; even though Isla had pushed him away in anger she did not do so for a second time, for something was soothing and familiar about his action.

'You must trust me. Now is not the time, but hopefully, one day it will be. But Ilarya is your name. That is who you are – don't ever forget it.'

'In here – I saw them go in here.'

They both jumped, breaking the tender moment between them.

Bang! Bang! Bang! They were trying to break down the door from the outside.

'Quick, you must go – your necklace.' Elston ran to the door; he tried to barricade it with whatever he could find and held his body against it. 'Go! Go!'

Isla pulled the necklace out from under her dress; immediately it glowed and the mirror changed, just as it had done before, only this time she could actually see what was on the other side. *The Manor.*

Miss Sparrow was at her desk; Mr Stopes was pacing. Could this really be happening – after all this time, was she really looking into the Manor? Isla took a step closer but stopped short of crossing the threshold. She paused at the sight of her own reflection and she realised something: the eyes, what he had been calling her. *Could it really be?* She turned round to face Elston, if that was even his real name, his body being thrashed about as he tried to keep whoever was on the outside from coming in.

'Isla.'

She heard the shocked voices of Mr Stopes and Miss Sparrow; they could obviously see her too. She turned around to face the mirror, and there they were, staring straight back at her. *Has time ever stood as still as this?*

They were calling for her to walk through, Elston was shouting for her to go, they all wanted her to go, but she was torn: should she leave or should she stay? She wanted to do both, but how could she choose? Before she had the chance to make the decision for herself, she felt her body being pulled. An invisible force had wrapped itself around her, and she was gone.

Just as her body collapsed to the floor in Miss Sparrow's office, the door to the room she had been in was burst open and Elston went flying.

Mr Stopes ran towards the mirror and uttered one word: 'Nycolas.'

It was barely a whisper, but Isla heard it: the final link, her story, it all made sense now; it all made perfect sense. She stared up from the floor, but before she could do anything about it, before she could say that she knew, it was taken away from her.

She saw the exchange; the look on both their faces spoke more than a thousand words.

Elston was the first to turn away. 'Look after my daughter.' It was a clear instruction, then Elston, or Nycolas, picked up a spear. He raised it high, yelled and brought it down hard and fast; the tip of the blade wedged itself into the middle of the mirror and it smashed into a million pieces, as did Isla's heart.

CHAPTER FORTY-FIVE

Was it her or did this place no longer feel like home? Isla recalled the many times when she'd longed for the comfort and safety of the only place she had ever known to be home, but now, stood in her room, staring at her bed, all her belongings exactly how she had left them, it was if she was standing inside a stranger's house.

To the far side of her she heard a rustle; it was Christmas morning and still dark outside. She could see the night had brought a layer of fresh snow, and tiny flakes still fluttered down past the window. She didn't say anything, for she didn't want her presence to be known just yet. She knew the story that had been told to everyone – Miss Sparrow had informed her of that. However, she wasn't sure that she too could say the same lie if questioned.

But as she continued to stare out to the grounds, reminded of the many years of memories and back to her own birthday, when the chain of events had all been set in motion, she too understood the need to keep it a secret. She did not just have a responsibly to help those of Westoria but also those of the Manor, and, as she had learned, some secrets were there for protection.

She heard the rustle again; this time it was followed by a little groan. It was Lexi waking up; she rubbed her eyes and mumbled something that Isla couldn't quite catch, then sat up in her sleepy state. Something clicked, and she fully awoke in excitement that it was Christmas Day. She scrambled on her hands and knees in her nightie to the end of her bed expectantly, hoping that the stocking she had so diligently hung the night before would be full of presents.

She stopped short of her bed, and Isla knew she had been rumbled; there was no point trying to hide her presence, so she spun around and faced Lexi, who was poised on her knees like a meerkat, momentarily frozen until, at full speed, she leapt off her bed, arms splayed, wrapping them tightly around her.

Elizabeth awoke almost immediately from the commotion and she too looked happy to see Isla's return, or was it relief? Isla wasn't sure. Sissie, however, not one for mornings, rolled over, putting her pillow over her head and blocking out the noise of her sister at such an ungodly hour.

'Leave me alone, Lexi, it's too early. Go back to bed,' moaned Sissie.

But Lexi did not listen; she kept poking at her sister's head until she relented and removed the pillow. Lexi didn't say anything but pointed gleefully in Isla's direction; Sissie squinted, her eyes trying to focus while feeling around for her glasses, not being able to see properly until she had put them on.

'*What the hell—*'

Elizabeth cut Sissie off. 'Isla, what an amazing surprise this is! We have all missed you – the room has not felt the same without you.'

'I knew you would come back,' cried Lexi. 'I told everyone you would. I said there was no way she would never not come back to see us.'

Isla felt a rush of guilt. Lexi had had that much faith in her, that she was sure that one day she would return – if only she knew she was that close to never seeing them again, she might not have felt the same. Still, she did not want to destroy her little bubble, on Christmas Day of all days, so she confirmed that she always had the intention of coming back to the Manor, but that time had just kind of escaped her, which wasn't entirely untrue; she just couldn't believe how much time.

Wanting to take the focus off her return, Isla motioned towards the stockings generously stuffed with presents hanging at the bottom of their beds. The distraction immediately worked, and Lexi joyously rummaged through what seemed to be a bottomless one.

Of course, not knowing that she was going to return, Isla didn't have one, although Lexi thoughtfully offered for Isla to share hers, and that innocent little girl melted her heart once again.

'Oh my God, wait until Will sees you – he is going to freak!'

'Lexi, do not use words like that, they're not very nice,' said Elizabeth.

'What? I didn't call him a freak, I just said he's going to, which he will. He's not been the same since you left, you know.' Lexi, oblivious, didn't know what she said, but Isla knew all too well that he hadn't been. She had seen it for herself, and the look on Elizabeth's face said that she knew more than what she was saying too.

The morning went by in a blur, with children running around playing with Christmas presents, comparing and trying each other's out; it was a bit wild, until Ms Pepperin ordered everyone to get washed and dressed before they were to have any breakfast. They all walked into the dining hall, where breakfast was already laid out on the table, which was more than their usual porridge and toast. There were pancakes, mince pies, fruit, steaming cups of cocoa, all there for the taking, and though she had missed the food of the Manor, Isla found she had no appetite at all.

It did not take long for the whispering to start and for the children to notice that Isla had returned; Lexi made it pretty obvious with the way she kept proudly announcing it to anyone that walked past, and if anyone missed that, then Jimmy Jameson blasted her name out so loud across the room that it was impossible for anyone not to know.

Before the chatter could continue to rise Miss Sparrow approached the front of the hall and addressed them all.

'Now, before you start your gossiping I am sure that most of you have not failed to notice that we have a familiar face back with us this morning. Before you all inundate Isla with the same monotonous questions, I shall tell you. She has been away reconnecting with her roots and will be staying for a while before her permanent residence is secured. Now, she arrived in the early hours of the morning. I am sure you are all happy to see her again, but let's keep the questions to a minimum until she settles back in – is that understood?' Miss Sparrow was unusually light in her deliverance. Perhaps it was the joyous festivities rubbing off on her or Isla's safe return, she didn't know, but only Isla knew the significance behind her words and she appreciated her efforts to keep the questioning to a minimum and her skill at essentially keeping it quite close to the truth.

'Now, I will not tolerate tardiness. We shall all be ready by 10am to head down to the village and give to those less fortunate than us. Ms Pepperin will be in charge today, and I expect you all to do as she tells you, so eat up and let's get moving.' Miss Sparrow walked away, glancing momentarily at Isla. She no longer feared her as she used to; in fact, in a strange way, she now admired her, or respected her at the very least. Especially now that she had found out exactly who she was, her guardian: everything she had sacrificed and given up to keep her safe, her dedication to her parents. She did not like that it had all been kept a secret, but it was no longer a secret now. She knew who she was, she knew where she came from and she knew she would find a way back. But now was not the time; today was about enjoying the company of the people she had always considered to be her family, to feel somewhat the old version of herself for a day.

She grabbed Lexi and gave her a squeeze; Lexi smiled back, then dived into all the glorious-looking food. Isla looked around and caught Elizabeth's eye, for she could not see the most important person of all, and mouthed, 'Where is he?'

'Come on, I'll show you,' Elizabeth said, getting up from her seat.

They left, quietly grabbing their coats, and made their way out of the Manor, following a single set of footprints.

'He kept saying he saw you, so he's come down here every day since. I'm not sure what he saw, but either way, he convinced himself he saw you. I tried so many times to get him to come back inside, but whatever the weather he'd just sit and wait.'

The two of them looked at each other, Elizabeth somewhat territorial. *Have the roles reversed? Is she the one that now looks out for Will?* Elizabeth cared about him, that was for sure – she could see it in her eyes – but had she cared this much before Isla had left?

'I don't know what happened, Isla, and perhaps it is not my business to know.' Elizabeth stopped Isla in her tracks. 'Do not misunderstand me – I am happy you are back, I am happy to see Lexi and Sissie so happy. We have all missed you dearly.'

Isla smiled back to confirm that she too was happy to see them again.

'But what I do know is that you were not with family, and wherever you were, whatever you have been doing, you have hurt Will in the process, whether it was intentional or not. He is not the same person you left, and you should know that.'

Wow, Isla was shocked to hear Elizabeth speak so plainly, and it stung. She was right, of course: Will had been through a lot. Isla had to take responsibility for the way she had left, the way she had treated him, but within the words that Elizabeth spoke she also felt that there was a warning, a warning not to hurt him any further, but she needn't have worried: Isla had no intention of hurting her best friend any more than she had – that was, if he was still her best friend.

'I'll let you go by yourself, give you your privacy.'

Isla said thank you to Elizabeth and watched her walk away; she definitely knew something – she'd pretty much told her as such. *What does she know?* But that was something to worry about for another day. Today was all about building bridges and making amends – it was Christmas, after all.

She knew exactly where to go, for she carried on following the foot-sized imprints in the snow, and though it had stopped snowing it was still cold, but not as cold as it looked. The fields of the Manor were exactly how she remembered them to be, and it was always particularly charming this time of year, the reason being that they were the only ones for miles, so the hills were left looking like rolling sheets of white silk.

She entered the garden, her heart starting to race a few beats faster; she was so nervous to see him after all this time. She didn't know what to say, she had so many things she wanted to say, but what should she say first?

She saw him and didn't hesitate; before she knew it she had blurted out his name and waited. When he didn't react she took another step closer and said it again; this time she could see her own face reflect back at her.

'Will.'

His eyes locked with hers and they both stared at one another, neither of them showing any emotion. *It can't be real, after all this time?* After what felt like a very long ten seconds, Will spun around as quickly as his body would allow him to, yet to utter a single word.

Isla held up a shy hand. 'Hi,' was the only appropriate thing she could think of saying. His eyes were as warm and as brown as she remembered; she barely had the chance to say another word before she was almost knocked off her feet and Will had her firmly wrapped within his arms. He had definitely grown since she had last seen him and she happily allowed herself to sink into them; she never knew how much she had missed him until this very moment.

When they finally pulled away, she saw his face properly for the first time; she saw the stress and the worry, all the things that her disappearance had done to him, and it broke her to see what her actions had done. Elizabeth was right: he was not the Will she had left behind, but then again, she was no longer the Isla that had vanished. She doubted that either of them would ever be the same people again.

'So, Mr Stopes?' She knew what he was implying. 'It seems you have family after all.' He smiled.

Isla had found out that not only was Miss Sparrow her guardian but Mr Stopes was also, in fact, her godfather – quite a lot of information to take in, so she wasn't sure it had fully sunk in yet.

'That's not the only family I have.' Isla took a deep breath. 'I also met my father.'

'*Your father?*'

'Yep, apparently I have one, and he is still alive.' Isla started walking, not liking being stood still, and Will followed.

'What? How? I mean, are you sure? This is huge.'

Isla laughed, not at all surprised at Will's reaction, she too had felt the same as she watched the mirror shatter into a thousand pieces as she finally joined the dots together that the man staring back at her was quite possibly the most important man in her life.

'Well, where is he?' Will asked, curious to know all the details.

Isla had done all her sobbing on the floor as she lay surrounded by shards of glass and couldn't bring herself to say the exact details there and then; she just wanted to enjoy being reunited with her oldest friend. She did not want it to be spoiled by retelling her story again – not for today, anyway.

Will pushed, not noticing that she didn't want to talk about that part of it. 'What are you going to do?'

Isla stopped and looked back towards the Manor, placing a hand across her chest, looking down at the shiny object that hung around her neck. She had a father and now also a piece of her mother. She looked at Will, back at her necklace, then back towards the Manor and smiled.

CHAPTER FORTY-SIX

It was a surprisingly mild evening for the middle of winter, and Isla had something she needed to do that she had been putting off. Though they had spoken when she first came back, she wasn't sure how she had felt about someone that was family – maybe not by blood but by choice, and the choice of her parents, no less – having been a part of her life her whole life and she hadn't even known it. It felt like a massive betrayal of momentous proportions, and it hurt.

Though she understood what they had done was in order to keep her safe and protected, she also could not forgive them for it either. And though there had been some relief to discover who and where she really came from, it also highlighted the fact that for ten years the very people that knew the truth had lied to her face every single day. She understood Miss Sparrow, as she naturally had a hold on her emotions, but Mr Stopes – how he could see her, knowing the truth and not once breaking, not once attempting?

She swallowed her sentiments; she needed a clear head for this. She wasn't entirely sure what she was going to say; she just knew she didn't want to cry.

Tap! Tap! Tap! Isla hit the knocker; it felt like ages she waited until he arrived, looking a little more dishevelled than usual. It was clear they both felt uncomfortable now the truth was out in the open, and it was obvious that neither of them knew what the new protocol should be, so they both chose to ignore it and sat down in further uncomfortable silence.

Mr Stopes, Isla noted, was drinking whisky rather than his usual tea and looked as if he had not slept for days. She felt sorry for him but then quickly reminded herself that she shouldn't: he was not the one that had spent the majority of his of life being lied to. He took another sip of his drink, then staring into the open flames, he finally broke the silence.

'I don't expect your forgiveness. I understand what it is that we have done to you.' He stopped, still not taking his eyes off the glow of the fire.

'Why? I don't understand how you could have known all this time and never said anything.' Isla found she was not so angry anymore; she just wanted to know the full truth. 'I understand why you always kept your distance from me now, why you always put more effort into everyone else but me. Was I too much responsibility for you? Did you regret ever saying yes to my parents?'

'No.' He raised his voiced then lowered it again and looked at her. 'That's not true. Don't ever believe that is true. I was always looking over you – Christ, we started those lessons because of you. I made sure every time you would get it, but you have to understand, Isla, I couldn't… I couldn't get too close, but I was always there – please believe me, I was always there.'

This was true. She may have not had the funny, jokey kind of relationship that he most certainly had with Sissie, where he helped her with all kinds of crazy experiments, but he had always been there; he had always made sure she understood, that she learned, that she was capable. He had, after all, probably let her spend more time with horses than anyone, homing in on her skills, letting her somehow still be a part of the person she was meant to be. But still, she had lost out on all that time, time when she should have been the one that he joked with, created memories with. She felt she didn't know him half as well as she should. A lie was one thing, but to then be denied a relationship with the last remaining relative she had was hurtful.

'I just don't understand why you still couldn't have had more to do with me, take me under your wing like you did with Sissie. She got to know you, and I didn't.'

Mr Stopes understood what it was all about now. It was not the lie at all; it was the feeling of further abandonment by the people who should have been there for her the most. 'You're right, I have no excuse for that. I guess it was easier, and now I see it was easier for me, not for you. It's just, you remind me of them so much. I promised them I would keep you safe, and I thought you would be better off to be free to grow up in your new life, to be happy, to have no link to your past.' He looked down again, ashamed that he had gotten it so wrong.

'We could make up time.' Isla could see in his face everything he had done he really had done so because he thought it was for the best. She could also see that it hurt him too, and after all, it was him that gave her her mother's necklace; it was him that wanted her to find her true self.

Mr Stopes smiled. 'I would like nothing more.' He looked a little closer to his old self now.

'What were they like?' Isla did not know much about her parents; she had never known anyone who had known them before, but now she did, and who better to ask than her father's best friend?

'This could take all night.'

'It's okay, I've got nowhere to be – have you?'

'No.' He smiled. 'I have nowhere else to be.' *Even if I did*, he thought to himself, there's *nowhere else I would rather be.* So they sat for hours, Mr Stopes telling stories of when they were younger, all the mischief the two of them used to get into, how her father fought for wanting to have a normal life, and then his duty of being the son of a king and the expectations that he would replace him one day, which had happened far sooner than anyone had expected.

'He only admitted his insecurities to me. He didn't think he was ready, but I never doubted him – your father was such a fair man, and even though he couldn't see it, he was built for being a king.'

Isla couldn't believe it. Elston, the man she'd met, was Nycolas Blackbourne, the man Alfled had spoken so highly of, who so many others had spoken so highly of, was her father, and not only that: according to Mr Stopes, he also struggled with self-doubt too. She could see why they all thought so much of him; even though the man she had met was a dirty, overgrown fragile mess, was he really? It's what the eye instantly saw, but he spoke with experience, he acted with power, he had saved her life, put her own life before his without a seconds' thought. Isla felt sick. The tears were starting to prickle, but she wasn't going to let that happen; she couldn't let it happen.

'And what about my mother? What was she like?'

'Oh, Aurelia.' This was the first time she had ever heard her mother's name; she had always been referred to as just that, her mother, and in recent times the queen. She repeated her name in her head: *Aurelia.* She had never had her own identity until now, and Isla liked it; she thought it was a beautiful name.

'Everyone loved her – there was nothing not to like. Aye, she was sweet and gentle, but she didn't take no crap either, that was for sure. She certainly gave your father the run-around, but we all knew that they were meant for each other. It was only a matter of time.'

'How did they meet?' Isla liked listening to all the stories about her parents; it helped fill in the gaps that she had felt for so many years.

'Well, your mother was on a visit to the City of People – all the territories had come together for some celebration. I really can't remember what it was now, I had drunk rather a lot. And just by chance they bumped into each other in the street. We came out of an inn – we really should not have been drinking because Nycolas and I were in the middle of our training for the king's guard, but being your father's best friend came with certain privileges. We walked out; he was first and bumped straight into her. She was doing a tour of the city – it was the first time she had ever been there. He apologised profusely; she seemed to find it funny and I teased him for being soft, but he didn't care – all he cared about was finding out who she was.'

Isla was so excited by their story; it felt as if fate really had intervened. 'And you did, you found out who she was?'

'Oh yes – that day, he asked around everyone. I gave up and left him to it, but he never stopped, and eventually, someone knew. Oh, that's Australd's daughter, he got told. I laughed, of course, when I heard – that was not going to be an easy challenge. You see, as great as your mother's family are, they are not known for their pleasantries. They prefer to stay with their own kind; they are highly intelligent and, justified or not, very proud people. Though your mother was different; other than her looks you would not think she was Valeyan at all, and though mixed marriages were not completely unheard of, they preferred to keep with their own kind.'

'And then what happened?' Isla was hooked.

'Your mother somehow convinced her father to let her stay for the summer – she said she was learning about different cultures, the way people lived, and it rounded her as a person and improved her intellect. Me, I say she felt just as much for your father that day as he did.'

'I can't believe it. So how did they finally get together?'

'Well, it just kind of happened. Like I said, she did not

make it easy for him – he had to work hard for her hand – but in between life and studies we all just kind of hung out like normal youngsters, and the rest is history.'

'Yes, but what did their parents say?'

'Well, as you can imagine, her father was not so pleased, but I believe her mother had a hand in persuading him and Nycolas's parents – well, they could see he was happy, but they just had one condition: that he was to put in serious effort and to finish his training with the king's guard before marriage. Anyway, they were both from highly respected families, and, while not your usual match, it brought the two most powerful families together from the northern and western quarters.'

'It sounds perfect – they must have loved each other very much.'

'Yes, they did. Everyone could see they were in love, but then your father was crowned king before his time, and though some thought that would put a strain on their relationship, it only seemed to make them stronger, and as Nycolas flourished into his role as king they took the next natural step, then you were born.'

It shocked her to hear her name, though she knew they had been talking about her parents, it also felt like she had been listening to a fictional story about someone else's life, someone that was nothing to do with her entirely, but hearing her name brought all the pieces of the puzzle together; it was a story about her parents, how they fell in love, and she was a product of that love.

Mr Stopes noticed Isla had gone quiet. 'What is it?'

'Oh, nothing,' she replied.

'You can speak to me, you know. You can ask me anything. I won't hold anything from you.'

'It's not that.'

'Then what is it?'

Isla hesitated, but she didn't need to keep secrets around him now, did she? 'My memory, it's not coming back.'

When Isla first arrived at the Manor all those years ago, she had just turned six, old enough to have already accrued some memories in her short life, but she remembered none of them. When she questioned Miss Sparrow about this, she had informed her matter-of-factly that they had been wiped, or rather blocked without a moment's hesitation. Isla had not felt that Miss Sparrow had said this so clearly to hurt her. Rather the opposite, really – for transparency. And as Miss Sparrow had informed her, the worst was yet to come, so she was best focusing on the here and now, not the past. There was small hope, though, that in time they would come back – exactly how much time no one knew, but Isla hoped soon, for they were her memories and not anyone else's to take.

'Spit it out.' Mr Stopes was looking at her with a knowing look. 'There's more.'

'Miss Sparrow.' *What the heck?* Isla thought. This was what confused her the most about everything. 'You're my godfather, yet I was put in Miss Sparrow's care – why would my parents do that?'

'Ah, first of all, I know she is a bit... well, not the easiest of people at times, but she really was the best fit. You should count yourself lucky – you could not have done better.'

Isla snorted; she wasn't sure about that. She had been even more distant to her over the years than Mr Stopes had been, but at least she was consistent with it. However, despite her refreshed respect for Miss Sparrow, their choice of guardian was still a mystery to her.

'I wasn't exactly in the best position.' He paused. 'I had other responsibilities, plus I was always on the road. Miss Sparrow was there from the day you were born; she was your mother's oldest confidant and a good friend to them both. You should know they both thought very highly of her.'

'They thought highly of you; they chose you as family. They made you my godfather – I presume I have a godmother, but Miss Sparrow is not it. Do you know who it is?'

Mr Stopes ignored her question. 'Isla,' he continued gently. 'Just give it time – when you get to know her like I know her, I think you will agree with your parent's decision. There is more to Eliza than what you see, and there were more factors involved than what you know, and, well, she is capable of making the hard decisions. Believe it or not, she has always put you first, and I will not hear a bad word about her.'

'I saw a picture of you, the two of you, when you were younger. She has it in her drawer,' Isla pointedly told him.

It clearly took Mr Stopes by surprise, for it was written all over his face. 'Oh.'

'You have a history, don't you?' Isla remembered the fleeting comments between the two now, the arguments (though most likely to do with her), but she joined the dots, and it was clear that some kind of past connected the two of them together.

He regained his cool. 'A history would be a pretty accurate description of sorts. But like other things, Isla, that's best left in the past.'

Isla felt weirdly satisfied with his response, and to be honest she didn't want to get into the ins and outs of their past. If that was where he wanted to leave it that was fine by her.

'So are you saying that Miss Sparrow was actually friends with my mother?' Isla said, moving the subject along in a jovial mocking tone.

Mr Stopes laughed. 'She really is not as bad as you think. She had a lot in common with your mother, and she'd kill me for saying this, but sometimes she even laughs.'

They were both laughing now like it was a casual evening reminiscing about some family get-together, and in a way it was, her family, her somewhat very odd, dysfunctional family, but it was hers.

'Right, time to hit the hay now. I think I've had far too many of these.' He pointed to the empty glass on the table. 'But first things first: you are to come down here whenever you want. You needn't even knock – this is your home as well now – and second of all, I think this is long overdue.' He stood up, and Isla did the same, thinking he was about to walk her to the door. 'I think your father would have wanted me to give you this a long time ago.' And he hugged her, the fatherly figure kind of hug, protective and reassuring. She'd promised herself she wouldn't, but there was nothing she could do; it was too late as she felt the first drop of warm liquid silently roll down her cheek, followed by another and another. She let the gates open, and even though she was crying, she finally felt content as she silently sobbed into the arms of the man who had sacrificed more for her than she would ever know.